DUDLEY PUBLIC LIBRARIES

The loan of this book may be renewed if not required by other
readers, by contacting the library from which it was borrowed.

SHATTERED DREAMS

Vivienne Dockerty

Matador
9 Priory Business Park, Wistow Road
Kibworth Beauchamp
Leicester LE8 0RX, UK
Tel: (+44) 116 279 2299
Fax: (+44) 116 279 2277
Email: books@troubador.co.uk
Web: www.troubador.co.uk/matador

ISBN 978 1780881 706

British Library Cataloguing in Publication Data.
A catalogue record for this book is available from the British Library.

Typeset in 11pt Aldine401 BT Roman by Troubador Publishing Ltd, Leicester, UK

Printed and bound in the UK by TJ International, Padstow, Cornwall

MIX
Paper from
responsible sources
FSC
www.fsc.org   FSC® C013056

To my niece Cathy, with gratitude for your support and interest in my work.

AUTHOR'S NOTE

I wrote this book with a lot of tears and heartache in the memory of my parents, who only looked for happiness as we all do, but their dreams were shattered by the Depression and the onset of the Second World War. They were a couple whose destiny was shaped by the decisions of weak and posturing politicians and a man named Adolph Hitler (the Devil Incarnate), who lived at that time on the earth.

I am grateful to my mother, Kathleen, an aspiring author, who left me a manuscript "Ted's story" written at my father's request. He said that there were so many recordings of the bare historical facts, that it would be good if a real soldier told his story. I have tried to adhere to it as much as possible, but some of the story has been fictionalised.

CHAPTER ONE

The young man turned his back on his father and walked to the door, temper making his body tremble whilst he fought to keep his feelings under control.

"I've told yer before, son, everything will be yours when I die. Now stop whining and get yerself down the lane and make a start on them footin's."

J.C. Dockerty, a small, grey haired, well-padded man in his fifties, sat back in his favourite chair and took a large swig from the glass of Guinness that his wife had placed on the table beside him. It had been a long day and he was looking forward to his dinner. Eddie, his eldest son, could be a right pain in the arse sometimes, always complaining about something or other. It had been the lorry this morning and now he was on about the deeds of the bungalow.

What more did the little bugger want? Everything that J.C. owned would be Eddie's one day, with him being the elder son. *Though it wasn't strictly true was it?* said the man's voice of conscience. He had promised the bungalow that Eddie was building in his spare time to his older daughter, Caitlin, who was to be married in the autumn to the son of a farmer from over Shropshire way. J.C. couldn't let it be seen that a wealthy man, such as himself, would be paltry in his wedding gift to the young couple. A brand new house was the least he could give, if he was to keep his standing amongst the other members of the Rotary Club.

Young people got it so easy these days, he thought to himself. When he was the same age as Eddie, he'd had to serve an apprenticeship in the family business too. Rising at cock crow to get over to the quarry, loading up the horse and cart with the small stones he had broken up himself, a process called 'knapping', from the rocks the previous day. Having the stone on the building site,

1

used for the footings as there was no cement in his day, before the brickies arrived to start their work, then having to hang around in all weathers, whilst learning the tricks of the trade. At least Eddie got to ride around in the lorry, was paid three half crowns on a Saturday and had use of the family car. It was more than his other sons were getting. Terry, Sam and Mickey only got bed and board.

Eddie hurried down the dirt track to the plot of land at the bottom of the family's garden. Anger had brought on a rush of adrenaline making him suddenly feel full of energy, even though he had been working since six that day. Though his father had just announced to him that everything was to be his one day (wouldn't that wipe the smile off the faces of his siblings who all toadied up to their father), the fact was his father wouldn't listen if he tried to talk to him man to man. It irked him greatly. He wasn't a snot-nosed schoolboy, he was an adult now, capable of going out into the world and earning a man's wage. But if he had to buckle down and take the curses and sometimes the blows from his tyrant of a father, so be it. His sisters and his brothers would all be dancing to their big brother's tune when he inherited the lot in years to come. And it was a lot to inherit. Father had a large stone quarry, a big eight-roomed house here in its own grounds, row upon row of terraced houses in Birkenhead that he got the rents from and soon a large estate of middle class dwellings that his workforce was about to make a start on. That was without the two-seater Ford that his father had recently taken delivery of. The first one of its kind in the district and J.C.'s pride and joy. It was Eddie's job to keep it maintained for his father. Keeping it topped up with oil and petrol, washing and polishing it, so that all J.C. had to do was jump in and drive himself anywhere he wanted.

Eddie had every reason to feel proud of himself. Being given a piece of land by his father was quite a responsibility, but as his father had said, if he was going to be the boss of the company in the future, he had to learn how to build a house from the bottom to the top. That meant digging out the footings, laying down the base and working on the brickwork. Later he would be given help by his brothers, as Terry had been trained in carpentry, Mickey was a plasterer and Sam, still a schoolboy, had recently been shown how to key in the roofing slates. All Eddie would have to do then was ask his girlfriend, Irene, the girl of his dreams, to marry him and then they could move in! He was certain she would say yes when he proposed to her. They had been courting for two years and it was time they settled down.

Eddie's anger towards his father ebbed away as his mind dwelt on his beloved. He would have another word with his father tomorrow over the lorry. The tipper had broken on it and the loads had to be taken off manually, the back lights were not working and he'd been stopped by the police again. J.C. had called it whining when Eddie had broached him about buying a new lorry, but none of it mattered really. He would order a fleet of lorries, when the business passed to him.

In the kitchen of her aunt's small bungalow a few miles away, Irene finished helping to clear away the dishes after their evening meal. She felt tired after her ten hour day working at Saltbury's department store and was looking forward to an early night. Her job as an apprentice shop assistant was poorly paid and she was given all the chores that the older girls didn't want.

Today had been a disaster from the very start. First the bus was late taking her into Birkenhead, causing her to be reprimanded by the floor manager. Then she was sent to assist the window dresser, a complaining, grumbling little man for whom she could never seem to do right. Then because he made her feel nervous, she had knocked over a pedestal, which in turn had crashed into some glass shelves. The sound of smashing glass and the man ranting and raving at her was still a recent memory resounding in her ears.

Irene was looking forward to doing what she always did when life at work got too much for her: a good book and a small bar of chocolate always seemed to do the trick, putting her in a relaxing mood when it was time to go to sleep.

"When are you going to see your young man again, Irene?"asked Aunt Miriam, a thin lady in her early sixties, with snowy white hair that she wore in a bun under a navy blue, Chinese style hat. They were sitting enjoying a pot of tea after the kitchen had been tidied and her niece had changed out of her shop uniform of a white long-sleeved blouse and black calf-length skirt, into a flowery poplin summer frock with short, puffed sleeves.

"I don't know really, probably at the weekend. He's very busy at the moment preparing the foundations of a house that his father has set him to building. Eddie sees it as a challenge, to show his father how well he can do."

"I bet he's a handsome boy, your Eddie. And fancy you having the attentions of the son of a wealthy local builder. One day you might be riding round in one of those big silver cars!"

"A Rolls Royce, I think you mean, Aunty, but I don't think that will happen. He's not even taken me to meet his parents yet and you'd think that he would have done, since I've known him for two years. Though I think Eddie may be wary of upsetting his father, because I'm a Protestant and his family are Roman Catholic, though they don't seem to be practicing, as him and his brothers went to Thurstaston school. I suppose if we did get married one day we wouldn't be allowed to marry in a church."

"I don't think that not being the same religion would stand in the way of a man in love. You're a lovely girl and as pretty as a picture. He would have to go a long way to find someone as loving and kind as you are. I should know. I don't know how I would have got over losing Tom, if it hadn't been for you."

"Oh, Aunty, that's a lovely thing for you to say. I'm glad that Father suggested I come over to keep you company. Since Isabel got married again and moved in with us at Peartree Cottage, the place has become rather crowded, with the two children as well. But, I like being here anyway. I like living here in the country."

"Your sister wants her bottom smacking. She'd only known that man for two minutes and now there's a baby on the way. How your poor father puts up with that man living there, I just don't know."

"Father's not in a fit state to do much about it, as you know. The doctor has told him that it will only be a couple of years before he's totally blind. They need Isabel's husband's wages to keep the household going. That and what I can give them when I visit at the weekend. I've been thinking, Aunty, that I might try for another position at a different department store. They've built a Cooperative store in Grange Road and there might be a bit more pay."

"That reminds me, I keep meaning to tell you, Irene. I got a letter this morning from your Aunty Jenny. She's retiring from her job near Lancaster and wants to know if she can set up home with me. What do you think? We can still have a bedroom each, because we can turn the parlour into a place for her and her money will come in handy, take the pressure a bit off you and me."

"Oh, that sounds wonderful, Aunty. I remember Aunt Jenny from when I was a little girl and Father used to take me to visit her in Liverpool. Didn't she used to drive a taxi in the Great War? I used to think she was a real pioneer. A lady driving a taxi. Father used to chuckle when he told me about her exploits."

"Well, as you know, my sister has been working for a well-to-do family as a housekeeper. It's time for her to put her feet up, especially as they have offered her a small pension. I'll write back and let her know that we'll be happy to have her company. Perhaps you could post the letter for me on your way to work."

"I still think I'll apply for a new job anyway, Aunty. I don't like the way the senior buyer has been looking at me lately. Sort of leering and watching me closely when I walk by. He gives me the creeps and he's never put my name forward for a promotion. A girl who started after me is already junior buyer on the clock and watch counter."

J.C. sat at the kitchen table next morning eating his large breakfast of sausages, bacon and eggs. He was wearing his pyjamas and dressing gown, feeling too bleary-eyed and hungover to bother yet with a wash and shave.

"Did Ellen press my good suit, Glad?" he asked, as his wife, Gladys, placed a rack of toast and a dish of marmalade before him.

"Only I've an appointment at the bank at eleven, bloomin' manager wants to see me again."

"Yes, it's hanging up in your wardrobe if you'd been bothered to look. Johnny, you really must cut down on your drinking and I wish you would try to make yourself presentable for breakfast times. The girls have only just left for school. Anyway, if you're going into town you may as well give me a lift. Save me waiting around for a bus in this hot weather."

"What is it this time? Another frock, a pair of shoes? I've not seen you wearing the dress you've got on before."

J.C. eyed his wife of twenty-five years with appreciation. Even after bearing him seven children, her figure was still slender and firm. Her glossy chestnut hair had not faded, though her once bright hazel eyes had lost the sparkle in them.

"I'm meeting Hilda. You know Charlie Pollitt's wife from the Rotary Club? She telephoned yesterday and asked could we meet up for lunch. We may have a wander around that new store that's just opened and I'll open up an account with them if anything catches my eye."

"Well, as long as you're back before Ellen starts on the dinner. Those potatoes were a load of watery mush that she put on the table last night; she hadn't drained them properly again. Maybe we should get rid of her and tell one of the girls to help you in the kitchen. Lord knows I've spent enough on my daughters' education, for one of them to be able to cook well."

"They've only been shown how to make sophisticated dishes, nouveau cuisine, or something like that, Johnny. I can't see Sheena turning out a decent steak and kidney pudding or Caitlin wielding a rolling pin. Anyway, leave Ellen and the kitchen alone. It's my domain is the kitchen. You just go and see what the bank manager wants you for."

J.C. already knew what Mr Martin, the bank manager, wanted

him for. It was about the loan that he had asked for to fund these new properties he wanted to build. J.C. couldn't see a problem. Let's face it, the building trade was in his very veins. Wasn't he descended from the family who had founded the biggest property company in the district? The Sheldon Property Company: started in 1849 by his Aunt Maggie and still going strong.

J.C. forced down the resentment that always appeared when he thought of the family history. A resentment learnt from an early age at his mother, Hannah's, knee. His Uncle Michael had diddled his half sister Hannah out of a fortune because of her illegitimacy, leaving J.C.'s father, Eddie, to struggle on and begin a rival firm. Eddie had been successful, but never as successful as his brother- in-law had been, finally passing on his business to his four grown-up sons. In time the business had come to J.C., when his unfortunate brothers had died on the Somme. Now he also had four sons to pass the trade onto, but lock, stock and barrel would go to his eldest son.

Eddie had his head under the bonnet of the lorry. He was stripped to his vest, whilst sweat poured down his legs underneath his cavalry twill trousers. Damn the thing! It had been tearing along quite happily from Buckley where he had been loading up the bricks and then the engine had conked out again.

Drat. This copper must be stalking him, Eddie could hear heavy footsteps a few yards away from him.

"Morning, lad. Broken down again, have yer? When's yer father going to get a new lorry; this one's only fit fer scrap as far as I can see."

"Morning, Officer." Eddie sighed and turned to look at the police constable. "Dad doesn't want to listen as long as the lorry's bringing him the loads."

"Well, I think we'll make him listen, young sir. This vehicle is dangerous. I've told yer before about it. Not only are the tyres bald, your back lights don't work and it's not up to carrying heavy loads. Look at that back axle, looks warped ter me and the hinges on the tipper are corroded. This time I'm going to talk ter my sergeant about you getting a summons. Being in charge of a dangerous vehicle will be enough ter do it and you'll have to appear in the County Court."

"But Officer, that's not fair. The lorry belongs to my father. I'm just his driver. Why are you going to summon me?"

"Because you, young man have been entrusted with the vehicle and it's up ter you to refuse to take it out if it's not fit for the highway. Now tell your father this and maybe he'll cough up for a new lorry. Now do yer want a push, we can jump start it down the hill?"

Irene was late again for work next morning, due this time to having forgotten to iron her white blouse the night before. She had watched her bus disappearing down the hill. She decided to walk. It was a pleasant sunny day, though there was a promise of another hot one if the lack of clouds above were anything to go by, but if she hurried she could be in time to catch the Crosville coach that passed along the bottom road. Irene found she was in luck and sat back breathlessly after she had paid her fare.

"I thought it was you, Irene."

She turned to see a pleasant faced young woman sitting on the seat behind her. It was Josie, a friend of her sister's: newly married and living out in the country, or so Irene had heard. Josie came to sit beside her.

"I haven't seen you for ages, Josie. We used to have a lot of fun when you came over to ours."

"No fun now, Irene. I've been married to Lennie for three months. In fact this is my last week working. I'm picking my cards up on Friday. Lennie says I've not to work anymore."

"Oh, is that because of the rule that married women have to give up working?"

"Not really. The manager said I could stay as long as I want to because they're a bit short of typists where I work. But Lennie says I should be expecting by now and it must be because I'm rushing off to work every day that I'm not. Anyway, he's put his foot down.

Master in his own home and all that business. How's life treating you, Irene, and how is Isabel, to change the subject? What are you doing so far from home?"

Irene explained that she was keeping her Aunt Miriam company because her uncle had died recently. She went to work every day from Irby, where before she used to travel from Wallasey. That she had met a young man who lived locally and she hoped to marry him one day and Isabel had divorced her husband and was seeing another man.

It appeared that Josie earned her living as a typist and Irene asked if typing was difficult to learn and were there better wages to be had? Better than a shop wage had been the reply, though boring as hell as Josie was a copy typist and you had to go to night school to learn the skill.

Her half hour break at lunchtime found Irene in a long queue at the Employment office in Hamilton Square that day. Full of hope that she could be directed to a new job with better pay had spurred her to scurry along the high street, eating the sandwich that her aunty had made as she ran.

"Do you have qualifications?"asked a superior young female clerk, glancing over her spectacles at Irene, as they faced each other through the glass panel later. "Did you pass your Matriculation? Speak a foreign language? Employers are being rather choosy at the moment. We are starting to have a worldwide depression as you probably know."

Irene didn't know, although the signs were there to see if she looked around for them. There were more men hanging around on street corners, the bus that brought the workers to the flour mill opposite her house wasn't as full as it had been and Saltbury's, being a department store that sold a lot of luxury items, wasn't very busy either.

The clerk suggested that she looked for a different kind of shop work. It was said that the new Co-op was incorporating a food department and, if she still wanted to improve her future prospects, there was always night school, though it didn't come cheap.

Irene left the place feeling quite despondent. She blamed her mother for her lack of qualifications, not having the good education that her sister had had at the convent, when her father had been made redundant at the nearby shipyard called Cammell Lairds.

Eddie's mother, Gladys Dockerty, sat with her friend, Hilda, in the restaurant at Saltbury's department store. They were drinking coffee from dainty china cups and chatting about mutual friends from the Rotary Circle. Both women wore expensive coats trimmed with fur tippets, over smart ankle-length dresses and T bar shoes. Their shingled hair was covered with neat cloche hats and both wore gloves on their manicured hands.

"My dear Gladys," said Hilda, elegantly dabbing at the corners of her mouth with a snowy white napkin. "How are the plans for the wedding progressing? You were telling me last time we met that it was to be held at St. Winefreds in Neston and afterwards at the Victoria Hotel."

"Yes, that's right, Hilda. Of course it is too early to put the invitations in the post, but naturally you and Charles will be there."

"A wedding is so exciting. Have you decided on what you will be wearing? It is so important, isn't it, when you are the mother of the bride? I can't wait for Emily to find herself a beau. What about Eddie, your eldest? Is he walking out with a young lady yet?"

"I have heard from one of my daughters that he is seeing one of the shop assistants that works here."

Gladys lowered her voice and looked around in case someone could hear.

"Hardly marriage material. She's not a Roman Catholic and Eddie is only nineteen, whilst she is twenty-one. Rather young I think to be settling down. I'm going to invite Marjorie Buckley around for Sunday tea as soon as I can get around to it. You know her father, Alfred Buckley, don't you? One of the leading lights at the Amateur Dramatic Society and a member of the Rotary. She is a lovely girl, educated with my daughters at the convent and pronounces her words so beautifully, puts my Welsh inflection to shame."

"Oh, Gladys, I think your accent is enchanting and you've managed to hold on to it all these years. Now shall we order some little sandwiches? They'll put us on until supper time."

The shop assistant to whom Eddie's mother had been referring was on her way back to her post on the hosiery counter. She had been given the job of counting stockings, then neatly folding them back into the wooden trays. Sarah Petey, who had been promoted to assistant buyer, though she had started her apprenticeship after Irene, was nowhere to be seen. It had been arranged that the two girls would liaise at one' clock to see if more stock was required.

Irene stood behind the counter waiting patiently. There was only so many times one could count stockings; she had already tidied the new fangled brassieres and the glass shelves were gleaming from when she had dusted them before. She kept her eye out for the floor walker. He was known to tattle tale to management if he thought a girl was not doing her share.

Boredom began to set in. There were no customers to be served and the girl from the millinery counter opposite was busy arranging her merchandise on the wooden hat stands. Irene stared glassy eyed towards the window. Was this what she was going to have to do for the rest of her life? Standing for ten hours a day, watching the minutes on the department clock tick by. Even if she did apply for a job at the new Co-op, would her day be any different? She could still be watching the clock in another store up the road!

Oh, where had Sarah got to? At least counting stockings in the girl's company would alleviate the boredom and they could have a laugh together as Sarah usually had a joke to tell. Finally Irene decided to go to the senior buyer's office. Mr Fielding would know where Sarah had got to.

Her mind in a whirl, Irene forgot to knock at the door of his office, but she soon discovered where Sarah was. Sitting on the senior buyer's knee! She couldn't say who was the most embarrassed, though Sarah managed to conceal her shame whilst doing up the buttons on her blouse and the man pretended he was about to sharpen a pencil.

"So this is how you got your promotion," Irene managed to splutter before leaving as an uncomfortable silence was beginning to fill the air.

With her mind made up she put her hat and coat on and walked up the road to the Co-op and, with the knowledge that she was sure to get a glowing reference from the senior buyer, Irene was given a job.

J.C. sat in the bank manager's office, whilst Mr Martin, a thin studious looking man, was busy studying his client's file.

"I have to tell you the truth of the matter, Mr Dockerty, you'll have to cut down on your expenditure or your workforce. There's too much money going out and not enough coming in."

"But I don't know what you mean by that," J.C. answered, sounding puzzled. "I've the rents from Conway Street coming in and that brings a tidy income as you know."

"But, you are spending more than you should do. Do you need twenty wages going out each Friday, when you've only just started putting the foundations in? If I were you I would lay off your workforce until they're needed. Then there's your lifestyle also. Drawings for self of fifty pounds each week is a bit over the top, surely?"

"I have the girls' education, a servant, a gardener, my wife's household expenses and the car. I'll need a new lorry shortly and I've my elder daughter's wedding. All got to be paid for somehow."

"Can I give you a word of advice, Johnny? And this is between you and me. That pair of semi's you own on the corner of your avenue, sell one of them and put the other in your wife's name. I have it on good authority that unless things improve in the economy, the bank will recall your initial loan. It's not just *your* business, it will be all sorts of businesses that will be going to the wall. I think there could be another depression in a year or so and it would be wise to draw in your horns. Perhaps cut the size of the development down, or make your men work twice as hard."

J.C. walked back to his car in a daze. He lit a cigarette with trembling fingers as he took in the import of the manager's words. It wasn't possible. The man was scaremongering; he'd been reading the wrong sort of broadsheet. It was propaganda in the newspapers that had caused him to speak as he had. This was the 1930's. Hadn't they built a new world fit to live in, with the blood of his brothers shed in the Great War? Still, perhaps he should restrict his spending a little and maybe follow the advice on the semi's he owned. Gladys would be delighted when he presented the house deeds to her and he'd get a decent lorry for Eddie to drive.

Gladys. It would break her heart if they had to change their lifestyle. Last time there had been a recession, she had sold her little sweet shop to pay his builders merchant bills. It had been her bit of independence, something she could call her own. Though he could say this was her repayment, a house that would be in her name. She'd like that, something to tell those friends of hers, how generous her husband had been. What a loyal and supportive wife he had in Gladys, or Glad as he liked to call her. Bearing all his children without complaint, running the house like clockwork, always up at the crack of dawn. And they'd had a good marriage, J.C. thought to himself. He had been an adequate provider most of the time and a devoted husband to his admirable wife. *But don't forget that other matter,* the voice of his conscience said, *don't forget that other matter that made you fall from grace!*

CHAPTER TWO

Irene was thinking about the coming weekend. She usually met Eddie at the local dance that was held in the village hall on a Saturday night. She would have liked him to call for her at her Aunt's bungalow, but he always gave some reason for why he couldn't. She had asked him once why he didn't come and collect her? His answer had been a jokey one. Why bother, when she knew the way to the dance hall without him herself! That was Eddie all over she had found. No commitment, no promises for the future, just took it for granted that she was his girl.

She remembered back to when she had first met him. Aunty had worried that Irene had no social life, so had asked her neighbour's son where the young people of the village went on a Saturday night. There had been various answers; the tennis club, or go to see a show at the Argylle Theatre, drinking in the local pub or visiting the houses of friends. Though he sometimes went to the village hall where there was a social evening. At the moment they danced to the music from a gramophone, but the committee there were thinking of inviting local bands. Would she like him to take her niece there?

Irene had danced with the boy when they had got there, but unfortunately he had spotted a few of his friends and disappeared from her view. She had been left to watch, as others twirled on the dance floor, wondering if she should make a quick exit. It was embarrassing sitting on her own, not knowing another soul.

Eddie had come to her rescue. He was the most handsome young man she had ever seen. Taller than her, slim but not scrawny, dark brown hair slicked back, cut short in army style. But what she noticed more than anything was his brown twinkly eyes, full of fun and good humour, as if the world could never get him down. He was dressed in the very latest men's fashion: a double-breasted pinstriped suit that he wore with a white starched collared shirt. A tie of bright yellow completed his outfit and she couldn't help noticing his patent leather dance shoes. What a dream boat. As he smiled and asked could he request a dance from her, she had felt very privileged to do so.

Eddie was the best of dancers, taught by his mother who liked nothing better than waltzing with her son around their large kitchen with its highly polished wooden floor. Luckily Irene had attended her cousin's dancing school when she had been younger, so they had made a very accomplished pair. She had been glad that she had worn her pink taffeta dress that had frills cascading from the waist to the hemline and still remembered the envious glances from the other girls as she and Eddie glided by.

That had been over two long years ago and the pattern had hardly changed in their courtship, if that was what she could call it. Dancing at the village hall on a Saturday, sometimes meeting up again on Sunday and going for a walk.

The area where Aunty lived was beautiful. The bungalow looked over farmland, which stretched for mile upon mile to the Irish Sea. It wasn't far from Thurstaston Common, which had wonderful views to the mountains of Wales. Sometimes Eddie would hold Irene's hand as they wandered along slowly, breathing in the fresh, iodine air, but he never wanted to find a sheltered spot in order to do a bit of canoodling. The best she got was a quick peck on the cheek before she walked down the lane to her home.

He had told her a bit about his background, of his snooty snobbish sisters, with their clever know-all ways, of how hard he and his brothers had to work and that the business would be his one day. And he often spoke proudly of his marvellous mother, who seemed to be the best parent in the world.

The following day was to be the last for Irene at Saltbury's. She had given in her notice and was set to start work at the Co-op the following week. There hadn't been a problem trying to avoid the eyes of her colleague Sarah while she had worked her week out. Sarah had been kept busy planning a new accessory counter on the ground floor. Seeing the senior buyer on a daily basis was not a problem either; he always walked around as if he had a smell under his nose.

Irene had spent a lot of her time thinking, as she stood at the back of her counter willing for the days to pass quickly so that she could start the next phase of her life. Was this it then? Was she destined to spend her life as a shop girl? Have a career like Hilda Makin from millinery, a spinster in her fifties who lived alone with her cats. Or was this just time she had to spend before Eddie decided to propose to her? If that was so, he was being very cautious. It could be years before she became his wife!

Perhaps she should force the issue? Start dating someone else. See how Eddie would feel about that. It wasn't as if she was short on admirers, Graham Edge from Packing was always asking her out. Then of course there was Evan, her first ever boyfriend. Their courtship had started when she was only fourteen, but he had blotted his copy book by taking Emma Fuller out from Victoria Road. He had sworn there was nothing in it. It was Irene he loved and would do so until his dying day. He still sent cards to her mother's house at Christmas time and birthdays, with little notes pleading that he be given another chance.

Irene knew she was fairly pretty. Though her face was rather rounded, she had peachy skin and lovely curly chestnut hair. Her eyes were hazel and her full lips were certainly kissable, so what was the matter with Eddie, that he didn't want her in a certain way? Well, now she had made her mind up. This weekend was Eddie's last chance to do something that proved he had some commitment. She would invite him to tea at her Aunty's house and if he declined her invitation she would pack him in there and then. With Aunt Jenny coming to live at the bungalow in the not too distant future, Aunt Miriam would have company, so she could move back to her old room at home. Isabel, her elder sister, now a mother to two children and one on the way, was going to move to Southport where her new husband had got a job in a pub. Irene was sure her mother would love to have her younger daughter back, if only to help with her poorly dad.

Eddie's thoughts were also on the weekend. He was hoping to borrow the Ford and take Irene somewhere special on Sunday. He planned to tell her all about the bungalow and how one day when they married it would be hers. With a bit of luck, the roof would be on in a month or so, then he and Irene could get engaged. Though he wasn't looking forward to telling his parents: Eddie knew his mother had her heart set on him marrying a Catholic girl.

J.C. was in a terrible rage. His lorry was laid up, Ellen had burnt the sausages and, to top it all, the dealer from where he had ordered the new lorry had rung to say there was some delay. That meant they would get behind with the bricklaying. The men would be idling around, but still wanting their wages, damn it. He spied Eddie munching on a sandwich in the kitchen. The lad turned to greet him as his father walked into the room.

"Oh, Dad, I'm glad you're here still. Can I borrow the car on Sunday? After you've come back from church of course. I want to take a young lady out for a spin in the countryside."

He should have noticed the warning signs. His father always limped when he was angry. For some reason, the wound he'd got when he was gored by a bull always flared up then in his leg.

"No yer can't, lad, and what are yer doin' here anyway? You should be out there grafting. Not sitting around eating yer head off. How the hell I'm going to get them houses finished? Bloody lorry's not coming 'til Tuesday, but that lot will still want paying. I bet they're all up at the pub!"

"Can I make a suggestion, Father?" Eddie tried to ignore the outburst, as J.C. swung himself onto a chair and mopped at his brow with a napkin. "What if the men spent their time at the bungalow? It would keep them busy for a while."

"Yes, and you would have more time to spend with yer lady love. Is that it? Can't wait to get into her drawers?"

"Father, that's enough!"

This came from Gladys, who had been listening nearby in the scullery.

"There's no need to be so coarse."

J.C. had the grace to look sorry and apologised profusely to his wife. He meekly agreed that Eddie's suggestion was a good one and was to go up to the pub and drag his men out.

While his mother was with them in the kitchen, Eddie thought it was a good time to tell him that a summons to the Court was on its way.

"What do yer mean, a summons?" J.C. looked as if he was about to have a heart attack, whilst loosening the collarless shirt that suddenly felt too tight for him.

"What have yer been up to? Oh hell, can this day get any worse? Is it that bloody policeman again? The one that told yer off months ago about yer speeding? I told yer to watch out fer him. He's after promotion of course. Gladys, do yer still see that woman at the Rotary? Yer know, the wife of that fellow that's high up in the police force. What's his name? Spencer something or other. Ask them round fer dinner, will yer? We'll soon get this sorted lad, or my name's not J.C. Dockerty. And Gladys, give Ellen the night off when you have them round fer dinner. She's burnt the bloody sausages again!"

Irene spent some of her final pay on an elegant ankle-length dance dress that she had seen in the fashion department. It was made of pink chiffon, decorated with pretty black velvet flowers and a black velvet trim on the hem. Her eyes had been drawn to it each time she had passed the display model as she had made her way to the canteen. The dress and a new pair of silver open toe sandals, were just right for what she had in mind.

It was Saturday night at the village hall and the dance floor was crowded with couples looking for a bit of fun. There was a small band playing called 'Horace and his Thingamajigs'. It comprised of a saxophone, a pianist and a violinist.

Irene was dancing with Leonard Stanton, a pleasant enough young man with an attractive smile. They were engaged in a fancy tango, when a voice bellowed across the room.

"You can let her go now, Stanton, I'm here to dance with my girl."

The couples around Leonard and Irene stopped and looked in horror or amusement at the scene. It was Eddie Dockerty, wasn't it, drunk as a mop and swaying by the door?

Irene excused herself to poor embarrassed Leonard and hurried over. She grabbed Eddie by the shoulder and hustled him out of the village hall.

"How dare you show me up in front of all those people? I'm not your property, you don't own me or tell me what I'm to do."

He had the grace to look ashamed, but said with drunken authority.

"You *are* my girl, Irene, and you shouldn't be dancing with another fellow. I'm only a bit late anyway, had to go on what's 'is name's stag do. But I'm here now. I came especially to see my wonderful girl. You know, Irene, I've been thinking. If you ever consider marrying someone, would you give me first refusal?"

So it had worked then, she thought triumphantly, Eddie had been jealous enough to ask the question. It wasn't quite how she had wanted his proposal to be, but it was good enough that he had asked her!

J.C. went with his son to court and pleaded with the judge on Eddie's behalf. He was sorry, but business was booming at the moment and he hadn't got time enough to keep an eye on his lad. The lorry was to be scrapped immediately, as there was a brand new one being delivered any day. The judge wasn't to blame Eddie and J.C. was there to pay any fine that he decided to give.

He chuckled when he and Eddie walked out of the court room, the fine was a pittance, but then again hadn't old Harry Spencer said to him on Saturday night over dinner that it would be.

"I've something to tell you, Dad, now that the court thing is out of the way," said Eddie.

"What's that son? Make it snappy, I've got a bit of business to do. I thought you could take the car home and I'll come back by train."

"I've decided to get married."

"Oh, that's nice for you, who's the lucky girl?"

"You don't know her, her name is Irene and we met at the village dance in Irby. She's lovely, Dad, so pretty and really good at dancing. She lives with her Aunt down Seaview Lane."

"Have you told your mother?"

"No, Dad, because she won't approve. She wants to fix me up with Marjorie Buckley, but you've seen what she looks like, she's a horse of a girl."

"I wouldn't go against your mother, son, yer know what she's like. Has this girl's family got any money? What does her father do?"

"As far as I know her father's an invalid. He used to work on submarines, got made redundant by Cammel Lairds and now he's beginning to go blind."

"And what religion are they?"

"Protestant, but that shouldn't make any difference. We love each other, Dad."

"As far as I'm concerned you can forget her, lad. I could put up with the fact that the family is penniless, though I would wonder if she was after you for your money, but if she's not Roman Catholic, you've no chance. Your mother wouldn't let her over the door. Forget her, son, and go out with Marjorie Buckley; she's from a good family. A Roman Catholic and, her father's a good friend of mine. Anyway, I must be off, see you later when I get back home."

Eddie was left feeling angry, but despondent. Though he was in love with Irene, was falling out with his mother worth it in the long run?

J.C. got on the train at Chester Station. He wasn't going far, just down to Queensferry, but he had this urge to go and visit a little cottage on the main street. He was sure of a welcome there, it was the place he went to when he needed a bit of affection.

He lit a cigar as he sat back in the First Class carriage and thought about Alice. No one loved him as Alice did and he was sure he loved her in return. She had been the family Nanny when the children were younger and of course he hadn't meant to put her in a compromising position that night, but Glad had gone back to stay with her mother for a few days in Holywell and he always knew that Alice worshipped him. He could tell from the way she always had his slippers warming and a nice cup of tea ready for him when he came in from work.

Things had gone on from there and they snatched what happiness they could over the next year or so, until she had come to tell him that she was expecting. She'd asked him to leave Glad and set up home with her somewhere that no one would know them. Maybe in the Welsh countryside, where he could perhaps buy a bit of land and work a small holding. Alice, though, was happy enough when he said he'd buy her a little house, somewhere he could visit and get to know their baby. She'd been happy with that, Alice adored him and would never have resorted to blackmail, when perhaps another girl would have done.

Gladys Dockerty was running over the list of wedding invitations with her daughter, Caitlin. Caitlin was a small chubby girl who had never lost her puppy fat and was too fond of cakes and steak and kidney puddings to ever lose her weight.

"I've decided to invite Marjorie Buckley to be Eddie's partner at the wedding, Caitlin. I would have asked you to have her as one of your bridesmaids, but with you having all your sisters that should be enough. Your father has told me that Eddie has proposed to a most unsuitable young lady. She's a shop assistant for heaven's sake, not quite what we were wanting for your father's son and heir."

"And you think that by throwing Eddie and Marjorie together is somehow going to make him un-betrothed, Mother? You don't know our Eddie very well then."

"Caitlin. I know your brother very well, he is my first born son, after all. I know that he's expecting to inherit everything from your father and will change his mind when I tell him that he will get nothing if he disobeys me."

"And does Eddie know that the bungalow he's working on is going to belong to me and Larry? Because if he doesn't, I'd like to be there to see his face when Dad tells him."

"Oh, you can be so heartless, Caitlin. No, he hasn't been told yet and I think it was quite underhanded of your father to pretend that the bungalow was going to be his."

"Well he'd better tell him soon, because Eddie's nearly got the roof on, he's been working every night on it. Probably that's why he's proposed to the shop girl, so that they can get married when he's finished it. Anyway, Mother, will you telephone Miss Clarence in Chester for me soon, because I'll have to go to a dressmaker for my wedding dress? I've looked around Liverpool and there's nothing suitable in the department stores."

Aunt Miriam's face was wreathed in smiles when Irene told her that Eddie had proposed.

"And when is he taking you for your engagement ring, dear? He's bound to get you a solitaire, not like this little thing that your uncle gave me. Still, I know they say that opals can bring bad luck for the wearer, but we had a happy marriage for nearly forty years."

"Oh, I don't mind what Eddie gets me, Aunty. I'm so pleased that I'm going to marry him, I could burst. I'll be able to leave work and set up home in a nice house somewhere, maybe even in West Kirby where the toffs live."

"Well, Heswall is quite a nice place to live too, Irene. Maybe you'll live down Mount Drive and have a view across the River Dee? Has he said when you'll be getting married? Is it to be a short engagement or a long one? I know most couples have to save up to get married, but with his background, the family will probably make sure you have everything that you need."

"I think there may be a little problem, Aunty. We haven't talked about it yet, but Eddie's family are Roman Catholic. He'll have to wait until it's the right time to tell his parents because they probably won't accept a Protestant like me."

"Surely that won't be a problem, Irene. Once they meet you, they'll see what a lovely girl you are and then religion won't come into it. I have heard that their eldest daughter is getting married. Miss Smith told me the other day when I went into the Post Office. She said she'd seen the announcement in the *Wirral News*. 'Caitlin Dockerty marrying Lawrence Davies from Shropshire'. She won't have to change the initial of her surname, will she?"

"The other thing, Aunty, is that Eddie is only nineteen, so he will need his father's permission to marry. If his father says no, we'll have to wait another two years and that will be four years in all that I will have known him."

"Well, that isn't such a bad thing, too many marriages falter because they've rushed into it. Remember the old adage of 'marry in haste and repent at leisure'."

On the following Saturday after the dance, Eddie walked Irene as far as her Aunty's gate.

"Would you like to come in and have a coffee before you go home?"she asked eagerly. "Aunty will probably still be up and she's dying to meet you."

"It's all right, Irene, I'll get off home if you don't mind, I'll see you again next Saturday."

"Eddie, I hope you don't think I'm being forward or anything, but last week when you said about us getting married, you did mean it, didn't you?"

He laughed nervously and looked a little sheepish, not being able to meet her eyes.

"Is this because I had a bit to drink, that you think I wasn't being serious?"

"Well you did say I was to give you first refusal if I was thinking of marrying someone. I suppose it was a bit of a cockeyed proposal, but you haven't mentioned anything since."

"It's difficult, Irene. Of course I would like to marry you, but there are so many hurdles to get over before we can be officially engaged. My parents won't be happy because we aren't the same religion. I would need their permission to marry as you know I'm only nineteen. But in two years time I'll be old enough to marry without their consent. So it's probably best if we keep our engagement secret for the moment, but you know and I know that we'll get married one day."

"Oh, and do you love me, Eddie?"

"What do you think, Irene, and I know you love me too."

She closed her eyes and lifted her face for him to kiss her, but he only kissed her lightly on the cheek, then walked away.

Gladys walked down the dirt track to the bungalow. She carried a small wicker basket that held a round of salmon sandwiches, an apple, a piece of chocolate cake and a Thermos flask of tea.

"Cooee," she called, as she daintily tiptoed in her cuban heels over the plank of wood that served as a ramp to the doorway.

"Eddie, are you there, darling? Mummy's here."

Her son swung down from the loft, where he had been busy checking that the roofing felt was secure enough.

"I thought I heard someone and it's you, Mum. Oh good, you've brought me some lunch. That will save me some time not having to come up to the house."

"Have you somewhere I could put a tablecloth down and Eddie, is there somewhere you could wash your hands? I brought enough tea for the both of us because I'd like a little talk as you're eating."

"We could use that work bench over there, Mum, and I'll just nip over the fence and wash my hands in the water butt. Sit on that crate, you should be comfortable enough on that."

He rushed off and was back in five minutes, while Gladys sat on the crate and rehearsed what she was going to say.

"Darling, you know how I hate to interfere in any of my children's business, but a little bird has told me that you are thinking of marrying a girl that you have met at the village hall dance?"

"Yes, Mum, her name is Irene. I haven't brought her home to meet the family yet because I've been busy getting this place ready, so that when we're married we can move in."

"This is why I wanted to talk to you, darling. Do eat that apple, Eddie, before you eat the gateau.

I'm afraid that your father has not been entirely honest with you. He has given you the impression that this will be your bungalow when it's finished. As you know, Caitlin and Larry will need somewhere to live when they're married because the house that they were going to have in Nutmeg Avenue has fallen through."

Eddie's face had been getting redder and redder as he listened to his mother's words. The bastard, the effing bloody bastard, he'd been working on this place for months and now it was being taken away!

"Where is he, Mother?" he asked in a dangerously calm voice.

"Who dear?"

"My father, of course. I'll bloody well swing for him. I've worked on this place in all my free time, given up going out with my mates, only seen Irene on Saturday nights and here he is saying I'm not getting it!"

"I think I would calm down if I were you, Eddie. I wouldn't go doing anything hasty. I know it has come as a shock to you, but your father is allowed to do whatever he likes with his land and property and remember you only work for him. Nothing will be yours until he dies."

"The way I'm feeling, Mum, I could choke the life out of him. But you're right, all of this is his anyway. I'll go and speak to him straight away, because I'm not doing another hands tap for him again."

"Just be careful what you say to him, darling, he's not in the greatest of moods at the moment, I'm not sure why. Something to do with that appointment he had a while back with the bank manager. Did I tell you that your father is putting a house in my name? Well, it was going to be a pair of semi's in my name, but your father has decided to sell one of them and raise some money for Caitlin's wedding."

"Bully for Caitlin. I bet he won't do anything for me and Irene."

"I'm sure he won't, dear. You'll have to make do with a civil wedding if you marry a Protestant and I'm sure you won't want that to happen, will you, Son?"

There was no answer from Eddie. He had shot off out of the bungalow and left Gladys to clear up the picnic.

J.C. was locking up his car on the driveway as Eddie ran through the gates and caught him by the shoulder. His father looked in surprise at his son's belligerent face, then brushed his hand away resignedly.

"Someone's told you then," he sighed. "What can a man do, when it comes to keeping his head up high in the community? I promised the girl somewhere to live and the bungalow will have to do."

"Have to do?" snarled Eddie. "You've loads of property you could put them in. Why pick the one that I've worked on since the footings? Let me tell you, Dad, if you give that bungalow to Caitlin, you and me are finished. I'll walk out of here and you'll never see me again."

"Hah, brave talk from a young whippersnapper, who's relied on me since he's been dirtying his cloths. I'll find you another plot of land and you can start building something else and be damn grateful I'm letting you."

"What!" Eddie exploded. "So you can give the next one away to Sheena or Rosalind? I don't think so. What do you take me for, I didn't come down in the last shower. No, I keep that bungalow or I'm out of here and, like I said, you'll never see me again."

"Go and pack your suitcase then, Son, because you're *not* having the bungalow, do you hear?"

"Johnny!" cried Gladys as she ran into the garden where her husband and son were having their row. "Eddie is not leaving this house! It's his home and you must settle your differences man to man, both of you. Now come into the kitchen and I'll make you both a nice cup of tea."

"No, Mum, I'm going. I'll not spend one more night under the roof of a man who could swindle his own flesh and blood. I'll find somewhere to stay and I'll find it easy enough to find a job in the building industry. Seeing as Dad has given me such a good apprenticeship."

Eddie ran swiftly up to his bedroom and packed a few things into the suitcase that was on top of his wardrobe. He had no idea where he was going, but it would be many miles from there.

CHAPTER THREE

"Good afternoon, I hope you don't mind me calling, but this is where Irene Wilson lives, isn't it?"

Eddie stood on the doorstep of Irene's aunt's bungalow feeling very dejected after the row with his father earlier.

"Why yes, though Irene isn't here because she's working today. Can I help you?"

"I'm Eddie Dockerty, her intended. Would you allow me to come in and wait for her if it's not too much trouble, as it looks as if it's going to rain?"

"Oh, Mr Dockerty, Irene has told me such a lot about you, I was hoping that we would meet one day. Do come in and I'll put the kettle on. Go through into the parlour, I've got a fire in there."

Aunt Miriam led the way down the tiny hallway and showed Eddie into a neat and tidy room, though it was cluttered with furniture and nick-nacks. She pointed to an overstuffed horsehair sofa, where he sat waiting for his hostess, still with his suitcase in his hand.

"Chilly day seeing it's almost June, isn't it?"Aunt Miriam said chattily, bustling back into the room a few minutes later."I've put the kettle on, but the gas seems to be very low at the moment, so it could be a while before I make the tea. Are you going somewhere, Mr Dockerty? I see you have a suitcase with you, would you like me to place it in the hall?"

"That would be very kind," Eddie replied, though he went ahead of her, carrying the suitcase himself as the lady looked quite frail. She was a tiny person with her white hair pulled back under a Chinese-looking hat, wearing a black ankle-length dress with a long floral pinny and black pointed slippers with pompoms on the toes.

"That's why I've come to see Irene," he said, after settling himself back onto the sofa, while Aunt Miriam fluttered in the doorway.

"I'm going away and we usually see each other at the dance on Saturday nights, so I wanted to let her know."

"Are you going on a holiday, Mr Dockerty? It's a very nice time of the year for a holiday usually, but perhaps the weather will perk up once you go."

"No, I'm not going on a holiday, I'm going to Liverpool to look for work. My father and I have had a falling out and I've decided to seek my fortune elsewhere. It means I'll only be able to see Irene now and again, so I've come to tell her that."

"Tell me to mind my own business if you want to, Mr Dockerty, but would this have anything to do with the fact that you and Irene are different religions?"

"Partly that, but no it's a bit more complicated and perhaps it's time I flew the nest. Stood on my own two feet as it were."

"Ah, I hear the kettle singing. I'll go and make us a nice cup of tea and perhaps you'll relax a little, my dear."

J.C. sat in his chair amongst the opulent furnishings of his sitting room. His leg was hurting and his breathing was laboured. He took a small sip of the whisky that he had poured himself a few minutes before. What an insolent young pup that son of his was, he thought wryly, though really Eddie was a chip off the old block. J.C. had been the same with his father all those years ago. Wouldn't listen to anything that his parents had said. He'd gone against their wishes and married his childhood sweetheart, the lovely Rosalind, who was the illegitimate daughter of his Aunt Maggie and her lover Johnny. His action had caused a family rift that hadn't been repaired until years later.

J.C. had been brought up with Rosalind. At one time he had thought that she was his sister, as he had lots of sisters younger than him. The pair of them had rough and tumbled together in the open fields that surrounded Redstone House at the bottom of Mill Hill Road, but curiously she always disappeared from their home for a few of the summer months. A lady would come and collect her, then bring her back at the start of the next school term. When he'd grown older, Rosalind told him that her mother owned a big business in Neston and she came twice a year from Ireland to put her finances in order. In the intervening time, Rosalind lived in a place called Killala, where she was allowed to run wild on the headland there.

At the age of sixteen, Rosalind was an attractive young woman with shoulder-length, curly auburn hair, a curvy body and hazel eyes that always seemed to be twinkling with mischief. J.C. was smitten with her and at the age of nineteen years, he had all the stirrings in his body of a young man wanting to fall in love. That year she had told the family that she wouldn't be coming back to England again that summer, as her father had died and her mother was now on her own.

J.C. had missed her presence so much that he had asked his father if he could follow Rosalind to Ireland and that was when the truth came out. A closely guarded skeleton in the Dockerty family cupboard.

His Aunt Maggie had given birth to Rosalind while she was still married to her husband, then had run away to be with Johnny, her sea-going lover, leaving the business in the hands of Michael, her son. Eddie and Hannah, J.C.'s parents, had been forced to leave their home at Selwyn Lodge and start a business of their own. Rosalind had stayed as part of the family to get an education in England, as Ireland was still in turmoil after the famine had caused havoc in that cruelly mistreated land. J.C. had been told not to embroil himself with the Irish branch of the family. Yes, they'd treated Rosalind as one of their own, but they wanted a better marriage for their son.

"But I love Rosalind," J.C. had cried with certainty. "She's the only girl I will ever love and I want to go over to Ireland to marry her. It's not her fault that her parents lived in sin and it's not as if I'm related to her."

His father had said be it on his own head, so J.C. had travelled to Killala. He married his sweetheart in the local Catholic church and stayed on to work as a stonemason.

But no children came from their union. Though Rosalind conceived many times, the babies were still born or an early miscarriage and it was a great source of sadness and pain to them.

When J.C. was twenty-nine, Maggie, his mother-in-law, passed away and a great deal of problems were caused by her death. Though her Will was straight forward, her son Michael meanly contested it in regards to the residence called Selwyn Lodge. Maggie had left it to Eddie and Hannah, but Michael went to court and unfortunately won. Hannah was given an annual bequest and Rosalind was left possession of the little house in Killala. Johnny, her father, having been drowned at sea.

Then one fateful night, a year after Maggie had passed away, Rosalind had a fatal haemorrhage and lost her life. J.C. was heartbroken and went back to make things up with his family and with the proceeds of Rosalind's cottage he bought himself a terrace house. He went back to work for his father, but Eddie was getting old and the business was being run successfully by his other three sons. J.C. was resented, the prodigal son had been given the fattened calf, but he managed to get along with them before marrying again and settling down.

His new wife's name was Gladys; a girl of tender years who had trained to be a nurse in her native Wales and had been visiting an aunt, who lived in the village up Mill Hill Road. J.C. was a friend of her aunt's son and love blossomed between them from the start. Well it did on Gladys' part anyway. J.C. was only looking for a wife to replace Rosalind, but he was an attractive man with property, which made him suitable marriage material in Gladys' eyes.

J.C. came back from his memories and lit a cigarette, though he knew he would be in trouble with Gladys. She hated the smell of smoke in her house and said that it lingered on her furnishings. It couldn't be good for her husband's lungs, if the ash was anything to go by in the saucer he used. He wanted to be careful, he wasn't getting any younger and if he wasn't careful they'd be burying him in a couple of years.

Nag, nag, nag. He didn't have that problem when he went to visit Alice in the little house in Queensferry. She had bought some pretty ashtrays made out of bone china painted in pink and white and had them dotted around her living room so that he would always have one to hand. And he never had any problems with back chat from his son who lived in the house with her. Stanley was only twelve, but he had the most impeccable manners. He didn't know that J.C. was his father, of course. The lad thought he was an uncle and that his father had died just after the War. That was the story that Alice had invented. She was a widow of a soldier who had been gassed while serving in the Great War and J.C. was kindly Uncle John, who had helped them in their hour of need.

Irene's eyes widened with horror when she heard Eddie's story later that day. She had been surprised to see him when she walked through the hallway of her aunty's bungalow and saw him chewing on one of her aunty's homemade scones.

"So has your father thrown you out then? Is there no possibility of you making friends with him again?"

"No, Irene, he's got to learn that he can't treat me in the way he has. That bungalow was for me and you. I hadn't told you as I wanted it to be a surprise, but now it looks as if we'll be living in a couple of rented rooms."

"Oh we've plenty of time to save up for something better than a couple of rented rooms, Eddie. You probably wouldn't get permission to marry anyway now, so we've still got a couple of years."

"That isn't the point, Irene. It's going to be hard to find a job when I say that I'm the son of J.C. Dockerty. Everyone knows him on the Wirral and they won't give a job to someone who's had a falling out with him. I'll have to find something different I suppose, unless I move to Liverpool, but I'd be paying most of my wages out on somewhere decent to rent."

"I'd say you could stay here with us," Aunty Miriam piped up, who was listening from the doorway whilst she waited for the kettle to boil to make Irene a cup of tea. "But it isn't done to have two young people living under the same roof and really we wouldn't have the room once Jenny moves in."

"You're okay. I've got a mate who lives in Chester who can put me up until I find a job, but I'll need to get off now to see him soon. Irene, we won't be able to go dancing tonight."

"I've just had a thought, Eddie. Listen to this, Aunty. What if we ask my parents if he can go and live with them? He could have my old room for the time being. I know they need a bit of income with Dad only getting a bit from the N.A.B. and you'd be a Godsend for my mother, Eddie, because she needs some help with the garden now that Dad's losing his sight."

"But I thought Isabel and her husband were living there," said Aunty, looking puzzled at her niece's suggestion. "There won't be any room for your fiancé with the little ones as well."

"Ah, but they won't be there much longer. Mother came into the shop and told me that they'd found a place to rent in Southport, that's where Isabel's new husband comes from and they want to make a fresh start there."

"I couldn't possibly, Irene. I haven't even met your parents, what will they think when I turn up on the doorstep?"

"You didn't know Aunty Miriam either until you turned up here today. I'm sure Aunty will let you stay one night on the sofa and then we can go tomorrow and I'll introduce you."

Irene and Eddie caught the bus from Woodside terminus to Wallasey. They got off on the corner of the dock road and walked up Poulton Bridge Road to Peartree Cottage. It was a four square building made of sandstone and in the small front garden stood the tree that gave the house its name.

Irene's sister answered the door. She looked as if the baby she was expecting was due for arrival at any moment, with her bump in front looking incongruous on her tiny frame. She'd had to wear a big coat for her recent registry office wedding.

"Irene," she said smiling, as she looked beyond her sister and saw she had a young man with her.

"Is this Eddie you've got with you? I wondered when we were going to meet your fiancé, you naughty girl."

"Yes, this is Eddie. Eddie, this is Isabel, my sister. I only told Mother yesterday that I was engaged to be married and she said I was to bring you over straight away. I bet they didn't think I'd be bringing you over so soon, though."

"Who is it, Isabel?" asked a feeble voice from within.

"It's Irene, Dad. She's brought her fiance over to meet us. I'll just go and put the kettle on the hob and I'll make us a cup of tea."

"Hello Papa," said Irene, walking into the rather sparsely furnished room, where her father lay on a sagging blue moquette-covered sofa.

"I've brought Eddie, my intended, to meet you. This is Eddie. Meet my father, Charlie Wilson."

Eddie nodded politely, putting out his hand to grasp the man's in his, whilst feeling sorry for the poor old bugger.

"Is Mother about? I suppose she'll be in the garden, that's where I'd expect her anyway."

"She's out there with Isabel's husband bringing in the new potatoes. This is the first time they've had the opportunity, I could hear the rain lashing on the windows yesterday."

"Poor Papa, is your eyesight no better? Is there nothing more they can do for you? What did the hospital say?"

"Stop worrying over it Irene, what will be will be. Eddie, come over and sit by me. I've still a little sight left enough to take a good look at my future son-to-be."

"Pleased to meet you, Sir," said Eddie, sitting down beside the man and staring into the pale, lined face. "I believe you used to be a sparky, working on those underwater machines."

"Submarines, Eddie. I think that's how I began to lose my eyesight. Being under water for long periods makes a body think they're a mole."

There was a titter of polite laughter from Charlie's daughters and Eddie, but all of them felt compassion for the man.

"And are you going to be old-fashioned, Eddie, and ask me for permission to wed my daughter?"

"Of course, Sir, that's why I'm here today to ask for your daughter's hand."

"I'm sure whoever our Irene falls in love with will make her happy. She's a practical girl with a good head on her shoulders and won't have chosen the first man who came along. Come here both of you and let me give you my blessing."

He took both their hands in his and gave them a wry smile.

The couple looked upon him sadly. Though Eddie had never seen him before, the man seemed to be wasting away. He'd heard from Irene that Charlie had never been robust after having spent a long time underwater marooned in a submarine, when the propeller had got stuck in a sand bank out in Liverpool Bay. It was a wonder the man was still living as he took huge gulps of breath and turned his head fretfully towards the open window. Though the day was fairly mild, the room was rather chilly, not helped at all by the miserable fire in the fireplace.

"Can I get you a blanket, Papa?" asked Irene, perturbed by the racking coughing spell that had followed his gulping and the thinness of his features since she had seen him last.

"If you would, Irene. I don't seem to be able to get warm nowadays."

"Sit down, Irene, I'll go and get him one," said Isabel, who had brought in a tray. "You and Eddie drink the tea I've made you. There's a blanket in the lobby that I can fetch him."

A noise from the back kitchen made Eddie and Irene prick up their ears.

"It's your mother coming in with Robert," gasped Charlie. "Don't tell her that I've had a coughing fit or she'll have me taken to hospital. I had to sleep down here last night because I was keeping her awake with my breathing."

"We won't say anything, Papa," Irene promised sadly. "But maybe you should be in hospital after all."

Lily Wilson, a woman in her late fifties, came stomping through to the living room in an old pair of men's socks, with a grubby blue mackintosh over her ankle length dress. She still had a floppy woollen hat on over her grey tangled hair and she looked askance when she saw she had visitors.

"Irene," she said. "Why didn't you tell me you were coming today? I only saw you yesterday, you could have told me then."

"I thought I'd bring over my fiancé to meet you, Mother. This is Eddie."

"Caught me on the hop, haven't you? It would have been far better if you had told me yesterday and then I could have got something in."

"We've got a seed cake that I baked yesterday, Mother, and a batch of scones that I made this morning."

"Yes, Isabel, I know that," Lily snapped. "But I'm sure Mr Dockerty is used to something a little grander, with him coming from a better class of family."

"Mother!" said Irene, feeling uncomfortable with her mother's attitude towards Eddie, though understanding as she knew that Lily herself had been born into a well-to-do family.

"I'm sure I didn't come here to be fed on the fat of the land, Mrs Wilson," said Eddie smiling congenially. "I came to meet my future family and I love to eat seed cake, it's my favourite food."

"Huh,"said Lily, though she began to feel mollified, seeing he was a handsome chap without any airs and graces. "I'll go and get Robert, he's in the garden. I've got to get those potatoes in while there's a bit of sun around."

"I'm here, Lily," shouted Robert, Isabel's husband, from the kitchen."I'll just bring us a couple of teas in and we'll put our feet up for a little while."

"No time for putting our feet up, Robert. Get in here and meet Irene's fiancé and then we'll get back to it, shall we?"

Robert came into the room. A big strong man, whilst Isabel was little and normally dainty. He had to duck to walk under the lintel before he greeted Eddie with a ready smile.

"Slave driver your mother," he said to Irene. "Has me working from dawn to sunset, all day and every day."

"Rubbish," snorted Lily. "I was up at six this morning, while you were turning over in your comfy bed."

"Mother, before you go back to the garden, can I ask you and Dad something?"

Irene wanted the question of Eddie's accommodation sorted, before her mother got stuck into the garden again.

"Yes?" Lily asked, one eyebrow raised in question. "What is it, you're not in the family way?"

"Lily," tutted Charlie reproachfully. "There's no need to take that tone, she's been a good daughter."

"I'm only asking because she wouldn't be the first daughter to tell me that she was expecting." She looked meaningfully at Isabel, who was expecting her third child.

"I wanted to ask you if Eddie could move in here with you? He's had a falling out with his father and wants to find some work locally. It will only be until his father says he's sorry for the way he's treated Eddie, but I thought he could have my old room, especially with Isabel and Robert moving soon."

"Well, I don't know," said Lily, pretending to consider the situation, but ready to jump at the chance of another strong muscled body. "It must have been a big row for your father to throw you out, Eddie."

"It wasn't a big row, Mother. It was a misunderstanding, which I'm sure Mr Dockerty will apologise for when he's thought it through."

"He didn't throw me out, Mrs Wilson," said Eddie quietly. "I walked out because he had made a promise, then didn't keep it. A man's word is his bond as far as I'm concerned."

"Very well, you can move in with us, but Irene you'll stay put at your Aunty's. I'm not having people thinking I'm running a bawdy house with all the comings and goings here."

"Shall I help Isabel with making afternoon tea then, Mother?"

Irene felt so relieved she wanted to kiss her stony-faced mother, but knew that the physical contact wouldn't be welcome. Mother kept everyone at arm's length if she could.

"Of course you can, Irene. Eddie can sit and keep your father company. Robert, two more of those trenches will do it, then I think I'll set up my stall again on Monday."

Irene stood behind the clock and watch counter at the Co-op, looking with pleasure at the little 'wigwag' clocks she had been allowed to order. They were charming time pieces. Each clock face had it's own character; a smiling clown, a marionette, a Cheshire cat or a leaping frog and underneath set in a small casing was a pendulum that merrily swung from side to side like a happy dog wagging its tail. The supervisor, an old man in his sixties, had told her that they wouldn't sell, but had given in to pleas of ordering some to prove to Irene how wrong she was. But the box she had just opened was the third in three weeks to be delivered, they had been selling like hot cakes at one pound, six shillings and nine pence.

It was only ten minutes away from her lunch break and Irene planned to eat her canteen meal of fried fish and mashed potatoes as quickly as she could, then amble around the market to look for a present for Isabel's new baby. Isabel had given birth to a daughter only days after she and her husband had moved into the rented house in Southport. Eddie and Irene were planning to visit that weekend.

The ping of the lift signalled that it had stopped at the first floor and a lady who looked to be in her late forties walked along to Irene's counter. She began to look into the display cabinet where Irene had placed a small array of wristlet watches on a satin covered tray. The lady was very smart in a blue, lightweight, ankle-length dress, a matching long-sleeve jacket, white cotton wrist-length gloves, white high heel pumps and a matching handbag. Her short shingled hair was pushed under a white crocheted hat.

Irene cleared her throat nervously. This was a woman who looked as if she was used to having the very best of everything, but the wristlet watches were eighteen carat gold, so Irene thought it would be helpful to point that out.

"Excuse me, Madam, may I help you? Those wristlet watches are the very latest from London, eighteen carat gold and very expensive, naturally. Would you like to try one on, Madam?"

"I haven't actually come to purchase a watch, young lady," the woman replied haughtily, her face grimacing in distaste as she looked at the shop girl before her.

"I've been told that Irene Wilson works on this floor and I would like to give a message to her."

"I'm Irene Wilson, Madam," Irene said, wondering who this elegant woman was, though it was beginning to dawn on her who she might be.

"I believe you may be able to get a message to my son. I'm Mrs Dockerty. Could you please tell Eddie that his father is ill and it's imperative that he comes back home to be with him. Thank you Miss Wilson." With that Irene's future mother-in-law walked back to wait for the lift.

She was left with a feeling of disbelief. What an arrogant woman. She had known that Irene was Eddie's intended, but she couldn't even be bothered to make some kind of effort towards her.

Irene, who was always slow to anger, felt her face begin to go hot and her body trembled with emotion. Give Eddie a message indeed. Who did his mother think she was, a telegraph woman?

It spoilt her day. The pleasure she'd had when she saw that her wigwags were selling and picking out a present for the baby didn't make up for the distress she felt by meeting Eddie's mother in the way she had. She was still feeling bitter as she climbed onto the bus that evening to Wallasey. No one deserved that kind of treatment just because she was the girlfriend of her son.

Eddie wasn't in when she got back to Peartree Cottage. No one was at home, but her mother had left a note on the kitchen table saying that her Dad had been rushed into hospital, as he couldn't get his breath. All thoughts of the sour-faced woman flew out of Irene's head as she ran the mile and a half to Victoria Hospital, only to find when she got there that her lovely father was dead.

Her mother was inconsolable. She babbled inconsequentially of how she had never loved him enough, how she hadn't really wanted to marry him because she had been in love with somebody else. Irene put it down to the grief that mother was feeling, after watching her terrified husband trying to get air into his lungs. She brought her mother back home in a taxi, which both could ill afford.

Eddie was waiting for them on their return, neatly scrubbed from his ablutions in the water butt outside. Peartree Cottage had neither bathroom, gas or electricity and kettles had to be boiled on the kitchen fire if anyone wanted a wash. He had known something was wrong because he had seen Lily's note when he had got in from work. He couldn't read the note because Eddie couldn't read, having spent a lot of time as a truant in his childhood, but he knew the word Irene at the beginning and Mother at the end.

He made the two sobbing women a comforting cup of tea, then set about frying eggs and bacon for everyone's supper. Irene and Lily said they couldn't eat, but Eddie insisted that they ate something, because they would need to keep their strength up over the next few days.

After they had finished their meal and Lily decided she would go to her bedroom, Irene suddenly remembered that she had promised her Aunt Miriam that she would be home on the ten o' clock bus.

"Eddie," she cried. "I can't leave my mother, I won't be able to go to work tomorrow either, but Aunt Miriam will be worrying where I've got to. Oh I wish we had a telephone."

"I'll go if you want and stay at your aunt's tonight, then if you write me a note I'll drop it through the Co-op letterbox on my way to work in the morning. They'll understand why you've not gone in."

"Oh thank you, Eddie, and what shall we do about Isabel, she'll have to be told that Papa has gone?"

"You'll have to send her a letter or maybe we could tell her together when we go over on Sunday."

"I don't know what to do, Eddie. I suppose a letter will be a shock to her, though, so perhaps we'll wait until Sunday. You're such a comfort, Eddie, thanks." She leaned over and gave him a kiss on the cheek.

"Well I suppose I'd better be off then. Strange to be going back to the village and not seeing my parents anymore."

"Eddie, oh Eddie, I'm sorry, I've forgotten to give you a message. Your mother came into the store today and told me to tell you that your father's ill."

"How did my mother know you worked at the Co-op?" asked Eddie, puzzled. "I've never told anyone where you were working or if I had I would have told them it was at the Saltbury's store."

"I don't know how things get round, Eddie, but it was definitely your mother, though I thought she was rather rude."

"No, it's just her way, Irene. My Mum is a lovely person, but she can be like that with people she doesn't know. One day you'll grow to love her like I do, I'm sure."

Mmm, thought Irene. *His mother is all fur coat and no knickers as far as I'm concerned.*

Eddie set off to travel to Aunt Miriam's by walking along the roads to Woodside Terminus, as it was light enough to see in the middle of July. He wanted to have some time to think about his mother's message. It must be his father's ticker that was giving him trouble: too many fags, too much alcohol and not enough exercise. His father never walked anywhere, everywhere he went was by car. How would the old man receive him if he turned up just for a visit? Probably throw something at him for leaving him in the lurch.

Eddie had got himself a job at a scrap metal merchants. The boss, Gerry Fielden, put him in charge of the float money. Two other men went ahead of the scrap wagon knocking on doors to drum up trade. Then Eddie would appear and pay the housewife for her rags, or her old dolly tub, copper boiler or mangle, paying as much as five shillings for a mangle because in some of the better off areas they were very much in demand. At the end of the day, the scrap metal and rags were weighed in the yard and each man then received their pay. The work took Eddie around the posher areas of the Wirral and sometimes he went through the Mersey tunnel to Liverpool.

He missed the familiar tinkle of trowels, though, the sound he'd grown up with since he was a boy. Sometimes if he passed a building site, he would stop the wagon and watch the brickies at their work. Maybe he'd been hasty, should he give it another go, perhaps his father was sorry and he'd move back home again?

By the time he'd caught the Heswall bus, Eddie had made his mind up. He would move back into his parents' home if they gave him permission to marry Irene. If not, they wouldn't have a son and heir, because he wasn't going to give up his girl.

CHAPTER FOUR

Eddie didn't turn up to his parent's house until Saturday afternoon, by which time his mother was beginning to think that the dratted girl hadn't passed on her message, but Eddie had to be there for Irene and her mother. He had taken Friday off work after staying over at Aunt Miriam's home, delivered Irene's note to the Co-op, then made his apologies to Gerry Fielden saying he had to take time off for family reasons.

After checking on Irene, he then went to the Funeral Directors to make arrangements for Charlie's burial. Neither of the two women felt up to doing that. Irene was heartbroken at losing her Papa and spent the day with her mother talking over old times.

Irene remembered how, as a little girl she would climb into one of the pear trees that they grew in the orchard. The sturdy branches had become a refuge from when her mother or sister wanted her to run a message up to the nearest shop, or worse still want to brush her long hair and twist it into ringlets. Papa always knew where she would be though and would creep stealthily under the trees, then catch her unawares. When she was a teenager he made her a bench to sit on, and on many a fine weekend in the late Spring she would do her sewing, watching the pear blossom blowing about as if it was snow.

She remembered how distressed her father had been when he was made redundant from Cammel Laird shipyard and he could no longer afford her school fees. It was if he had diminished in front of her eyes as man of the house and provider. His wife's tone got sharper and she'd had to sell her garden produce from a stall on the dock road outside. That was when Charlie Wilson's health started to go downhill, the shock of losing his employment brought his illness to the fore.

Around two o' clock on Saturday afternoon, when Eddie had

made sure that there was nothing more he could do for the bereaved women, he caught the bus to Whaley Lane, which was just around the corner from his parent's home.

Gladys was sitting in the morning room, which looked over a patio and a small pond in the large back garden. She was reading a fashion magazine wondering what style of outfit she was going to wear at Caitlin's wedding and whether she should wear pale blue, which was her favourite colour, or lilac, which was quite a modern shade.

Ellen, the maid of all work, met Eddie in the hallway.

"I've just put the kettle on, Eddie, shall I bring yer in a cup of tea?"

Her tone was as if he hadn't been away for more than an hour or so. She nodded in the direction of the morning room and then pointed up to the ceiling with an exaggerated sigh.

"Himself's poorly, have yer come to see him then?"

"That will be all, Ellen," said Gladys, after she heard her maid talking to someone and had walked into the hallway to see who had come to call. She looked delighted when she saw her eldest son.

"Darling, you've come back home again. Isn't it strange that I told Ellen only yesterday to make up your bed again? Come into the morning room and let me have a proper look at you. Where have you been, you silly boy?"

"It's only a flying visit, Mum, sorry. I've got to get back to Wallasey, Irene's father died the other day."

"You mean you're living at this young woman's house?" said his mother aghast, ignoring the mention of Irene's father having passed on. "Such impropriety, Eddie, I never thought it of one of my sons."

"We're not living together, Mother," he answered sharply. "Irene stays at her aunt's in Seaview Lane, I've been living with her Mum and Dad."

"Oh, well never mind, you'll be coming back to live here soon, won't you, Eddie? Now that your father's ill you must come back and see that the business is running properly."

"I'm only coming back if I get permission to marry Irene, otherwise one of my brothers will have to do the overseeing. Terry or Mickey will have to do."

"No, no Eddie. Your brothers are far too young to have such responsibility. No, it must be you and I'm sure your father will agree with me."

"Here's your tea, Eddie," said Ellen, her ears flapping as she brought in a silver tray with a china cup and saucer. "Coming back to stay are yer? Missed yer while you've been away."

"Seeing as the kettle has boiled you can make me a cup of coffee, Ellen, then get back to whatever you were doing before Eddie came."

His mother raised her eyebrows upwards and shrugged her shoulders.

"What can you do? Are you going to see your father now that you're here?"

"I suppose I'd better. Shall I go up on my own or will you come too?"

"No, you go darling, it's probably better that way."

Eddie drank his tea, then bounded up the stairs two at a time. His father sat in his bed hunched up on a pile of pillows, his breathing sounded harsh and his face was red and blotchy.

"So you're back then?" he growled, as Eddie put his head around the door. "Come to say you're sorry now your daddy's at death's door?"

"That bad is it?" said Eddie lightheartedly. "I thought you might be skiving, taken to your bed for a few days."

"Always the joker. Anyway it's yer mother that wants yer back. She misses you, it's not me."

"Oh, so you're quite happy to let the business fall around your ears, while you sit in bed letting it happen?"

"I agree Terry and Mickey have no experience in dealing with the men, but seeing as you've made the effort, it looks to me as if yer want to come back again. If yer do, though, it's on my terms. I'll not give you permission to marry, as far as I'm concerned you're far too young."

"But not too young to be running your business for you?"

"You're quite the clever dick, aren't yer son? This is just a bout of indigestion I've got 'cos of that bloody Ellen and her cooking. Doctor's told me to rest in bed and lay off the cigs and whisky, so I'll be right as rain in a couple of days."

"Fine, then it looks as if you don't need me."

Eddie went back down the stairs again.

"Still in a grumpy mood, is he?" asked Gladys when her son returned to the morning room. "Look, Eddie, I've had a word with the doctor and he thinks your dad is troubled with his heart. He wants to have him in hospital for tests, but your father won't hear of it. Your father really needs you here, but of course he'll never say."

"I told him I won't be coming back to work for him, unless he gives me permission to marry Irene."

"Oh darling, you both can be so stubborn. You've eighteen months to go before you're twenty-one, then we can't stop you marrying this shop girl. Come back home. Do it for me and then we'll see what happens. Please, Eddie, I've got Caitlin's wedding to see to and I really don't want the family disunited at this moment in time."

Eddie looked around at the spacious room with its elegant furnishings and the French windows that looked out onto the lovely garden and its little pond, then thought about Peartree Cottage with it's sparse interior, lack of facilities and the problems of keeping the place warm. It would be good to get back to some home comforts, even if Ellen's cooking left a lot to be desired. Irene could move back from her aunty's to keep her mother company and they could have a proper courtship from then on.

It was like living a nightmare for Irene after her father's funeral. Her mother would not be consoled and wandered around the house in a daze, whilst Irene did her best to comfort her. Eddie had left the day after he and Irene had gone to Southport to break the news to Isabel, so it was hard being left alone with Lily, who constantly cried that she hadn't loved her husband enough and that he would still be there if she had.

Irene was worried. She didn't want to leave her mother on her own, but the Co-op would be expecting her back as soon as possible and she wasn't getting any pay. Her mother took no interest in her garden, though the Victoria plums were falling off the trees and the cabbages were beginning to bolt in the ground. She wouldn't be cajoled into manning her produce stall outside the front gate, even if Irene were to offer her a hand. It was Eddie who came up with the solution. Why not take in lodgers again? Put an advert in the local shop and hopefully that would bring in a much needed income for the old dear.

And he had been right, for within a few days a local man with Irish relatives who visited Wallasey for a few weeks every year, answered the card that had been placed in the shop window. He was looking for somewhere for them to stay, as his cottage was too small to accommodate them.

The Kelly family consisted of mother, father and Kathleen their daughter. They were a lovely, happy trio, who brightened up the days of the two grieving women while they were there. Kathleen borrowed Irene's old tap dance shoes and Mr Kelly played the fiddle, and evenings were spent watching the young girl perform Irish jigs or listening to old Irish melodies.

Eddie, meantime, had begun to take over some of the responsibility of running his father's firm, though he found it rather difficult because J.C. still had his fingers in many pies. There was a lot of bitterness between them still, especially when Eddie attended the lavish wedding of Caitlin and Larry, then had to watch as the couple moved into the bungalow that should have been his.

One morning Eddie was eating his breakfast in the kitchen, when J.C. staggered down the stairs.

"You'll have to lay the men off on Friday," he said, pinching a piece of his son's toast, as Eddie sat munching on his breakfast. "I've a bit of a problem with the bank at the moment, I've spent all night worrying, but I can't see any other way."

"What kind of problem, Dad? Cash flow problems? I thought those rents that you got from town covered the workforce's pay."

"It's none of your business really, son. Just do as I say and tell the men we'll get in touch when we start the building again."

"I think it is my business if I have to go and tell them. I know there's a bit of a slump on in the trade, but I was under the impression you could weather it with all the rents you're getting in."

"I've had a lot of expenses what with Caitlin's wedding and our Sheena's walking out with Harry Bennett now, so she'll be looking for a big wedding before long."

"And a bungalow no doubt, but don't expect me to build it for them."

"Cheeky sod. Think of all the experience yer got in building that one. Anyway I've got to see the bank manager again today, so let's hope he's got some better news."

To cheer Irene, Eddie decided to take her to the Argyle Theatre. He couldn't afford the best seats, because his dad was back to paying him three half crowns again, so they made do with the nine penny seats in the gallery.

The first act was Max Wall, a young comedian who had the audience rolling in the aisles, then Tubby Turner whose act was wrestling with a deck chair, and a singer named Donald Peers, who was billed as the Laughing Cavalier. His songs were very catchy, especially the one that became his signature tune, 'By a babbling brook.'

Eddie took Irene to the Blackpool Supper Bar on Conway Street and treated her to a plate of fish and chips.

They waited by the Wallasey bus stop later and Eddie moaned about how nothing had changed in the Dockerty household since he decided to go back again.

"There's Caitlin and Larry lording it up in that bungalow, Dad's still an old cuss, Mother's spending money like it's going out of fashion and here I am, still only seeing you once a week like I did before."

"I know, Eddie, I thought things would have changed for the better when you went back there. I wish we could get married, then we could live together with mother instead of having all these different lodgers all the time."

"I've been thinking that maybe we could get away one weekend, Irene. Just the two of us in a nice little hotel."

"Oh I don't know about that, Eddie, it sounds a bit naughty. Anyway neither of us could afford to find the money for a hotel bill."

They said goodbye as the Wallasey bus drew up, both reflecting sadly on the situation they were in.

J.C. sat in his bedroom with his head in his hands. It was worse than he had thought. The bank was drawing all his loans in and the houses from which he got his rents were all to be sold. He was told to file for bankruptcy, losing the quarry, the house and all the land that his father, Eddie Dockerty, had acquired the generation before. He glanced at the pills that his doctor had given him. Should he take the lot now with a bottle of whisky and be done with it, or face his family and rescue what he could? It had to be the latter, he was a Catholic wasn't he and didn't want to roast for eternity in a fiery Hell.

J.C. chose a Sunday afternoon to tell his family. He could guarantee that they would all be there because Ellen had the day off and Gladys cooked a roast dinner with the help of Sheena and Rosaleen. They all usually sat around in the sitting room later, the girls to relate a bit of gossip and the lads to discuss football and who was going to win the Cup.

J.C. cleared his throat nervously, looking over at Gladys who was resting her legs on an upholstered stool.

"I've got something to tell you all."

His family looked at him expectantly. Maybe Sheena had announced the date of her wedding, another good do like the last one they hoped.

"I'm afraid I've got to file for bankruptcy."

He could feel the heat of his body pouring into his brain as he said it and through the mist that seemed to envelop him causing his eyes to fill with tears, he saw the shocked faces on all of his children. There was a silence for a moment, then Gladys came over with a handkerchief. She stood in front of him while he wiped his face and so his children couldn't see him disgrace himself.

"It's a joke, isn't it, Dad?" said Sam, the youngest, who went through life with his head in the clouds and never worried where his parents got their money from.

"No it isn't, son," answered J.C. morosely. "The slump's affecting all sorts of people and I had a lot of loans that the bank's called in."

"Does that mean that I have to get a job now, Dad?" asked Rosaleen, who had just left the Ladies College in Chester and had a small allowance given to her.

"Yes, Rosie, I'm sorry, but you're very good at flower arrangements, maybe a florist will take you on."

"And I suppose that goes for the rest of us," Eddie put in bitterly. "Us lads will have to scrat around for a living like the rest of the men in the building trade, fighting for anything that we can turn our hand to."

"We could ask Uncle Michael if he'd set us on at Sheldon," said Terry. "Seeing that it was our Great Aunt Maggie that started the company, we're entitled being family."

"Don't even think about it. You're not going cap in hand to that two-timing sod, begging your pardon, Glad."

"He may have a point, though, Johnny. Sheldon Properties will weather the storm like they always have and now Michael's sons are at the helm, surely they would take some of their kin on."

"Gladys! Michael will probably buy everything I owned from the bank at a knock down price. No, they go to work for him over my dead body."

"So when is this all going to happen?" asked Sheena. "I won't be getting my big white wedding then, Dad?"

"No, sorry Princess and your poor mother is going to lose this house, cancel her accounts at all the department stores and probably have to resign from the Rotary Club. Isn't that right Glad?"

His wife nodded at him glumly.

"So where are you going to be living then?" asked Eddie, thinking that he may as well move back to Wallasey, at least he would get a welcome at Irene's home.

"On the corner. I put a semi in your mother's name on the advice of Mr Martin last year. That's where we'll be living. It has three bedrooms, so you lads can sleep in one, the two girls in another and me and your mother in the double room."

"But those houses only have a box room for the third room," wailed Rosaleen. "Sheena and I can't possibly share a bed."

"Then you'll have to find a husband like Sheena has. Sheena, you'll have to push your beau to get wed."

He left his family then and limped back to the bedroom where he lay on his bed in turmoil. The kids would hate him now, though they would soon get over it. It was Glad, his wife, he felt sorry for. She'd gone from rags to riches and would be going back to rags again.

Eddie found his mother in the kitchen later where she was tidying away some of the dinner plates that had been left to drain on the rack.

"You didn't seem surprised, Mum," he said, thinking sadly that out of all of them she was the one who was going to suffer, having to give up this house and the lifestyle she had grown to love.

"I wondered, Eddie, when your father put that house in my name. He never does anything unless there's a reason behind it. That's why you never got your bungalow, because he wanted to play the big man and give it as a wedding gift to Caitlin. I had nothing when I married your father. As you know I was working as a nurse in a cottage hospital near Llangollen and never dreamt that one day I would live in a big house like this one. It's your dad's dreams that have been shattered, losing all that he's built up since his father passed away, and you children who will have a share of nothing. At least the girls will make good marriages, but you lads are going to have to make your own way."

"Oh I can get a job easily enough, don't you worry about me. I was working for a scrap dealer when I lived away before and the bloke would give me my old job back if I asked him to."

"No, Eddie, not a rag and bone man! Surely you could use your expertise in the building trade. With your experience you could easily become a foreman."

"Too young I think, I've only just had my twentieth birthday. Anyway, Mum, you've enough to worry you, so let me do the worrying about my life."

"You're not going to leave me again, are you Eddie? Your dad will need you and the boys to keep the home fires burning. He's too ill to find himself a job, so we'll need all your wages coming in."

Eddie sighed to himself inwardly. Irene and him would never marry the way things were going on.

Irene couldn't help but feel a little smug when she heard of the Dockerty's downfall. What a come down for Gladys, Eddie's mother, having to leave her great big house and slum it in a small semi. Though maybe some good would come out of it. At least now a lowly shop girl would be on an equal footing with them.

Work had started on a flour mill near to the dock road where Irene lived. She told Eddie about it when he came to see her one evening to report that he hadn't found any work. The situation in the building trade was getting worse, no new estates were being built and what little building there was had queues of men like Eddie wanting to be taken on.

He visited the flour mill site the next morning, but the only vacancy they had was for laying drains. "Not a problem," Eddie had told the foreman, his spirits soaring as he felt he'd got the job, but then he was asked if he was in a trade union. Eddie shook his head; his father had never employed union men because he had the fixed idea that they would disrupt the job.

"Sorry," said the elderly chap. "No union card, no job."

It posed a problem for Eddie, as he was fed up with trailing about looking for work on the Wirral and his next port of call would have to be Liverpool. His brothers had taken temporary work in a factory in Bromborough, but Eddie hated the idea of being cooped up inside.

As he walked along the dock road dejectedly, a flash of inspiration came. He'd travel over to Neston and see if his uncle would give him a hand. Not take him on as a workman, no that would surely give his father a heart attack, but maybe the Sheldon work force belonged to a union and he could help him get a card?

Eddie caught the train from Woodside to Neston. Luckily he had the fare, as his mother had given him a little money that morning. Selwyn Lodge, where his uncle lived, was near to St Winefred's, the church that the Dockerty family sometimes attended. Though Eddie had never visited his uncle's home, he certainly knew where it was.

"Yes, Mr Haines is at home," said the maid as she answered Eddie's tentative knock on the front door. "Whom shall I say is calling?"

"My name is Edward Dockerty, would you tell him it's J.C.'s son."

"Certainly, Sir, just a moment." And the maid disappeared down the hallway.

Eddie stepped back to look in appreciation at the old house that belonged to his uncle. He knew the story of the split between his Uncle Michael and Hannah, his grandmother. Sometimes J.C. would bemoan the fact that if Michael hadn't been so greedy, it would have been them that lived at Selwyn Lodge and they would have had all the advantages that Michael's sons had. But maybe his uncle had more of a head for business, thought Eddie disloyally. His father was never thrifty and spent money as it came along.

The maid came back and announced that Mr Haines would see him in the drawing room. With a sigh of relief he followed the woman, glad that his uncle hadn't turned him away. He was shown into a large room that was beautifully furnished and sitting at a mahogany bureau near the window was Maggie's son. A stooped man in his late eighties, white haired with a ruddy complexion and wearing what Eddie knew to be a dark red quilted smoking jacket.

"Well," said Eddie's uncle. "So you're one of J.C. Dockerty's sons. Didn't ever think I'd meet any of Hannah's issue, can't say I blame her for never speaking to me again. All long dead now, my enemies, though I'll probably have to answer to Him upstairs when my time comes. Come over in the light and let me take a look at you. Legs have gone now. Have to use them dreadful sticks or be pushed about like a baby in a damned basket chair."

Eddie walked over with his hand outstretched. His uncle's grip was firm and there was nothing but pleasure in his rheumy eyes when he said he was glad at last to meet with one of his own.

"I'll ring the maid and ask her to bring in some refreshments. Pity you didn't come and visit me last year and you could have met your Aunt Kate before she died."

"It isn't really a social call, Uncle, though I've always wanted to meet you, but my father told us to keep away."

"Yes, I've seen him from time to time at St. Winefred's, but he's always snubbed me and I can't say I blame him in a way. But you're here now. Ah, thank you Mary, I was just going to ring for you. Just leave the pot of tea near Eddie, I'm sure he will pour."

Eddie pulled up an upholstered chair after he had poured the tea, so that he could be on the same level as his uncle, who was sitting on something like a piano stool.

"I'll come straight to the point, Uncle Michael. Dad has had to go bankrupt. It wasn't his fault, but he had taken quite a few loans out and with there being a slump in the building industry the bank has called in his loans. So, my brothers and I have had to take work elsewhere. We've all been apprenticed to father, but now my brothers have decided to take factory work. I've got the chance of working on a flour mill down in Wallasey, but I need to be in a trade union for them to take me on. I wondered if you had a union work force and if there's any chance you could get me a card?"

Michael looked at Eddie for a moment considering the young man's request. He owed the family something, didn't he, and perhaps this was a way that might give his troubled soul some peace?

"You could come and work for Sheldon, Eddie. I'm sure my sons would find a place for you and as we haven't been troubled much by the slump, there'd be plenty of work for your brothers too."

"I don't think my father would be happy with that, Sir, he would see it as being disloyal to the Dockerty name. But if you could see your way to getting me in a union I would be very much obliged."

The old man reached into one of the cubicles in a bureau and brought out a sheet of Sheldon Property headed writing paper. He wrote something at length upon it, then handed it to Eddie with a wry smile.

"It's a pity that is all you're asking me to do for you Eddie, but this letter will see you right with the union branch in Birkenhead."

He reached into the inside pocket of his jacket and pulled out a five pound note.

"And this will help you with expenses until you earn a wage again."

Eddie was over the moon now that he had got his job laying down the drains in the foundations of the flour mill. He was able to go to Irene's house for his evening meal, then walk along later to the bus stop.

One evening in February the snow began to fall with ferocity, just as Eddie was about to take his leave and say goodnight to Irene.

"You can't go home in this, Eddie," she said, looking fearfully at the inch of snow that covered the ground already along the dock road. "They might stop the buses when you get to the terminus or maybe in the morning you won't be able to get into work."

"I don't think they'll expect us in if it continues to fall like this, Irene, but I agree, I might have to walk it home if they stop the buses at Woodside."

"I think you'd better stay over then. You can stay in the spare bedroom, as you know we've no lodgers here at the moment. I'll just ask mother for her permission, but I'm sure she'll agree that you can stay given the circumstances."

Lily agreed reluctantly, but warned that there was to be no shenanigans under her roof.

The couple laughed and agreed there wouldn't be and around about ten they all went to bed.

It was around two o' clock in the morning when Eddie heard a noise coming from the landing. Stealthy footsteps trod on the wooden staircase, then silence as the sound disappeared into the night. He was dying for a pee and felt around under the bed for a chamber pot. There wasn't one, was he to do it out of the window instead? He groaned inwardly, then putting his overcoat on over his vest and long johns, he went down the staircase, intending to go through the kitchen to the outer door and relieve himself in the garden privy.

Irene was sitting in her blue heavy quilted dressing gown by the dying embers of the kitchen fire, as he crept past the back of the sofa that she sat on. He signalled that he was off to the privy and she whispered that she would make him a cup of tea.

Her body was warm as he pressed his shivering one against her later. Her lips were velvety and inviting and he couldn't help himself. Nearly five long years of denial for each other's bodies was long enough. They helped themselves to each other, fulfilling a need that would satisfy until the day they said "I do".

CHAPTER FIVE

Eddie was kept on at the flour mill site after the drains and footings had been completed.

The foreman liked the way he worked, not always looking for breaks from his toil like some did, so Eddie was employed on the brick work later, a job that he really enjoyed.

He would call on Irene each evening after she had returned from work. Lily was now in charge of cooking and a hot meal was what they both needed at the end of the day.

The events of the snowbound night were never repeated, Irene being fearful that she might get pregnant and Eddie wanting to show his respect and regard for his girl.

So it came as a bit of a shock for both of them when Irene didn't get her monthly. Eddie had thought that a girl couldn't get pregnant the first time they had intercourse. Irene knew you could because it had happened to her sister Isabel, but had hoped that lightning wouldn't strike in the family twice. Lily was going to be mortified that it had happened to both her daughters, especially when she had given permission for Eddie to stay that night.

"Oh well, at least your father will give his permission now," said Irene thankfully after she told Eddie that she thought she might be expecting. "Perhaps you could arrange for me to come and visit your family. It will be the first grandchild, won't it, so they're bound to be pleased?"

"Not the first grandchild, Irene, Caitlin gave birth to a daughter the other day. But I know my father, he still won't give his permission even if it means you having the child out of wedlock. He can be stubborn, as you know, and this won't change his mind."

"Oh no," cried Irene, putting her head into her hands as the import of Eddie's words sank in.

"Don't worry," he said, patting her shoulder awkwardly. "I'll be twenty-one by then. It's a good job that you're already over twenty-one, because I couldn't see your mother giving permission for our marriage either."

"Why Eddie, my mother thinks the world of you, at least she's never said anything different to me."

"She resents me, Irene. She's said a few things to me out of your hearing, thinks you should have married some other bloke instead."

"That'll be Evan, he was a distant cousin and he used to walk me home from school. His father's a professor over in Liverpool and when the family first came to the area from Wales, they lived in that old house across the road. When will you tell your family, Eddie? You never know they might change their minds and pay something towards the wedding."

"Don't bank on it, Irene. In fact there might only be me and you there and we'll have to bring our witnesses in off the street!"

J.C. went mad when Eddie told him that Irene was expecting and it brought on another turn, so that he had to take to his bed.

"See what you've done," Gladys said, after the doctor left a little later. "Don't you think we've enough to put up without you going and getting your shop girl pregnant. Don't think we'll give you permission to marry, Eddie, you'll have to wait until you're twenty-one."

"Exactly what my father said not an hour ago, Mother, and so you won't mind if I pack a suitcase again and go to live with my girl."

He'd had it with the lot of them, he thought, as he caught the bus down to Birkenhead. Even Sheena was to have a wedding, though this time it wouldn't be a grand affair. Eddie hoped that Irene had told her mother, because he was banking on her to give him a bed. It would be so easy too to get to work each day, because the flour mill was only across the way.

But Lily wasn't pleased to say the least and they had to endure her scolding for the next couple of days. It was separate rooms and separate beds, though as Eddie said jokingly to Irene, the damage was already done!

A few evenings later, when Lily was doing her rounds outside, checking the greenhouse and the hen house area for predatory rats, Irene asked Eddie when they would be getting married.

"I would have thought your father would have given permission by now, Eddie. Didn't you tell him I'll be nearly six months gone by the time you're twenty one? Why not ask your Mum to sign the papers? She's a woman, surely she'll have some sympathy towards me having to get married with a bump in the front?"

"Mum won't go against my father, Irene, and now I've left home he'll never speak to me again. No, unfortunately you'll have to find a dress that's got a lot of material in it, but will it matter, there won't be anybody to see us get married anyway?"

So Irene had to be content with that and carried on working for the next few months to bring some money in. Though Eddie was working and Lily now manned her produce stall outside again, they always seemed to be on the bread line.

A month before Irene was to give her notice in at work, a young lady stood before her at the clock and watch counter. She was smartly dressed in a calf-length floral summer frock, her dark hair was cut into a short bob and she smiled a little sadly at Irene.

"Are you Irene, Eddie's fiancé?" she asked.

"Yes, who am I speaking to?"

"I'm Sheena, his sister. I've got a message for him from my mother and I wondered if you would pass it on."

"Of course."

"Could you tell him that his mother wants to see him?"

"I can do, but I'm not sure that he'll come and see her. You can see the condition I'm in, can't you, and he's not happy he can't marry me until he's twenty-one."

"Yes, I'm sorry Irene, but my wedding has had to be postponed

59

also. I wanted Eddie to hear this from Mum, but Father passed away in the night."

"Oh," said Irene, wondering whether she should give this girl her condolences. It would be two-faced if she did, but it was only polite to do so after all.

"I'll let Eddie know when I see him this evening. I'm sorry, Sheena, I lost my father last year so I know what you must be going through."

The girl said thank you and turned on her heel to make her way out of the department store. Irene was left feeling disconcerted by her visit, she was going to be related soon after all.

Eddie was shocked and very bitter when Irene gave him the message.

"I could have been there for him if he hadn't have been so cantankerous, helped him with sorting out the finances if he had let me. But no, he had to be the boss, wanted no help from anyone and look what's happened now? Mother a widow, in that poor little house with no income that I know of. Who's going to look after her now that I'm not there?"

"I'm sorry, Eddie, but you have got other brothers who live at home, they'll have to take care of her. You've me and the baby to see to when it comes."

"Yes and that wouldn't have happened if I'd still been working for Dad and not at the flour mill. Once you've had the baby, there'll only be my money coming in."

"Oh so you're saying you wished I hadn't got pregnant and we could have waited another few years before we got married," said Irene defensively. "We'd already been courting for four years, Eddie, if that is what you could call it."

"What do you mean by that?" he said angrily.

"Well, for the first two years we only ever saw each other on a Saturday, that was if you deigned to turn up to the dance at all. You wouldn't come and meet my aunty and it was me who pushed for a proposal of marriage by making you jealous that night."

"Me jealous, never," he blustered. "Anyway, if we're going to start rowing I'm off to my mother's. I'll need to be there to help with arrangements anyway. Perhaps you'll be in a better mood when I come back."

He went to his bedroom and Irene could hear him throwing some things into his suitcase. She went into the kitchen and made herself a cup of tea.

Gladys sat in the small living room at the back of the semi, her face blank as she sat unseeingly and her children sat in silence not knowing what to do. Eddie was a breath of fresh air as he came in through the kitchen door, taking a look at their grieving faces, knowing that he would have to be the one to get them organised if anything was to be done.

"Right," he said. "What's been done up to now? Death certificate, undertaker, is Dad at the hospital or upstairs?"

Caitlin stood up and volunteered the information that their father had been rushed into hospital the night before and that was where his body was. That she had telephoned the undertaker and he was awaiting instructions as to where the burial would be.

"I should imagine he'll be buried at St.Winefred's then, unless anyone has any objections to that?"

His mother stirred herself and said that was what their father had wanted, then lapsed back into her silent state, just staring into space.

"Caitlin, I think you should get Mother upstairs and get her to lie down for a while. Has she had anything to eat or drink? Rosaleen you see to that."

Eddie spent the rest of the evening in charge, then spent the night on the sofa in the living room. It had helped to take away some of the ache of loss that he was feeling for his father.

The family stood in the churchyard a few days later, surrounding the hole where the coffin had been lowered. Eddie held up his grieving mother and the girls wept into their handkerchiefs. Terry nudged Mickey with his elbow.

"Do you see who's over there by the willow tree, Mickey?"

His brother took a quick peek over his shoulder."

"Yes, it's Alice, my old nanny. Wonder why she's bothered coming? I thought she'd had a falling out with my mother and that's why she left."

"Well she must be still nannying 'cos she's got a lad with her. Though he looks a bit too old, you'd think he'd be at school."

Gladys followed her sons' eyes to the woman who stood near the lych gate. *So she'd turned up had she and brought her bastard son with her?* Not entirely unexpected, though Gladys had been too upset to let it worry her. She remembered back to the day when the little tart had told her that she was expecting J.C.'s child. Alice had stood in front of her defiantly, saying that J.C. was going to marry her and they were going to move away. But Gladys knew he wouldn't, not when she, Gladys, had borne him four sons and three daughters, plus he was a Roman Catholic and wouldn't want to burn in Hell. To give J.C. his due, he had supported the child through his solicitor, though what was going to happen now that there was no money in the bank?

Gladys turned back to the proceedings with a sigh, which was taken by the family as a sign of anguish. Little did they know that she was thinking of J.C.'s sins that were now catching him up!

Later, as the family gathered to hear the reading of the Will by the local solicitor, no one was surprised to hear that there was no money left to be shared out. Though they were surprised to hear that a bequest *would* have been left to Alice Meadows and her young son.

Irene was getting worried. There'd been no word from Eddie since he had gone back to be with his family. She had left her employment now and had time to think. What was she going to do if he didn't come back to marry her? Lily said she was sure he'd be back, turn up like a bad penny and make an honest woman of her. Though he'd probably leave it to the last minute, a man would do that sort of thing. So Irene waited, but it wasn't until the middle of July that he turned up full of apologies. He had looked for work nearer his mother's house because he couldn't bear the thought of leaving her on her own.

"But what about your brothers, they're still at home aren't they and Caitlin only lives down the lane?"

Irene felt furious that Eddie had put his mother first and hadn't even told the foreman at the flour mill that he was leaving his employ.

"It's me my mother needs, Irene, she relies on me more than the others. Now are you going to place the banns at the Registry Office, or shall I do it on my way back home?"

Three weeks later Eddie and Irene were married at the Registry Office in Hamilton Square. The witnesses were Sheena and her fiancé Harry, no one else from his family bothered to come. Isabel came from Southport with her baby and Lily put her best hat on to attend, then after the ceremony they celebrated with fish and chips at the Blackpool Supper Bar in Conway Street.

Though when Eddie came to live at Pear Tree Cottage permanently, things began to change between Lily and himself. She began to treat him in a most unfriendly fashion, seemingly resenting that he'd taken her husband's place. Things were made worse because Lily had taken on a new lodger, a cantankerous old fellow for whom nothing was ever right. The couple desperately needed a place of their own, but Irene knew that her mother wouldn't be able to cope. The trio lurched from row to row, with Irene in the middle with divided loyalties. Eddie threatened to leave the lot of them, but he knew he couldn't with a baby on the way.

He had gone back to bricklaying, though his days were long as he could only find a job across the Mersey in Liverpool. He was working on an extension to a telephone exchange in Edge Hill and it was rumoured that the Postmaster General, Sir Kingsley Wood, was coming to lay the foundation stone. Eddie was very curious, as he had never seen that kind of ceremony before.

The men on construction were told to carry on working as the shiny black Daimler swept along the driveway carrying its distinguished passenger. Eddie, though, was determined that he was going to join the privileged few. He had heard that coins and some records would be laid under the stone for posterity. Unfortunately, a reporter and photographer were there from the Liverpool Echo, who snapped a picture of a brickie with his arms around two switchboard girls. Eddie was given his cards the very next day and he didn't get to keep the photo as a souvenir!

Irene was depressed when he told her what had happened; the baby was due in a couple of weeks and she worried a lot over money. It wasn't easy to get a job anymore, unemployment was high as the country hadn't recovered from the slump of the years before. She was annoyed with Eddie that he had disregarded the foreman's instruction.

Eddie landed on his feet, however, when, as he was travelling on the ferry boat the next day to start to look for work again, he spoke with an elderly man with whom he had become friendly on previous journeys. Not knowing what the man did for a living, he happened to mention that he had become unemployed and told him of the Kingsley Wood fiasco. As luck would have it the man was helping to build a new façade on the front of the Littlewood building near the telephone exchange. The job was only for a week or two, but it tided Eddie over until the baby came.

The baby showed signs that it was on its way on a rainy Saturday morning in January. The greengrocer van had just been to deliver a sack of potatoes, as the yield hadn't been very good in the Pear Tree Cottage garden. The bread boy had called to deliver their order, with Lily in two minds whether to get some cakes for Sunday tea, for she was certain the boy was licking the cream off before he handed them over. Irene had cleaned the house from top to bottom over the past few days and was busy emptying a bucket of water into the outside drain, when another stream of water made its presence felt as she stood there.

She called Lily to come quick in her panic, not knowing anything about signs to watch for or twinges that might occur. Lily stood rooted to the spot, while Eddie raced round, grabbing Irene's coat to sling round her shoulders, picking up her previously packed suitcase, then pushing her gently down the front path to the gate. He hailed the first vehicle that came along the dock road. Luckily for Irene it was a chauffeur-driven Bentley, had it been a coal cart she still would have been slung onto it. She was taken to the nursing home where she was booked to have her baby and her little daughter, Gina, made her appearance the next day.

But back home, when Irene should have been resting after giving birth to her baby, she found she was in the middle of a war zone between Eddie and his mother-in-law. They were quarrelling or not speaking alternately over petty things, like who was responsible for the garden, who should order the coal, who should do the heavy shopping, whether a crying child should be picked up or left to cry alone.

Irene felt that her wonderful dream of marital happiness was being shattered and wondered where it would all end.

One Sunday morning, Eddie decided to cheer Irene up and take her and his new daughter to be shown off to the family. The moment had come which Irene had been dreading. She tried to think of a reason why she couldn't go and let Eddie go on his own. She couldn't think of one, so that afternoon she found herself in the front room of Gladys' semi, being stared at rudely by the Dockerty family as a whole.

While Eddie's sisters clucked and cooed over Gina, Irene sat on the sofa, ignored by Gladys and snubbed by his brothers. It was an uncomfortable feeling and one she didn't wish to repeat again. Caitlin, though, was kind, presenting Irene with a baby coat and beret for Gina, which made her feel awkward, because she hadn't thought to buy anything for Caitlin's child.

The conversation between the brothers was either football or the German chancellor, Adolph Hitler. Neither things were of interest to Irene, but she listened politely anyway. It seemed that this man in Germany was a warmonger, who was threatening to roll his tanks into Poland and Czechoslovakia as an act of oppression. Britain's prime minister, Neville Chamberlain, had already come back from a meeting with the German chancellor saying he'd signed a peace treaty, but the brothers reckoned that Chamberlain was an idiot and the Second World War could start any day.

"I'll be the first one to enlist," said Terry. "Anything's better than working in that margarine factory. We'd whip Hitler back into his place within a month or two, they say that the British Army is the best in the world."

"Do you think they'd take me, Terry?" asked Mickey. "I know I'm only sixteen, but I look older than my age. I hate it where I'm working too. Being on that conveyor belt at Cadbury's is so boring. We could sign up together and be in the same regiment."

"So I'll miss it then," said Sam, the youngest, glumly. "But never mind, I'll get to see the Tranmere home matches while you're both away."

The Littlewoods job came to an end and Eddie spent his days traipsing around the building sites of Liverpool. It wasn't long before he found employment on a housing estate that was being built in the Old Roan area, so once again there was money coming into the Pear Tree Cottage household. The weather began to pick up again as an early Spring gladdened hearts and Lily began to spend her time sowing seeds and digging in the potato tubers. Irene spent her time keeping the house clean and walking Gina out in an old pram that somebody had given her. It was a time of peace and although there was widespread unemployment and threatened strikes by those in work, nobody believed that a second war was in the offing. To most people, Germany was a place over the water in a place called Europe and really had nothing to do with Britain at all.

So it came as a bit of a shock to most ordinary people, when the picture houses started showing scenes of this ruddy man called Hitler; goose stepping about with his army and threatening all the countries around him. The newspapers reported that Poland had fallen and soon Czechoslovakia would be governed with military rule.

Who was he? people thought, *what made him think he could take over the world?* The British Army would soon sort him out and give the swine a bloody nose. It was all so far away, though, and most people got on with their lives. It was only time to worry if the sod came over there.

Irene was out shopping one morning and, as she came out of the grocers, she saw a group of people standing together looking up at the sky. She glanced up as well and saw six tiny silver specks high up below the clouds. Someone in the group shouted that they were spotter planes, which caused widespread panic amongst them and they hurriedly dispersed.

Irene's heart thudded against her chest, as she ran as fast as she could with the pram and her shopping down the brow to the cottage, then trembled for the next half hour with thoughts of what was to come. She had only just read that morning in the *Daily Mail* that civilians in the captured countries were being massacred as they fled ahead of the advancing army of Germany and there were harrowing stories of refugees mown down by the aircraft above.

War had been declared on September 3rd and literature had been sent around to each household telling people what to do in the event of an air raid, but somehow it didn't sink in. It wouldn't happen in England, it was too far for a plane to come over from Germany and anyhow there wouldn't be enough fuel in the aircraft to get it over here. It was irritating that they were compelled to buy yards of blackout material for the windows, or affix some paper panels there instead. A typical war-time joke that began to circulate was:

Air Raid Warden: "Hey Missis. You've got a chink up there."

Lady of the house: "Nonsense officer, it's the Japanese ambassador."

A week later, though, as Irene was putting Gina to bed, the wail of the siren frightened everyone rigid as night raiders flew over

Merseyside, dropping bombs in their wake. The noise of the Ack Ack units added to the feeling that their world was going to be blown to pieces, so Eddie, Lily and Irene, who was carrying Gina, stumbled down the cellar steps to take their shelter there.

None of them had thought to provide emergency seating or lighting, there was no food or water and the place smelt of the recently installed gas supply. The cellar housed the coal and logs, a dank, cold place, the only air coming from the ill-fitting lid above the coal chute, and so they shivered together for what seemed hours until the All Clear siren sounded.

They crawled out of the cellar early next morning, as the first flush of daylight mingled with the clear cold air. Thrushes sang high up in the trees of the orchard, whilst the family looked around for damage to their home.

Thankfully there was none, but the bread man who came to call later that day reported that a number of civilians had been killed or wounded in the next street to him. The news on the wireless that evening said that Hitler was reported to be gloating because his Luftwaffe had bombed ports and installations in Britain and it wouldn't be long before the country was brought to its knees.

Eddie came home from his work in Liverpool one evening and announced that he and Irene were going to move to somewhere safer. Pear Tree Cottage was too near the docks for comfort and he had seen the devastation wrought on the city as he had travelled by bus to the housing estate.

Whole rows of buildings had been blown apart, shipping had been sunk in the river, people were homeless, wandering around with their possessions tied up in bundles. There was no way they were staying with Lily when they had a child to rear.

"So what am I supposed to do then?" asked Lily, bitterly. "Stay here and get blown up or catch pneumonia in the cellar?"

"I've thought of that too, you can go and stay with Isabel. Southport will be very bracing at this time of year and she'll probably need a bit of help with the children now she's got three of them."

Deep down Eddie was happy to use the excuse of the bombing to get away from his mother-in-law. He'd be back in familiar surroundings if they moved back to Irby. He was sure that Aunt Miriam would make room for them at her bungalow and he'd be nearer to his mother as well. He missed his mum. Even though he and Irene now visited each Sunday afternoon, it wasn't the same with his wife itching to be away again.

They left the following afternoon, Irene putting Lily on the ferryboat first, with her suitcase packed full of her clothes and any little ornaments that she could fit in. Lily wailed that her vegetables would rot in the ground and what a waste of all that time she'd spent with the planting, she was going to miss her rose bushes and who was going to pick the fruit from the trees? But before they'd left they'd had a visit from the landlord, he had wanted two months rent in lieu of notice before he would allow them to go.

Eddie had been out trying to get the loan of a handcart from somewhere when the landlord arrived, worried over his livelihood as he saw a mass exodus of his tenants trying to flee from the troubles ahead. He wasn't going to have one put over him by the widow who lived in Pear Tree Cottage and two months rent would tide him over nicely for the next week or so.

Lily had sat in the parlour frightened and intimidated by the pompous individual pontificating about his rights. She needed her money to get over to Southport and wanted to give Isabel a bit of housekeeping, as it didn't seem right for her to be an extra mouth to feed. Irene listened from the kitchen, where she was packing up some boxes with pots and pans, dishes, tableware and tea towels. It made her blood boil to hear the man having a go at her mother. Though Irene was usually even tempered, the stress of the air raids and sleepless nights were beginning to take its toll. She flew into the parlour and told the man to leave her mother alone.

"I don't know who's worse," she shouted angrily. "Hitler, who's responsible for driving decent folks from their homes, or you, whose only concern is making money for yourself. Have you no sympathy for someone like my mother who's lived in this house for thirty odd years and now has to leave it? Who has paid you on the nail all this time and never been in arrears. Have you no humanity for your fellow being? Shame on you and as for rights, we've all got the right to live in a peaceful world."

The man had sat there stunned by this young woman's outburst, then rose from his seat in defeat, though he reminded the two women that when the war was over, he wouldn't be allowing them back.

Irene caught the bus to Irby with Gina later, leaving poor Eddie the task of dealing with their smaller possessions. He couldn't get a handcart for love nor money and was left to pile the old pram up with as much as he could, then push it all the way to Aunt Miriam's, which was ten miles away. He decided that he would have to hire a van from somewhere to move the furniture, though where he was going to store the beds, the wardrobes, sofa, the chairs and tables and Lily's precious ebony cabinet and piano, he hadn't got a clue. Something would come up, it usually did and in that optimistic frame of mind he set off for Aunt Miriam's bungalow.

He trundled across the Penny Bridge, cut along by Birkenhead Park and was pushing the pram over Oxton Ridge, when an authoritative voice rang out through the stillness of the gloomy night and made Eddie jump with surprise.

"Hey you," the male voice shouted. "You can't go that way, an unexploded bomb's over in that woodland and it could go off any minute."

Eddie took a few seconds to reply. He couldn't see the speaker, though presumed it was someone from the Home Guard, but he wondered if it was a wind up, why hadn't the man appeared? He decided to take his chances, it was bad enough having to push the pram without looking for a diversion. It had started to sag to one side and one of the wheels was beginning to wobble dangerously.

He started to explain to the unseen guard that he still had another seven miles to walk, then offered the man two options.

He could shoot him or take his name to report him. The guard let him go, tutting impatiently.

When Eddie arrived at the bungalow he was in a very poor shape, the sweat was pouring off him and he was so tired he could hardly talk. He spent the next morning in the bedroom still feeling all of a tremble, but the pram wanted fixing for Irene to take Gina out, so he had to get out of bed.

Then that evening he went to visit his mother, who was all agog at the news she'd been hearing that the docks had been bombed again.

"When?" asked Eddie.

"In the early hours of this morning," said his mother.

"Oh no," said Eddie. "Which docks, not the Wallasey docks?"

"I don't know,"she said."All I heard it was the docks again."

Eddie had a horrible feeling. He didn't think he would be hiring a removal van. When he visited the house a few days later, everything had been blown to smithereens.

CHAPTER SIX

At first Gina thrived in the pure country air, she was a charming child and the aunts got very attached to her. It was a bit of a squash with all of them living in the bungalow together, especially as Aunt Jenny's bed had been moved into the parlour, so that Eddie and Irene could sleep together in Irene's old room and Gina had a borrowed cot at the end of their bed. It was only at the weekends when Eddie was home that things got a bit fraught between them. With him having the role of the breadwinner, he always wanted the final say.

The loss of the furniture and some of their wedding presents that had still been in the house caused Irene misery. It was one step back that the couple hadn't needed, so the drive was on to save as much as they could for when they managed to find a place to rent. They had registered with a lettings agent and waited in vain to hear from them.

Meantime, Gina was suffering from the war-time diet being fed to her. Her legs were not very strong and she wasn't thriving as she had initially. The Ministry of Health handed out free cod liver oil and orange juice eventually, but it was too late for Gina who began to develop bow legs. Irene took her to the hospital in Birkenhead, where she was advised to give her toddler a spoonful of malt each day. Whilst at the hospital, though, they both got impetigo, a skin disease that had reached epidemic levels in the war.

Irene managed to buy a pushchair from a neighbour whose child had grown too big for it. The doctor had said that she was to keep Gina off her feet as much as possible, which was very hard with a toddler. Irene walked for miles around the countryside, or across the hill at Thurstaston Common and sometimes as far as Thurstaston shore. As the weeks went by her child got stronger and Gina began to walk on her own again.

The search for a house to rent went on for a very long time. The phone box in the village where Irene telephoned Lobley's estate agents, became known to Gina as the 'Lobley' box, because her mother went there every day. Irene went there each morning with very little hope as she lifted the receiver. It was just a way of life now to give the agent a call and get a negative reply again.

Then one morning, to Irene's amazement, she was told there was a house to rent a few streets away. If she went to the office the following day she'd be given a set of keys. The wheels of the pushchair took wings, as she sped down the hill to give the good news to her aunties. They were just as pleased as she was, though they said they'd miss Irene and Gina if they moved away.

The rest of the day was a whirl, as the women discussed curtains and furnishings, while Irene couldn't wait until Eddie came home from work. As soon as they had finished their meal he wanted to go immediately to view the house. It was at the bottom of Whaley Lane; a house that used to belong to Eddie's father, which was bittersweet really when they came to think of it.

It was just around the corner from Acorn Drive where Eddie's mother lived. A small semi with a downstairs bathroom, so very different from the place where Irene used to live. It had two large gardens, one either side of the driveway and a small one at the back of the house, where grew a profusion of blackcurrant canes.

The couple stood outside the house looking at it longingly, hoping that they could afford the rent, planning the vegetables that they would grow and agreeing that the exterior walls could do with a coat of paint. Irene kept worrying: what if for some reason they didn't get the keys, what if they had to wait for something else? She really loved this place and she didn't want her dreams of a rosy future to be shattered. Eddie told her to wait for a moment and disappeared off to his mother's, coming back shortly with an old wooden coat stand. He stood it by the front door and used one of the heavy pegs to break one of the small glass panels in it, then hopped inside to claim his ownership. "Meredith," he shouted, using an old music hall expression, "Meredith, we're in!"

Irene paid the first week's rent next morning, collected the keys, then she and Eddie went round to the house again the following evening. This time they walked up to the door and opened it with the key. Eddie had brought some glass and putty and busied himself repairing his break in, while Irene measured the windows and looked around. This was to be their little palace, little being the operative word after having all that room at Pear Tree Cottage. The bedrooms were tiny, the living room was small and the kitchen shared its wall with the bathroom and toilet. But they had all the land, plenty of ground to dig over for the war effort and they could be self sufficient if they bought some chickens and a couple of sows. It would be wonderful to be together without others poking their noses in, they both felt happier than they had been since they were wed.

The nights were peaceful now, the Battle of Britain had been won and Winston Churchill gave his famous speech... "Never had so much been owed by so many to so few".

There was hope in people's hearts that things might start getting back to normal, although whole streets lay shattered, bomb craters were much in evidence and as the work force was being depleted daily with men enlisting to the Forces, not much building or repair work was done. But after people had mourned their dead, found somewhere new to live and got on with the job of living, the future looked a bit more hopeful for a while.

Eddie was directed by the Ministry of Works to help with the repair of bomb-damaged property in Liverpool. Though he didn't have much time after his day's toil, he worked enthusiastically on the house and the garden. The place had been neglected by the previous occupant; she had been elderly and couldn't do very much other than try to keep body and soul together. He filled the garden with vegetable seedlings that Irene had nurtured in the small wash house attached to the semi, then he dug out trenches for potatoes and onions, bought a couple of fruit trees and built a small wooden hen house. It was lovely working in the garden with the thrushes, blackbirds, robins and chaffinches whistling away merrily, as they waited for their share of worms.

Eddie was working in Liverpool again, as tradesmen were badly needed in the dock area that had taken most of the bombing during the blitz. Any house that could be repaired and made fit to live in was finished as quickly as possible, so that owners who were eager to return could move back again.

Irene never knew of the conditions that Eddie was working in, as he would strip all his clothes off in the wash house, then streak into the bathroom to scrub himself clean. It was only when she came to use the wash tub, that she saw the fleas jumping about all over the place.

But conditions were bad anywhere at that time. A friend of Isabel's had volunteered to work in munitions. She didn't have to because she had a family, but the thought that her efforts might bring the end of the war closer made her leave her children with her mother each day. One night she had come in from work exhausted, she slumped into a chair and put her elbows on the table. Her head itched and she rubbed it mechanically, but to her horror a little insect dropped out. Within minutes the table was covered with lice, something she had never seen before in her life!

One day Eddie was working in one of the back streets near the docks when a small boy approached him.

"Me mam wants to talk to you," he said.

"Oh," said Eddie. "Who is your mam and where does she live?"

The boy looked up hopefully, he was very thin and his large brown eyes seemed to occupy most of his face.

"Me mam's name is Mrs Brown and we live in that end house." He jerked a dirty thumb towards the end of the street.

Eddie felt surprised, he didn't know anybody around there and he was puzzled as to why the boy's mother would want to see him.

"Tell your mother that I'll be along at dinner time. Is it about your house?"

"Yes," the boy answered a bit uncertainly.

Eddie put his hand in his pocket and drew out a few coppers to give to the undernourished little soul. The boy's face brightened and he dashed off to the corner shop, coming out again with a bulging paper bag in his hand.

After Eddie had eaten his lunch of spam sandwiches, he walked along the street to inspect the house. He stepped into the road to get a better view of the roof; there was a gaping hole in it. The door of the house opened and a woman came out to talk to him. She had been pretty once, but time and suffering had taken its toll.

"Do you think you could mend my roof please?" she asked in a pleading voice.

"I'll have to ask the boss," Eddie answered.

"Please do it," she begged tearfully. "The rain is getting in and the children's beds are soaked. I'll pay you anything, only please mend the roof."

"I'll see what I can do, but like I said, I must square it with the boss first."

Eddie walked down to see the foreman in his office, feeling very sorry for the young woman and her children. Although the air raids were mostly responsible for the damage to the houses around there, a lot of the dilapidation was caused by years of the landlords' neglect.

The foreman looked at his list, only bomb-damaged houses qualified for repair, the woman's house was not on it.

"It's not on the list, so we can't do it," he said, pushing the paper under Eddie's nose for scrutiny.

"Then I'll do it in my dinner hour with the apprentice, it will be good experience for him to work on a roof repair. We can't have the children's beds soaking now, can we?"

The foreman shook his head and said he'd turn a blind eye.

Eddie spent his dinner hour next day mending the woman's roof with the help of the apprentice; he used second hand slates that he had picked up from a tip in the next street. She came to Eddie later and offered him payment from a slim and shabby purse, but he felt he couldn't accept payment and told her so.

A few days later he was working on another house and an old lady appeared by his side.

"Are you the fella that mended our Cilla's roof?" she asked.

"If you mean the roof on the end house, yes," replied Eddie.

"Then come along to the pub with me, I want to buy yer a drink."

"I'm working, I can't stop now," he said a trifle indignantly. "It'll be my dinner hour soon, I'll see you then."

At twelve o' clock, Eddie took his sandwiches and went along to the pub on the corner of the street. There seemed to be one on the corner of every street in Liverpool, this one was called The Clock. It was a spit and sawdust type of place where people didn't dress up to enter it, so Eddie didn't mind the fact that he was wearing his working clothes. He found the old woman in a wide circle of friends, they all seemed to be drinking glasses of light ale.

"Come over here," she shouted making room for him on the wooden bench beside her. "What'll yer have to drink?"

"I'll have the same as you," he said.

When he was seated comfortably, she lowered her voice and told him that if he went to the shop in the next street and mentioned her name, Mrs Cooper, he would be able to buy two pounds of sugar. Sugar was on strict rations then and if Eddie ever wanted his shoes mending, her old man would do them for him. He thanked her and continued to sip his ale, thinking what a pleasant woman the old lady was, but what she said next caused him to sweat with embarrassment.

"See that house opposite?"

Eddie looked through the pub's grimy window.

"I've got it all arranged for yer. Next time you're feeling horny, go over to Liz's house, she's our Cilla's sister, she'll see you're right and then I think we'll be square, don't you?"

Eddie was so relieved when he finished the work in that street and moved on to the next, though he kept looking over his shoulder in case Mrs Cooper appeared again!

Old ladies seemed to make a beeline for Eddie. One day a woman came up to him and asked would he fix her fire grate? She told him that she couldn't light a fire until it was repaired and the weather was getting chilly. So once again Eddie gave up his dinner hour and went to the house to repair the grate; he was rewarded with tea and cakes for his efforts and felt lucky that he wasn't propositioned again!

As the war rumbled on, a couple of local women started a Services canteen in Irby. They first got in touch with Northern Command and asked permission to do so. Their request was granted and they were given a permit for rations.

Their idea was to give service men and women, who were billeted in the area, somewhere to go in their free time. They were provided with a hot meal, table tennis for exercise and plenty of chairs by a warm fire. It proved very popular and a weekly dance, where an elderly band volunteered their services, was held in the village hall on Saturday nights to raise the funds to pay for it.

Eddie and Irene managed to find a willing babysitter in Rosaleen, Eddie's youngest sister. Now eighteen and with no love interest in her life, she was persuaded by Gina's happy smile and cherub ways to keep an eye on her, so they were able to attend the dance on that first Saturday. Unfortunately there was no M.C., so Eddie took the job on. He loved it: he'd announce each dance, popular then was the rhumba and bossa-nova, then leap off the stage to dance with Irene, or a young lady that he saw hadn't got a partner. He was such a good dancer that he developed a following, all the girls competed to partner him in the 'Ladies request dances'.

After the work finished on the houses around the docks, Eddie was directed to work for a contractor who made him a foreman over a gang of six men. It was further out of Liverpool in a place called

Litherland. Mostly it was clearance work, as a new estate was needed to house some of the blitz victims who couldn't return to their homes. The work was very tiring, dirty and dusty; the wallpaper that was hanging on the walls in some houses sheltered all sorts of bugs and the men went home in a terrible state with fleas bouncing off their clothes.

Most of the men liked to slake their thirst in one of the pubs nearby, as the enterprising landlord provided a range of delicious sandwiches and pies. The dinner hour was what it said; an hour and Eddie demanded that they started back at work at one o' clock on the dot. He was a fairly easy going boss, providing that the men did their work, so he turned a blind eye if one of the workers was five minutes late.

Curly Flanagan was one such worker, but he pushed the five minutes to the limit and arrived a little later each day. At the end of the week he was short by two hours, so Eddie decided to teach him a lesson and dock the man's pay.

"What's this?" shouted Curly as he flung open the back door of the house that Eddie was working on. He was a mean-looking man, with eyebrows that met in the middle under a narrow forehead; the type of man who would have been spending time in Walton Jail if it hadn't been for the War.

"I'm two bloody hours short in me pay packet, don't think yer goin' to get away with this."

Eddie carried on with his work and said over his shoulder, "You didn't show up for work at one each day like I told you to, so that's why I've docked your pay."

"We'll see about that," retorted the man and, gripping Eddie by his arm, he slung him against the kitchen wall. Next he picked up a lump hammer and brandished it in front of Eddie, effing and blinding, saying what he'd like to do to him. Eddie ducked as the hammer swung at him, then hit Flanagan squarely on the jaw. The man bounced with the force from Eddie's fist through the back yard door, then cracked his head on the stone flags there. He lay still with blood pouring out of the wound and Eddie thought that he had killed him. He ran with the labourer, who had been working with him and had seen it all, to check his pulse and to see if the man was dead. Thank God he wasn't, he began to come round and started mouthing obscenities.

Eddie sent his labourer to the telephone box for an ambulance, while the rest of the men in his gang crowded in. A violent row started, with all the workers taking Flanagan's side.

"Ted shouldn't have hit him." "Curly was only messing, he wouldn't have used the hammer." "He was only fooling around."

With the sound of the ambulance came Eddie's boss, who was told the version by his men before Eddie got a chance. Labourers were hard to find owing to the army conscription, which were decimating the work forces week by week.

"It's me that keeps yer out of the army," the boss growled at Eddie. "If I can't rely on yer to keep things going smoothly here, I'll have to get somebody else."

Eddie had no one to back him up because his labourer, his eyewitness, had disappeared.

"Right," he said, his anger getting the better of his judgment at the injustice of it all. "If that's the way it is, get my cards ready for tonight. I'd rather be in the army than try to get work-shy fellows like this one to do an honest day's work."

Then the eyewitness to Flanagan's attack came back, after directing the ambulance men to where the stricken man lay. He told the boss the story, but Eddie didn't stay for an apology. By then it was too late for Eddie and his pride; if the boss hadn't believed him in the first place, then he'd rather not be there in any case.

There were two losers on that day, besides the wounded Flanagan. The boss who would soon realise that without Eddie, the men could do what they liked with him; and Eddie, who through sitting on his angry pride, was destined to fight in the depths of Hell.

As Eddie travelled on the ferry back to Woodside, his heart was heavy as he realised what he'd done. His temper had cooled and as he stood on the top deck looking down the Mersey, he felt full of misery. He'd be leaving all he held dear to fight a war he had no stomach for. Deep down he was a pacifist, a country boy, it was just that sometimes his temper overtook him. He wondered how long it would be before he got his call up papers. Irene was devastated when he told her.

"Well you can just go back to the site and apologise," she said. "How are me and Gina going to cope without you being here? I'll have to go and get a job now, we can't exist on army pay."

"You're not getting a job and I'm not going back to apologise," Eddie replied stubbornly. "You'll manage, it's just a question of economising. You've got the chickens and they're laying plenty, and before I go I'll take one of the pigs to the abattoir and you can put it in a barrel of brine and leave it in the wash house."

"I'll have to have my mother back then, I'm not living here with just Gina for company. This is too bad of you Eddie, that job kept you out of the war and now you've chucked it away."

"Well tough," said Eddie, his temper rising again as he heard her condemnation. "I'm off to my mother's, she'll be happy I'm going, anyway."

Irene sobbed her heart out when Eddie flung out of the house in a fit of pique. It was the first real quarrel that they'd ever had; she usually kept her mouth shut if she didn't agree with him. But this time he'd gone too far, put his life in jeopardy, possibly putting her into early widowhood if he didn't return. Gina, who was now three years old and had listened to her parents rowing, flung herself on her mother's lap and cried along as well.

There was an uneasy truce between the couple for the next few weeks, Eddie not admitting the fear he felt, nor the annoyance with his mother when she had called him a fool. Everything had to go on as normal, keep a stiff upper lip, pretend that what he'd done wasn't going to ruin their happiness. It would all be over in a year or so, wasn't Winston Churchill saying that the war was nearly won?

He went to work on a local farm, the farmer was having difficulty getting his harvest in, where peace and quiet helped to settle his mind. The words of the boss still rankled though and he still clung on to his pride.

The dreaded Call Up papers arrived a month later, but it was still a shock to Eddie and Irene because they'd tried to push it out of their minds. He was to report to the Chesterfield barracks at the end of the week and a travel warrant was enclosed. That meant they only had three days left together and they carried on as if he wasn't going away. But the day before he was leaving, Irene broke down in tears.

They decided to have one last happy day together, something that they would remember for the rest of their lives, a day out in the lovely Autumn sunshine, picking blackberries in the fields of Barnston, a twenty minute walk away.

With Gina toddling beside them, they picked basket upon basket of the glossy sweet-tasting fruit from brambles low with the weight of their bounty. They laboured until sunset, picking with stained hands, popping the occasional large berry into their mouths, then back home where they both shared in the making of their meal. Afterwards, with Gina tucked up in her little bed, they set to work making jam, with the hope that it wouldn't be too long before Eddie was having the results of their efforts on a piece of bread.

It was not until they lay in bed later, that the enormity of what Eddie had done finally hit them. He was leaving early next morning and might not come back again. This was not a time for sleeping, nor even making love because if Irene was made a widow, she'd have two children then to rear. Instead, Irene lay in her husband's arms, cherishing each moment together, praying that one day, not so far away, Eddie would hold her in his arms again. If not, their dreams of a happy future would be shattered by the war.

CHAPTER SEVEN

Loneliness was the biggest problem for Irene once Eddie had gone. She was ignored by his family, unless she made the effort to visit his mother to show Gina off, or went to her aunties' bungalow to help them with work in their house. Nothing could be done in the garden as temperatures had plummeted and the ground was a solid block; rationing had begun to bite and Irene could only purchase what was in the shops. She was glad that the chickens were still laying and there was still a barrel of pork, but money was tight for the first few weeks until she was able to draw on Eddie's army pay.

Irene decided to invite her mother to come and stay. She'd be company, they could pool their ration books, Lily had a widow's pension and she would be happy to babysit Gina if Irene got a job. The problem was that Eddie had insisted that she stay home and look after their daughter, but he hadn't said she couldn't do voluntary work, so that had become her plan.

The government had built a barracks on the perimeter of Arrowe Park, it housed men from the Free French Army who had come over to help their allies with the war. They frequented the Services canteen in Irby and Irene had heard that volunteers were needed a few hours every day.

The soldiers were charming, courteous and extremely polite to the canteen ladies and Irene tried out her schoolgirl French to the amazement of the homesick men.

She had her favourites; there was Jean Pierre, Grand Pierre and Petit Pierre who gallantly vied for her attention when her shift came around. She felt flattered, skittish, unused to the compliments that were always coming her way, suddenly she felt alive again and not so lonely after all.

Like many of the call up men, Eddie was very unsettled in those first few weeks away from his family. He couldn't get used to the army discipline and being left-handed he found it awkward drilling and handling the weapons. He had hoped to be put into a regiment where his experience in driving lorries for his father could be put to good use, feeling that he would be more suited to a transport regiment than being assigned to become an artillery man.

One day, a man named Sergeant Miller unfortunately pushed Eddie to his limit, by sniping and picking at everything he did. He was ridiculed because of his clumsiness with a rifle, ridiculed because he couldn't seem to march in time and told off for not saluting an officer that had passed by.

That day Eddie saw red. His arm was aching with the pain of the injections he'd been given, but as he'd always had a short fuse anyway, he challenged the sergeant to a fight behind the tents. Miller was man enough to take him up on it and they were to meet that evening at seven o' clock, but some sneak told the Major and Eddie was thrown into the guardroom to cool his heels.

An hour later no one had come to lay a charge against him, the corporal who was on duty had gone for a cup of tea, so seeing the open door and an open gate beyond it, Eddie decided he'd had enough.

He walked until he reached the town of Chesterfield and passed a small white pub where he heard music being played. He was thirsty and thoroughly fed up with the way he was being treated, so in he went, thinking a few pints would make him feel human again and the army could do what it liked.

The pianist was a young lady, a pretty girl with a cheerful face, who was dressed in a green long-sleeved woollen dress and when she saw that Eddie was in uniform, waved to him merrily. "Don't bother to buy drinks, soldier," she shouted over, "help me by drinking some of these that have been bought for me."

He looked at the row of glasses lined up on top of the piano and gave her a broad smile. An hour later the glasses were empty and the world had become a better place.

Two soldiers came in and sat at his table, by this time everyone had become Ted's friend and he poured his troubles out to them in an inebriated state. They were sympathetic, but horrified that Eddie didn't know what was in store for him. To go was a great big sin, the penalty would be more than just an hour in the guardroom. They helped him up and, taking an arm each, walked the unsteady rookie soldier back to the camp.

The sergeant was waiting; Eddie hadn't turned up for their fight, so he sent him back to the guardroom and this time laid a charge on him.

Eddie spent an uneasy night feeling trapped and bewildered, his head ached from all the beer he had drunk and his arm throbbed from the injections he'd had. Not for the first time he realised how foolish he had been, he could have been home with Irene, home and free.

The next morning after Eddie had been given his breakfast he was escorted to the parade ground, where he joined six other men on a charge like himself. They were marched in single file down a steep hill to a school house that had been taken over by the army. The other men were taken in first, leaving Eddie to cool his heels with a corporal in charge. The man was sympathetic, hadn't he been a raw recruit like Eddie, confused and bewildered, not knowing any of the rules?

Sergeant Miller appeared, with a nasty sneer on his face, he grabbed at poor Eddie's forage cap and threw it on the floor. Then he yelled very loudly at him. "Quick march, quick march!" Eddie pretended to have a limp, which made the sergeant mad again.

In the bare room where three officers sat at a long table by a wall, Eddie was told to stand at ease. Ease was about the last word Eddie was feeling, his case had already been fully discussed; he was there to hear his punishment. He was told that he would be returned to his own country.

"Permission to speak, Sir?" Eddie addressed one of the officers. The officer gave a nod.

"Which country would that be, Sir, I was born in England and this is my country?"

"You will be sent to Ireland, Dockerty, you will finish your training there with the Irish Fusiliers. That is our decision and there is no right of appeal."

He was quick marched out of the school room, wondering as he did so what kind of looneys did they have in charge?

A few days later he was in Ireland, but in a state of total collapse due to a high fever as his body fought against his inoculations. The sergeant took in the situation at a glance, dismissed Eddie's escort, then put his new recruit to bed in his own quarters.

Sergeant Mannion was a compassionate fellow who had served in the army since the First World War, though his men had to be brought up to the best standard of training, he treated them as human beings. Next morning Eddie was given a superb breakfast and began to feel he could face the world again.

He did well in his training, he worked hard at being the smartest man in battle dress and the best at weapon drill, he was given special duties and made the 'stick man' for the day. When a soldier won this distinction he had to report to the office for any special messages or duties. Most days it was a mere formality and then he was free for the day.

In his leisure time he went to help one of the local farmers, who found Eddie to be a capable and willing man who also loved working in the farmer's fields.

In all this time he had not been given any leave to go home to his family. Christmas had come and gone, Spring was nearly over, so in desperation, Eddie volunteered to go on a draft which was going over to England. When he arrived in Ringwood, Hampshire, feeling low from an infection that he had picked up on the way back over, he intended to ask for permission to go on leave.

He decided to surprise Irene, thinking that a telegram coming out of the blue would cause her alarm at the sight of a telegraph boy. He was tired and very hungry when he got off the bus with his kit-bag, so began to walk to his mother's house where he could be sure of a plate of rib-sticking stew. His spirits lifted at the thought, as he walked along the leafy tree-lined Acorn Drive to reach his mother's semi on the corner.

"Eddie!" his mother cried with delight, as he walked unannounced into the kitchen where she was washing the plates from supper. "Why didn't you say you were coming? Does Irene know, 'cos she didn't tell me when I saw her this morning out with the child?"

"I thought I'd surprise you all," Eddie answered as his mother threw her arms around him and hugged him to her, like she had when he was a little boy.

"Where's Rosaleen and Sam? Have Terry and Mickey had any leave, or am I the first one home?"

"Put your kit-bag in the hallway first and then I'll bring you up with the news while you eat some dinner, Eddie. You look as thin as a rake, what's the army been feeding you? Mind you, you've never had much weight on, not like our Caitlin. You should see her now. Come, sit here at the table, I must have known you were coming because as usual I made too much stew. I got so used to cooking for seven children and me and your father that it's difficult to cook for just Rosaleen and Sam."

"How are you managing, Mum? I thought with all the rationing and the supply routes being knocked out by the Jerrys, that people were having it hard."

"Not when you live in the country, Eddie, not when there's so many farms around and of course we've all turned our gardens over to growing veg. Did you not notice my cauli's when you came up the side of the house?"

"Well yes, I gave our gardens over to vegetables too before I went off to the War, I hope Irene's been keeping on top of them while I've been away."

"Your wife seems to be busy with other things, Eddie, though it's not my place to say. It's a good job that Lily woman's living there, she probably sees to the growing of things."

Eddie put down the spoon that he had been using to gulp down the mostly vegetable stew.

"What kind of other things has Irene been doing?" he asked calmly, though his heart started beating madly as the import of his mother's words began to sink in. He had heard from some of his mates stories of going home to find that the missis had been playing away from home, or a baby being expected that wasn't his own.

"Oh I'm sure she'll tell you all about the job she has in the canteen in the village, serving the chaps from the barracks that they've built near Arrowe Park. Now don't worry your head about anything, just finish off your meal and then I'll tell you what the family are up to and I've also had a letter from the solicitor that I need to tell you about."

All the time that she was telling him that Rosaleen was going to join the landgirls if her application was successful, Sam was working for a local farmer while he waited to be old enough to fight in the War, Caitlin was expecting again and looked like a rain butt, Eddie was itching to get away and see what Irene had been up to. He hadn't the heart though to rush off and leave his mother, she seemed to have aged ten years since J.C. had died and her hair had gone white, which it wasn't before.

"So when I got this letter from Willerby Brough I was so annoyed with your father, I felt like stamping on his grave."

"Have you got the letter, Mum?" he said, forcing himself to listen to his mother. "You'll be pleased to know I can read now, the army taught me, within six weeks would you believe!"

"You were always a clever boy, Eddie. It was wrong of your father not to have given you boys a good education like the girls got. What use is that to Caitlin and Sheena now they've got married? Though they've both made good marriages as you know."

"Mum, the letter, do you want me to read it or not?"

"Oh yes, you'll be wanting to get along to that wife and child of yours. Here it is, it says that your father was paying maintenance to that Alice who used to work for us."

"What!" Eddie exploded. "Did you know anything about this? What was he paying money to Alice for?"

"Well, Eddie, you must be a man of the world now and know that maintenance payments are for the support of illegitimate children."

"You mean Father had a by-blow besides the seven children he had with you?"

Gladys nodded bleakly. "I knew about the baby, Eddie, I sacked her when I found out she was expecting. She thought that your father would up sticks and go and live with her, but I knew J.C. a lot better than she did and he would never have left us for that little tart. He went on his knees to me and begged forgiveness and I thought that was the end of the matter, but it seems from the letter he'd been paying out for the child for all these years, and even now he's dead she's still expecting to be paid."

"So what are you going to do about it?" asked Eddie, feeling shocked at his mother's revelation and wondering at her ability to have forgiven J.C.'s travesty.

"I was going to forget about it. The child must be fourteen or fifteen now and old enough to be supporting himself."

"Himself? So we've got a half brother somewhere. Have you any idea where he and Alice are living?"

"Now Eddie, I don't want you rushing off trying to find them and giving Alice the length of your tongue. I do know where they are because when I was going through your father's papers, it appeared that there was a house in Queensferry that belonged to him. He obviously bought it for them to live in, probably he was under obligation or she might have blackmailed him."

"But that house belongs to you now, you can throw her out, sell it and with the sale of this one you could afford a far better place."

"I'll have to think about it, Eddie. Obviously he didn't disclose the house to the people who were dealing with the bankruptcy or he had put it in her name. Anyway, I've told only you and I don't want the others hearing about it. I wanted you to know about the solicitor's letter in case one day you'll be seeing to my affairs."

"But what if they are in touch again?"

"Oh I'll tell them that there's no money left and they can go to Hell."

Eddie walked along to his own house, his mind reeling with what his mother had said. The thought of Irene being unfaithful to him seemed a lesser problem after being told of the infidelity of his father. Well the sanctimonious old lecher, such a pillar of the community and he was having it off with his brothers' nursemaid. How in heaven had his mother put up with it? She must be a saint.

He stood at the top of his driveway surveying the garden. It was dusk by now, but through the gloom he could see neat rows of cabbages, the white flowers on the green foliage of the potato plants, he could smell the aroma of the onion sets and the pleasant whiff of mint as he brushed past their leaves. To the right of him grunted Sally the sow, as she settled herself comfortably on the straw of the pigsty, her litter lying in a row at the side of her, sated from a recent feed. The hens clucked contentedly from their perches in the wooden coop, while the cockerel glared at Eddie when he had a look through the netting.

Eddie strode round to the wash house, taking off his army boots and leaving them by the door. There was no sound coming from the kitchen, and of course there were no lights visible from the windows, as the blackout curtains were drawn across each one.

He knocked on the kitchen door impatiently; surely Irene must be in there? It was growing late and she wouldn't leave young Gina alone.

"Just a minute," someone shouted.

Eddie groaned. He knew that voice, it was Lily, his mother-in-law.

"Oh, Eddie, you're back then," Lily said in a surprised voice, as she spoke to him through the window of the door, seemingly not in a hurry to let him in. "Why didn't you let us know you were coming? Irene would have stayed at home."

"Open the door will you," Eddie growled. "I'm not standing here on my own doorstep conducting a conversation with you."

"Sorry I'm sure," replied Lily testily. "It's because my fingers are having trouble with these fancy locks and knobs."

She eventually managed to get the door open and started to explain that Irene had got a neighbour to put a bolt and an extra lock on to deter a German from breaking in.

"Don't be so daft woman, if a German wanted to get in here he'd smash the glass with a bayonet. Well, where is she then and is Gina tucked up in bed?"

"That's where I was when you started your knocking," said Lily in an irritated voice. "The poor mite's scared stiff at the moment. She only has to hear a plane going over and she starts trembling. I've given her a bottle of milk to settle her down."

"I'll go and see her."

Eddie pushed his way past Lily and made for the bottom of the stairs.

"Don't be so stupid, man," cried Lily, rushing after him to grasp a handful of his jacket. "She hasn't seen you for months, how do you think she'll feel if she sees a strange man in uniform?"

He stopped in his tracks, then slunk into the living room. He sat himself down on the sofa and put his head in his hands.

"I didn't think of that, God what are these bloody Jerry's doing to people with families. I've waited for months to see Gina and you're right, she'll probably not even know who I am."

"Can I get you a cup of tea?" said Lily sympathetically, putting her hand on his shoulder. "You must be tired from your journey. Where was it, Chesterfield you were stationed at?"

"No, I'm based in Hampshire now, though I was in Ireland before that. Hasn't Irene been keeping you up to date with my manoeuvres then?"

"I don't think she knew where you were stationed, Eddie, the last she heard you were at the training camp. She was saying only the other day that she hadn't heard from you. She didn't know where to write neither, I think she was going to contact your regiment headquarters to see where you were."

"Oh, I'm not even with the same regiment now, I got transferred to the Irish Fusiliers 'cause my name's Dockerty. I was ill for a while, got some damned infection or something. Still I'm back in England now and managed to get a bit of leave. Anyway, where is she? Has she gone up with Gina and had an early night?"

Lily coloured slightly and said that she'd just go and get his tea. She seemed nervous when she returned with a cup and saucer and her hand was shaking as she passed Eddie his tea.

"The thing is, Eddie, with her not being able to keep in touch and you not being around, she decided to go and help out at the canteen in the village. It was set up as you know to give somewhere for the service personnel to relax at the end of the day and get a decent meal."

"I know that," Eddie cut her short. "I helped set the place up, I was the M.C. at the dances before I got my call up papers, but I told Irene that I didn't want her working. One of Gina's parents has to be here in her life to give her stability."

"It's only voluntary work. Eddie, she's not getting paid for it and I'm here to look after Gina anyway."

"Well what's Irene doing out at this time if she's just helping out with the cooking and things? Don't tell me she's attending the dances as well."

"There's a lot of clearing up to be done..."

Eddie stood up, feeling the rage inside him surging through his body, as it had once before that evening.

"I'll go and meet her, I'll see for myself what she's up to. She knows darn well she should be here looking after our child."

Lily heard him slamming out of the back door nearly putting the window in, then listened at the foot of the stairs for the sound of her grandchild's wail.

Eddie walked swiftly along the main road towards the village. His heart was thumping angrily. She should have been there, his wife should have been there for him when he came home on leave, not enjoying herself with other men, while he was away fighting a war.

"Come on now, Eddie," spoke his voice of reason. "Irene would never be unfaithful, sure she loves you and would never be underhand."

He skirted the old gnarled trees of Harrock's Wood, where owls hooted eerily and the rustlings from the bushes made the hairs on the back of his neck stand on end. Irene had to pass here, suppose someone jumped out and dragged her in? His vivid imagination began to make his stomach crawl. His beautiful Irene, he wanted this damned war to be over so he could love her, protect her, not have her frightened by the thought of Germans bashing in her door. He'd calm himself down, look forward to her delighted surprise when he walked through the door of the village hall, he'd take her home and make love to her, pretend that there was just the two of them in the world.

Eddie took some deep breaths to settle his laboured breathing and began to walk slowly up the hill.

From the top of the hill came excited, clamouring voices, men's voice, foreign voices, as Eddie found out, as they came towards him. A shambling group of French men appeared out of the gloom. Some wore unbuttoned navy jackets with ill matching trousers, while others had open-necked shirts on and the bottoms of their navy blue uniform. Most were drunk or were close to it and lurched towards Eddie as he stood in their way.

"Ah, good evening Tommy," said one in a friendly fashion "Sa va, comment allez vous?"

"Piss off, Froggies," replied Eddie. "Get back to your own country and defend it without coming over here and sitting out the war."

"Pardonez moi, could you repeat what you have just said?" the soldier said slowly, but menacingly in a heavily foreign accent. The others stopped in their tracks when they heard the threatening timbre of his words. What had this Englishman been saying to them?

"I said nice to meet you all, won't it be good when you can all go back to your own country?"

"Oui, tres bien, bon nuit," came the reply and the French men ambled off again.

Eddie heaved a sigh of relief, that was a close call. He hadn't realised that French people could understand English, the only French that he knew was "oui, oui!"

Thoroughly shaken by his encounter he loped off thinking how rude he had been, but he reasoned, as he approached the opening that lead down the short lane to the village hall, that if the French hadn't capitulated to the Germans, he wouldn't be trying to track his wife down, she'd be sat at home by the living room fire.

At the top of the lane Eddie heard more French being spoken, along with a woman's voice who was speaking English in reply. He ducked behind some bushes as the woman's voice sounded familiar. If it was Irene he'd swing for her, he wasn't going to let her dally with another man. To his horror he saw it was Irene, but if this was her boyfriend they didn't look as if they were having a fling.

He listened to the happy lilt in her voice as the pair past him by, thanking the man beside her for taking the trouble to walk her home.

"It's those woods at the bottom of the hill, Pierre, I always feel spooky when I pass them in the dark. I know there's no need to worry, if my husband was here I'm sure he'd be here to hold my hand."

The Frenchman replied to her in his own language and Irene nodded her head. It was then that he remembered that his wife could understand French very well.

He began to feel a fool then, Irene would be overjoyed to be able to use the language that she'd been taught in the convent school. What a suspicious fool he was. He kept to the shadows behind them, as the pair walked slowly down the main road, pretending that he was on night manoeuvres so that they wouldn't hear any noise.

At the end of Whaley Lane, the Frenchman took Irene's hand and kissed the back of it, then he saluted smartly and waited until she disappeared into her home. Eddie ducked down behind the bus shelter and watched until the man was out of sight. Now he had to think up a convincing tale of how he had missed Irene on his way to meet her from work. Something about a short cut would satisfy her, yes a short cut on his way to meet her across the farmer's fields.

"Eddie!" His lovely wife was waiting at the top of the drive for him, her eyes full of tears as he hurried to take her in his arms, while Lily watched curiously from a chink in the pantry window blind.

"Why didn't you say you were coming? I wouldn't have gone to the canteen tonight, I would have stayed at home waiting for you."

In a muffled voice, as he rested his chin in the collar of her lightweight coat, feeling her bony shoulders under his outstretched arms, he told her he didn't want her to have the worry of seeing the telegraph boy appearing on his bike. His throat was aching as he held her, he wanted to cry, releasing tears himself. Oh hell what a day, it had been nothing like he imagined, nothing like the homecoming that you saw in a romantic film, but at least Irene was his for a short while, 'til he was back in the bloody war.

The next morning, as Eddie looked forward to his daughter running into their bedroom to welcome him back with excited squeals, there came another shock for him. Gina stood shyly in the doorway looking at him with enormous eyes as she gazed at the strange man in bed with her mummy. Lily stood behind her, wrapped up in an all-enveloping nightgown, urging the child to run to her daddy and give him a kiss and a hug.

"That's not my daddy," lisped Gina, close to tears at the sight of Eddie. "My daddy's gone to fight the Germans, that's not my daddy in the bed."

She turned and ran back to her bedroom, as Lily raised her eyes to heaven and gave a shrug.

"She'll come round, Eddie," said Irene consolingly. "You have to remember it's been nearly a year since she saw you and a year's a long time for a four year old."

She snuggled down beside him, putting her hand in his to give it a reassuring squeeze.

"You never said how long your leave is, she'll probably have got used to you when you're going off again."

"Thanks for those comforting words, Irene. I have to be back at the barracks on Saturday evening. I only managed to get a bit of leave because I'd not been given any since I joined.

"You'll probably go to France then," Irene replied in a sleepy voice. "Pierre was telling me that the British and the Allies are all preparing to meet up on the beaches in France and give the Germans a bloody nose."

"What!" said Eddie looking down at Irene in horror. "Who's this Pierre and how does he know what plans the War Office is making? Irene that kind of information is privileged, he'd be shot if someone heard him telling you that."

"Oh he's the commander at the French barracks, Eddie. He sometimes walks me home from the canteen. It's probably all guess work on his part, though actually he was telling me that people like me were needed to help win the war."

"What good would a canteen assistant be behind the front lines in France, Irene? What would you do if you saw a German, hit him over the head with your soup tureen?"

"No, silly. It's because I understand French and of course speak it a little. They need women like me to be dropped by parachute into one of the major towns and report back to headquarters via a wireless. It sounds exciting and I told Pierre I'd have a jolly good think about it. Just think I might..."

"Stop right there, Irene. You are not leaving this house and traipsing off to heaven knows where. Have you lost your senses? You could be shot as soon as your parachute landed or, even worse, taken off by some looney and interrogated. Get back in the real world, Irene, you've been reading too many books and they must have gone to your head."

He sprang out of bed and stalked off down to the bathroom. What was it with some people and now his wife, full of desire to serve their country, thinking that one person could somehow alter the War? It was the bloody government feeding them on bullshit and propaganda, but the politicians weren't out there doing the fighting, they had a comfy bunker in which to lay their heads.

For the thousandth time Eddie wished he'd kept his temper on the building site then he'd still be on a cushy number sitting out the War, he'd still be close to his adorable little Gina and able to make love to his wife instead of settling for a cuddle, looking on a pregnancy with dread.

Lily was up and about already, feeding her little granddaughter with a spoon at the table in the kitchen.

"Isn't she old enough to be doing that herself now?" Eddie asked, as he passed them by on his way to the bathroom. Lily made no comment. She bit back an angry retort. Instead she smiled sweetly at her son-in-law and asked him what he planned to do with his day.

"I thought I'd have a look at the garden, see how that's progressing. Check over the livestock see that they're O.K. See if Gina wants a walk to see her Nana Dockerty, maybe have a few drinks at the Club."

Eddie set about his ablutions, then looked in the airing cupboard to see if there was any clean underwear. He found an old pair of underpants that had wedged themselves between the pipe work and a faded holey vest on a wooden coat hanger.

"If you're looking for anything you didn't take with you, everything's in the bedding box in the front bedroom. Irene had to make room in her wardrobe for my stuff when I moved in."

Bloody great, thought Eddie, *now I've got to go searching for me civvies to wear, 'cos I'm not manking around in that sweaty uniform.*

Eddie stood at the top of a row of cabbages watching a pair of white butterflies fluttering about on the leaves. He filled his lungs deeply with the healthy fresh air and wished yet again that he hadn't been so foolish. He could have spent his weekends helping with the digging, playing with Gina, holding Irene and loving her, instead of leaving her yet again in a few days time. He stabbed the hoe viciously into a lump of dry soil and swore at himself, what made him flare up the way that he did?

Out of the corner of his eye he saw his little daughter. She was hiding behind the corner of the wash-house, but every few minutes she'd pop her curly head round again.

"Peep po," shouted Eddie encouragingly. A broad smile appeared on Gina's face every time he said it.

She edged out uncertainly until she was within two yards of an old gnarled apple tree nearby. Eddie got down on his haunches and grinned, then put out his arms to see if she would run to him, but he had to be content with another smile.

"Are you going to show me those piggies, Gina? What are their names? Don't they make a funny noise?"

In answer his daughter ran across to the pig sty and stood on a boulder so that she could look over the wall, making little grunting noises in reply to the sow.

"His name's Sally and he's got all these babies."

Eddie laughed. "No, Gina, the pig is a girl and *she's* got all those babies. Have you given them all names yet?"

His daughter shook her head and looked up at him trustingly.

"Mummy said I had to wait until my daddy came home and then we could name them."

"Well, I am home now, Gina, I'm your daddy. I've been away training to fight the Germans, but I'm here until Saturday."

Gina got down from the boulder and put her arms up to Eddie for a carry. "That's what Grandma said and she never tells me fibs."

Eddie and Gina sat at the kitchen table in his mother's house a few hours later. Gladys had given the little girl a piece of bread to chew on, after she had poured her son a bowl of vegetable soup.

"Here, you can dip that into your father's soup, Gina, when it's cooled a bit," she said. "I won't give her any for herself, because I'm sure her mother wouldn't be pleased with me."

"You're probably right," answered Eddie distantly. "Mum, aren't you curious about Alice's lad at all?"

"Why should I be Eddie? Though actually I have seen him. He was at your father's funeral, sort of on the sidelines over by the trees."

"Did he look like any of us? Slim like Alice or a bit plump like some of the Dockertys?"

"To be honest I didn't get a good look at him. I couldn't stand gawping in his and Alice's direction, though it was Terry and Mickey who pointed out that Alice was there. I'm not going to do anything about that letter you know, Eddie, and I don't want you to either. Let her find out the hard way that her golden goose is dead."

"I might have a ride out to Queensferry and take a look around. I'll take Gina and Irene on the train for a day out, pop into Chester on the way."

"Don't you dare, Eddie, what would be the point of raking up the past just so that you can take a look at your half brother? I'll be angry if you start stirring up a hornet's nest. How do you think I'm feeling having to look at your father's infidelity in the face?"

"Yes I'm sorry Mum, I should be thinking of your feelings too. I'll just finish my soup then I'll take this one home. I fancy going up to the Club for a jar or two, 'cos some of my mates might be home on leave like me. Pity Terry's still in the thick of it, it must be scorching out in Greece."

CHAPTER EIGHT

Back at camp, based on an estate where a vast amount of land surrounded a lovely old house, Eddie could only mourn for home. His dreams at night were of Irene and Gina, and he could only think of what a fool he had been. He began to write to Irene, finding that putting things on paper helped his troubled soul.

One windy night, after he had been put on guard duty and had gone to relieve another soldier, he became aware of noises coming from the nearby wood. Being a country man he could identify the hoots and squeals from a hunting owl, the rustlings and snapping of twigs as nocturnal animals moved about in there, but that night everything felt eerie, perhaps from the whooshing of the waves from the sea nearby.

Eddie put the collar of his greatcoat up and tried to stop the feeling of lethargy that was beginning to envelop him as the first fingers of dawn showed in the sky. His relief was about to come at any moment and he looked forward to his breakfast in the next half hour. He blinked his eyes as he saw a movement on the front lawn of the house he was guarding and challenged the person in a loud voice three times. With no response to his warning of "Halt, who goes there?" he cocked his rifle then fired.

The camp came alive in an uproar of sound, as every soldier sprang to alert, dressed and ready for action in two minutes flat, but when the light of the day grew stronger and the reason for the shooting lay dead and bleeding on the lawn in front of them, Eddie became the subject of the soldiers' scorn. Two large rabbits ended up in the pot and by way of consolation, the cook complimented him on being a first class marksman.

There was not a lot going on at the camp while the company waited for their orders to go overseas. Eddie was often at a loose end and filled his time with reading, writing home and polishing his boots to a perfect shine. He was not given to spending his time in the local pub like so many of the men, as he was only a moderate drinker. He would go to the town if there was chance of a dance somewhere, but there were not many of these to go to, as they usually occurred at the local village hall.

One evening as Eddie settled down in his hut to read another chapter of his 'who dunnit?', a soldier came to say that there was to be what they called a 'bunfight' organised by the local vicar and everyone was welcome there. The villagers would provide refreshments; lemonade, tea and buns filled with cheese or ham and a group would play for them all.

This evening, however, the group hadn't put in an appearance and the vicar, embarrassed, but not wanting the evening to be a flop, asked if anyone would fill the gap until they came. Eddie suddenly found himself on the stage, volunteered by his fellow soldiers, who knew he could tell a bit of a tale.

Assuming an Irish accent, not difficult because his father had a bit of a brogue, he began by saying, "Me name's Dockerty, so I'll tell yer a couple of Irish jokes. Mick is driving his car past the bus stop and sees Paddy standing there. 'Do yer want a lift?' asks Mick. 'Better not,' said Paddy. 'I'll miss me bus.'

An Englishman, a Scotsman and an Irishman were all sat on the top of a building about to eat their lunch. The Englishman opened his lunch box and found he had some cheese and onion sandwiches, so he said, 'I'm fed up with cheese and onion sandwiches, if I get them again tomorrow, I'm going to jump off this building and kill myself.'

The Scotsman opened his lunch box and seeing that he had cheese and onion sandwiches, which he'd had every day for the past week, vowed if he were to get cheese and onion sandwiches the next day, he would jump off the roof.

The Irishman opened his lunch box and groaned when he saw that he had cheese and onion sandwiches too. 'If I find that I've got cheese and onion sandwiches tomorrow, then I'll jump off the roof and kill meself, so I will.'

The next day the three men were sitting on top of the building and the Englishman, when he saw he had cheese and onion sandwiches again for his lunch, jumped off the roof and killed himself.

The Scotsman checked his lunch box and seeing that he also had cheese and onion sandwiches for his lunch, jumped off the building and killed himself.

The Irishman took a sandwich out of his lunch box, checked the filling and then jumped off the building and killed himself.

Next day the police investigating their deaths went to speak to the wives of the workmen. The Englishman's wife verified that she had made her husband cheese and onion sandwiches as she normally did. The Scotsman's wife verified that she had made her husband cheese and onion sandwiches as she normally did.

And the Irishman's wife verified that the Irishman had made *his* cheese and onion sandwiches like *he* normally did."

Then Eddie finished off by doing a sand dance, made famous by Wilson, Keppel and Betty. It filled the gap and as he finished the missing players turned up.

Next morning as he sauntered along the village street, Eddie found he had become something of a celebrity. A woman patted his arm and said how much she had enjoyed his impromptu act and an old lady invited him into her cottage for tea and scones!

A few days later, Eddie and the rest of his group were sent up to the Scottish Borders to make up the numbers in a regiment there. He had trained with the Irish Fusiliers in Ireland, but he was sent to join the Royal Ulster Rifles and here he met up with regular soldiers, who were to be a great help to him in his army life.

The new regiment was all under canvas when Eddie's platoon arrived in the town of Hawick. Nissen huts were in the process of being erected, but with a shortage of tradesmen they were slow in building and bricklayers were in high demand. Eddie saw a notice pinned up outside the commanding officer's quarters, asking for any skilled artisans to report to him that day. He was assigned to the building of the guardroom, and a row of Nissen huts. For the first time in his life, he found that his expertise as a brickie was at last standing him in good stead.

It was at this time that Eddie got his first good pair of boots, courtesy of the Quarter Master of the regiment. He had rather small feet for his height of 5ft 8ins and in civvy street he could usually find a pair of shoes to fit him, but this was not the case in the army. Army boots brought tears to many a strong man's eyes, as the blisters caused by marching over many miles in them left an indelible memory.

Eddie was working for the Garrison Engineer during the day and not being used to army ways, he didn't know what to do with his rifle. He had wrapped it up in a piece of cloth and placed it in his bed. It was found there when the beds were inspected and he was reported to the Company Sergeant Major and put on a charge, despite his protests. This stopped the work on the centre, essential in the eyes of the Quarter Master who was responsible for the furnishing and equipment for the place. He sent a man to hunt for the missing bricklayer, who was found doing guard duty by the main gate.

Eddie found himself freed then from all duty except for building work and as it seemed that he was indispensable, asked the Q.M. for boots that properly fitted so that he could concentrate on his work. He was given free run of the store and chose the finest boots that the army could offer and nothing would part him from them throughout the duration of the War.

An unfortunate accident caused him to be sent to hospital a few weeks later. He and another soldier were carrying a heavy pallet between them when the other man slipped. The full weight of the load fell on Eddie's foot, causing it to be badly injured and in need of an operation.

The hospital was run on strict disciplinary lines and Eddie, on two occasions, fell foul of the Matron: once after a nurse had failed to make his bed and the Matron demanded to know the culprit and Eddie wouldn't say.

The second occasion brought consequences, when Eddie, confident that his foot was healing nicely, feet tapping to a catchy tune being played on the radio, waltzed around the ward with a nurse who should have been serving the lunches. He was sent back to camp with a barely healed foot, which got worse as he walked back along the country lanes, as no transport had been provided. The M.O., furious at the way Eddie had been treated, sent him back with a curt note for the Matron and he was operated on again without delay.

Eddie was allowed leave a few weeks later, he was of no use to the army whilst he was limping around unable to carry out any duties. He caught the first train out of the local station and was back in his garden by the next day.

It was Autumn again. The hedges were thick with blackberries that year and Irene made jelly with some of her precious sugar ration after she and Ted, with Gina and Lily picnicked and harvested in the Barnston Dales one day.

Eddie made Gina a swing in the back garden and built another hen house, then invested in some white Leghorn pullets which flew about the run like a cloud of delicate fairies, so he put up extra high wire around the place to keep the little egg providers from escaping.

He was busy that leave, though took to resting his foot as much as he could. He helped the elderly small-holder, Sam, who lived in a small, very old, whitewashed cottage at the top of the lane, travelling by the man's horse and cart to the U.S. base at Arrowe to pick up some packing cases that the place had no more use for. They took Gina that day and her two little hands were filled with American candy bars by homesick men delighted to treat her, as English sweets were hard to come by.

Sam also asked Eddie to repair his wife's washing boiler, as she took in washing from the better off ladies of the district. It was an old-fashioned type of copper, which sat on a crumbling brick surround, so Eddie took it out and built her a new surround which held the copper in better.

To make a little extra money, Eddie went to build a vault in Landican Cemetery at the request of a local builder. Skilled tradesmen were at a premium then, either away in the services or on essential war work. It was getting dark before he would finish and, as the funeral was scheduled for the next day, he asked the verger if he would fix up a light for him to continue to work by. The labourer whom Eddie had employed to help him made his feelings plain.

"When it's dark I'm off," he had said, his eyes round with the thought of having to be in such a eerie place, with the owls hooting in the dense dark trees that surrounded it and granite angels staring at him.

Eddie had shrugged, it wasn't the dead who could do you the harm, it was the living. Wasn't Hitler and his cohorts doing just that every day?

Returning to Scotland from his leave, Eddie was put on guard duty at the Main gate. There was quite a lot of traffic passing by at one point in his shift and he had failed to salute a staff car.

The senior officer riding in the back of the car was quite put out by this lack of respect by a lowly soldier and Eddie was duly reported. He had been quite unaware that a charge had been brought against him and was surprised when he was informed by a superior that he had to attend a Military Court.

His Major, a sympathetic soul, accompanied him and in his position as Eddie's defending counsel, pointed out that as the accused wasn't a regular serving soldier, but a 'call up' man, he was bound to get it wrong now and again. Eddie was let off with a caution, but after that episode he was always careful to salute anything or anyone who looked as though they warranted one!

He had started making friends amongst the soldiers in his platoon. Mick was one of the older time serving regulars, who advised Eddie to obtain a copy of the handbook, which laid out all of the rules and regulations of the army. He read it from cover to cover and found that he was entitled to a cup of cocoa every night. Armed with this newfound knowledge, obviously something that hadn't been made aware to the platoon, due perhaps to the cost of serving up the warming drink before lights out, he approached the cook in charge. He was perfectly correct and was entitled also to a wad (an army term for a piece of bread and butter), but woe betide him if he requested it and forgot to turn up for it each night.

One of Mick's pals in the company was a sergeant, a first class soldier, but liked to go on a bender occasionally. He would lose his stripes for this misdemeanour and be demoted back to rifleman. However, he was such a good soldier that he was soon given his stripes back again. On the other hand, Mick was a connoisseur of good whisky and with there being hundreds of soldiers in the garrison town of Hawick, the publicans had a hard job to keep up with the demands. Mick's continual complaint was that the Scottish whisky he was served was not as good as the taste of his Irish whiskey, which didn't go down at all well with the local men and often fights broke out.

The local women, though, did their best to make the soldiers of the garrison welcome by providing a library, a weekly dance and a drop in centre, where those who shunned the taste of alcohol could meet those who had a like mind and drink a warming beverage instead.

Eddie made full use of the library in his spare time and, now that he could read, acquainted himself with the works of many authors, including that of Robbie Burns. He was mindful of Mick's advice, in the infinite wisdom of a regular soldier, as he sat in the billet reading with his feet up: whilst his mates were whooping it up in the town, he should get all the rest he could now. He also signed on for a course in barbering, as there could be a call for his skill overseas.

Training had started in real earnest when all the men had come back from their various leaves. As it was a rifle regiment the men went out every day to practice on the range. Eddie had difficulty in adjusting to this as he was left handed, but he managed to be at the end of the line, which seemed to assist his aim.

They had been going to the range for a couple of weeks when the Major decided to accompany them to check on their progress. He dropped in beside Eddie and asked to borrow his rifle. He fired a couple of shots across the butts and then asked the soldier in charge to mark them up.

"Two bulls and a magpie, Sir," the soldier had replied cheekily, and the Major, knowing full well that he had deliberately fired over the target, was very upset at being given a false report and enraged by the men's apparent laxity. It questioned the sole idea of his checking the accuracy of the platoon's marksmanship and, crimson with rage, he stopped all further practice for the day. Dismissing the lorries waiting to take the soldiers back to camp he instructed them to march back over many miles to the depot, after lecturing them sternly about the ruthlessness of the enemy and that the only things they would have to rely on in action were their weapons and training should not be taken lightly.

It was a much more dedicated and sober platoon which set out to the range the next day, as every man had taken the Major's words to heart. This was training for the real thing, not a boy's day out on a rifle range.

CHAPTER NINE

Telegrams were something that people were very apprehensive about in war time, so when Irene saw the boy coming up her path a few weeks after Eddie had gone back from his leave, it was natural that her heart began to beat quickly with fear.

She opened the missive with trembling hands and, after telling the boy that there wouldn't be a reply, she watched him ride off on his red bicycle and then went indoors. There wasn't much to go on in the words that Eddie had instructed for the post woman in Hawick to write.

"Meet me in London as soon as possible", but if that was what her husband wanted, she would move heaven and earth to meet him there.

Lily, of course, was there to look after Gina and watched with trepidation as her daughter packed the small family suitcase with a change of underwear, a smart brown winter weight dress in case Eddie took her somewhere posh for a meal and took her navy and white checked two-piece suit, still in vogue as no one could afford to wear the latest fashions even if there were any, from the wardrobe, hunting as she did for her best pair of black shoes.

"Gina's been wearing them, look under the bed in our room," Lily had said, holding on to her granddaughter tightly, as Gina had spotted Irene's lipstick and wanted to try it on. She had caught the little monkey trying on her black straw hat only the day before, parading in front of the dressing table mirror with her mother's high heel shoes on.

"I hope I'll be able to catch a train," Irene had said, chucking Gina under the chin tenderly when she came back with the shoes, wearing only her full length petticoat and her navy blouse with the matching necktie. "They might be full, with the soldiers being moved around the country like they are. It must be something very important, though, for Eddie to ask me to go to London as quickly as possible. It might be that he's off to France, Pierre was saying that something was afoot only yesterday."

"We'll all be better off when we get France back off the Germans," Lily said grimly. "And then them Froggies and Yanks can get back to their families, we can get our loved ones back and that Hitler fellow'll get his just desserts."

"Oh Mother, I didn't know you cared," Irene said gaily, looking forward to her trip to London, a place she had been many times with her Aunt Jenny when she was younger. "I thought you were pleased to have the run of the house while Eddie was away."

"I'm talking generally, not just Eddie," Lily said diplomatically, who wasn't a great fan of the man that her daughter had married, but enjoyed having the company of Irene and the care of Gina. "This war's going on much longer than anybody thought."

Irene managed to get a seat on the train from Lime Street quite easily, after paying her ten shillings for her return ticket to Euston at the booth. Although there was a great presence of the forces personnel, a seat was found for the pretty young woman as she hovered in the crowded corridor of the train uncertainly. Of course she had to put up with a bit of banter from the men, most of them having said farewell to their loved ones in Liverpool and needing cheering up, but after a while when she purposely got an Agatha Christie book out of her handbag, she was left alone to read it.

It was late that evening when she scanned the crowds from the spot she had chosen, away from the main thoroughfare at the busy London station. Some were dashing along the platform to catch a train, some rushing out to hail a taxi, others like Irene waited patiently, sitting on their suitcases like she was, their faces grim or sad looking depending on their mood.

She spoke to a young woman who had introduced herself as Doreen, who had propped herself up against the stone wall of the building nearby and found that she too was waiting for her soldier husband to come and collect her.

There was a number of women military police walking around the station. One of these seemed to be watching Irene and her companion very closely. All was revealed when Eddie quickly appeared and, taking Irene by the arm, bundled her outside and began to hurry her along.

"Wait a minute Eddie!" she said, stopping resolutely on the pavement, fleetingly wondering why he had not taken her into his arms and kissed her, which most men would have done if he hadn't seen his wife for a while. "That girl I was with... she's been waiting all day for her husband to appear and she's travelled all the way from up north like I have. Would it be possible for us to take her with us, he might leave her there all night?"

Eddie moaned to himself. Here he was giving himself a last chance to say goodbye to his wife, after sneaking out with a few of his fellow soldiers early that morning, after the battalion had been sent in convoys to a field near Gravesend earlier that week, hoping that it wouldn't be noticed that they were missing that night, knowing full well that they could be court marshalled for going, but willing to take that chance. It appeared now that other regiments had received their marching orders and that was why there was a large presence of the Military, looking for absent men.

"Well, I haven't booked us anywhere, Irene, we might end up sleeping in a doorway. She'll be better off kipping in the station, at least he'll see her there."

"Don't be a meany, Eddie. You wouldn't like it if I was left on my own all night. Besides, I know of a place just down the road from here. It's not what you would call salubrious, but when aunty and I stayed there once it was nice and clean."

"Oh, go on then."

What else could he say? He wasn't going to start a row when in a few days time the regiment was being sent overseas. Not that Eddie would tell her that, not when there was a real possibility he may never see her again.

So the three of them slept in a small three bedded room, with a primitive toilet consisting of a bucket and a tap on the lower landing and listened to the young wife sobbing herself to sleep under her woollen blanket.

"Well at least it was clean," said Irene, as they stepped out into the morning sunshine on the way to find the missing husband. They had dressed hurriedly once the sun had come up and once Doreen had been reunited with her husband they intended to go to the The Lyons Corner House for their breakfast. He was there this time, had actually seen Doreen walk out with the Dockerty's the night before, but hadn't dared show himself, as he too had left the camp without a pass and was afraid with all the Military police around to come out of his hiding place and meet with his wife.

Irene stole an admiring look at Eddie when she heard his words. Rather than leave his wife in apprehension, Eddie had risked a court marshal to be with her.

After they had left the couple, they set off for the popular eating place, which opened early to cater for the many people from all walks of life who appreciated good food at a reasonable price. Irene having to manage on rations marvelled that it was possible to get a meal at all and was impressed with the service of the scurrying waitresses. Later they wandered around the shops together and Irene found a pair of gloves in Gallerie Lafayette for her souvenir of London.

In the evening, after spending the afternoon wandering hand in hand around a large park and doing a little sightseeing, they checked out what film was showing at a cinema in Leicester Square. They decided to watch 'For whom the bell tolls' starring Ingrid Bergman and purchased tickets in the circle costing three and sixpence each, expensive for a couple not accustomed to London prices. They agreed, however, as they came out of the cinema and made their way back to Lyons for their dinner, that the show had been worth every penny, based as it was on Ernest Hemingway's book about the Spanish Civil War.

Irene had been amazed that Eddie was spending his money as if he had won a sum on the horses, but what he hadn't told her was that his mates back at camp, knowing he was taking a big chance, but willing to cover for him, had all made a contribution towards his costs. She put it down to the fact that Eddie wasn't a big drinker, so had been able to save his allowance for a big night out.

Feeling troubled that he was leaving his wife alone, as he really needed get back to camp in case his whereabouts were discovered and Irene had planned to travel back early next morning, Eddie suggested that she went to stay with a cousin by marriage in the Chelsea district of London. The cousin was living in a large flat in Sloane Street with friends and Isabel, Irene's sister, corresponded with her now and again.

They located Sloane Street and found that the hallway, which the cousin invited them into, was bigger than their small house back home! Irene was made very welcome, as she had met her host and hostess on a previous trip to the capital, when they had lived on Highgate Hill. Perhaps the very hill where Dick Whittington had heard the bells tolling "Turn again Dick Whittington, Lord Mayor of London".

Eddie, satisfied that his wife would be well looked after for the night, made his return to the camp.

However his absence had not gone unnoticed, as his expertise with the field ovens had been required and the camp had been scoured for his whereabouts, though when he saw the sergeant cook and had got the ovens working satisfactorily, much to the men's delight, nothing more was said.

The loyalty and support of his mates touched Eddie deeply as he had never encountered men like these before.

Irene had been home four days before the news was released on the radio and in the newspapers that 'Operation Overlord' was to be a reality and not one of the best kept secrets of the war. The first wave of invasion troops had already landed on the French beaches.

She learnt later that her host in London was a war correspondent and he had been present at a meeting with Field Marshall Montgomery at the Savoy Hotel, only hours prior to Irene landing on the doorstep.

He had known and Eddie had known that the invasion of France was only days away!

CHAPTER TEN

On Eddie's return from London, a few days before that fateful invasion in June 1944, the camp was now under canvas and the battalion was being issued with new kit and equipment.

There were visits from distinguished army officers and the men lined up for frequent inspections, but it seemed that only the officers were given something to sleep on, ordinary soldiers were expected to sleep on the ground.

Bemused by this turn of events, Eddie and a few mates scoured the area and found a pile of duck boards in a corner of the field which they commandeered. A few blankets filched from the back of a stationary lorry, ensured their comfort for that first night. However, much later that night the sergeant put his head through the tent flaps and was horrified to find them sleeping in relative comfort, especially as it was the officers' duck boards they were lying on. They were ordered to take them to the officers' quarters the next morning.

Not that the officers had chance to make use of them, as it was on the next morning after breakfast that the battalion was ordered to line up and march down to the dockside, where landing craft waited, rocking gently in the swell of the English channel.

There was a silence amongst the men as they stood there; only the seagulls that circled above an incoming fishing boat could be heard. This was it then. All that training, all that discipline, being deprived of their loved ones to fight this bloody war. Stomachs rumbled as the cook had been stingy with their breakfast, presumably in case of sea sickness amongst them.

There were a couple of Wrens who had been pinning army numbers on the front of the waiting soldiers' uniforms. Eddie, trying to break the tension, though he felt it as much himself, jokingly asked one of the girls had she any food in her pockets? She ran to her billet and came back with half a leg of lamb! It still had fat clinging to it from when she had lifted it from the roasting tin. He blessed her and gave her a kiss, then jumped aboard his designated landing craft.

She had wrapped the lamb in some paper and the older soldiers in the craft, who had become Eddie's friends, looked on the parcel with curiosity.

"And what would that be under your arm then, Dockerty?" one of them wondered, as Eddie made himself comfortable and the smell of the lamb began to compete with the fishy smell abounding.

Eddie unwrapped the parcel enjoying the incredulous looks on the various faces as they stared at its contents. Out came their knives and each cut himself a shive and there was very little left when it came Eddie's way again. He liked to think that it took their minds off what lay ahead of them.

It was not so for the young soldier who lay huddled in a corner whimpering in fear. The men had left him alone, feeling helpless themselves, though they managed to conceal their terror of what might lie ahead of them.

Eddie shook his head and clambered across the others until he reached the young man's side.

"Come on, toughen up," said Eddie. "What would your mammy say if she could hear you?"

"Leave the poor lad alone, he's frightened," said a man from nearby, who was taking his mind off his own fear by playing a hand of cards with a couple of others. Eddie took no notice and hunkered down by the boy, who only looked to be about seventeen, a similar age to his youngest brother, and spoke to him gently.

"Look, don't be afraid mate. You stay by me and I'll see you're all right. Get your gear and come over to sit with me and my pals for the journey. We'll sing a few songs from Ireland and make you feel at home."

The Channel had been smooth when they had first set out, but it soon got choppy as they sighted the French coast. The less hardy quailed as seasickness pangs began to sweep over them and many hung over the craft as they spewed up their stomach contents.

They were a sorry looking bunch as the Normandy beach loomed up ahead, a pleasant place to spend a holiday in peace time, but all that could be seen was barbed wire entanglements looped and trailing over the sandy shore, breached at the cost of the first invasion, and casualties waiting with the dead for ships to take them back home.

Eddie took in the situation at first glance and he moved fast, not waiting for the landing craft to move forward onto the beach. He jumped into waist deep cold water as soon as the board was let down, struggling to carry with him the collapsible bicycle he had been issued with. With his mates shouting that he'd get himself killed and that he was a bloody eejit resounding in his ears, he left the bike behind and took off up the beach because his life depended on it. He could hear the drone of a plane somewhere in the distance and he wasn't about to wait like the others to be the subject of its aim.

Finding cover in a hole below a sand dune, which had been blasted out by a hand grenade but didn't contain a body, he saw that the plane was a Lancaster carrying troops who were to be landed a few miles away. He looked back with relief, as his mates, who had waited until the craft hit shallow water, jumped off rather cautiously without even getting their socks wet!

Their sergeant, who had been speaking with an officer on the beach front, along with another group of soldiers that had their rifles trained on three men in German uniform who had their hands on their heads, explained whilst he sat astride his bike in front of the assembled men now standing by the wall waiting for further orders, that the captured men were German snipers. Apparently during the enemy's onslaught only hours before, these snipers had used the cover of the empty and partially bombed out houses that lined the road to a small village and would be taken back to Britain to be incarcerated in a camp.

With mutters of, "I'd hang the buggers from that bloody tree," and, "Bloody Jerries, they get to sit the war out in sodding comfort", the men were put to work helping to put the dead and injured on the crafts on which they had just landed; a horrid job which made even the most hardened man in their platoon want to weep. When this was done, they got on their bikes and peddled along a narrow lane, except Eddie of course, whose bike had been carried out by a heavy swelling tide.

After an uneasy night, hidden in dug outs that they'd had to hastily dig themselves on a piece of wasteland that must have been an old rubbish tip judging by the various tins, bottles, pieces of rag and broken china that they kept digging up, the sergeant decided after all his men had been through they should get some rest, Eddie, who had an emergency ration pack with him, felt ravenous.

As they passed a field which an economical farmer had planted with alternative rows of corn and potatoes, he left his platoon, some who were peddling along the road at a slow pace as the bikes were quite small for a hefty man and others who had abandoned theirs and were ambling, and felt under the potato haulms for the small new crop. As he collected them, rubbing them with his camouflage netting to get them clean, he scraped them with his finger nails and filled up all his pockets so that he could have them cooked later.

It was a surprised Major who had arrived to regroup, whilst the men were gathering around the cook who had made a scanty meal at the roadside, with the potatoes as a supplement and was given a tasty morsel himself. Later, as he lined up the men, plainly delighted to see some of them that he had served with in earlier campaigns and had been briefed about the sad task they had had to perform on their landing, he was amazed when he got to the end of the line to find the man he thought the least likely to be standing there. He stopped short, disbelief showing in his face as he pumped the man's hand. "My God, Dockerty, you made it!" he said. "Well done man, well done."

Eddie felt a warm feeling growing inside him. He had been a most unwilling soldier since he had received his call up papers. He had found it had taken the utmost self-discipline to comply with all that the army had demanded of him and here he was being shaken by the hand by a fellow survivor. Eddie began to realise the true sense of comradeship which bound them all as one.

He smiled back at the Major, perhaps he had been rather good.

Many miles on, after many battles had been fought and won, the Major was still very thoughtful whenever his eyes rested on Eddie. He was heard to say on many occasions, "My God man, what makes you tick?"

As the Germans retreated inland and Captain Montgomery's men, of which Eddie's platoon was part, moved forward in their wake, they came to the village of Cambes, a place that was actually enclosed by two woods with ten feet walls around them, where they were told to halt as the place afforded some cover. The soldiers camped in a small copse close by, when food at that time, or rather the lack of it was presenting a very real problem.

Eddie and a lieutenant, who had recently joined up with them, went in search for food and luckily came across another platoon who were hiding out up a track that led towards a large forest. They were able to help out with a few tins of pork and a dozen eggs which the lieutenant loaded into his pockets.

The two men were making their way back towards the village when the enemy began to shell. Diving for cover, clutching his knapsack full of tins, Eddie managed to get behind a wall which had railings fixed above it and the lieutenant managed to throw himself into the nearest ditch, which luckily for him was a dry one. The shrapnel kept hitting the railings, giving Eddie some bad moments as he lay there, so when the shelling had subsided he quickly made his way to better shelter in a nearby wood, with the lieutenant rushing to join him. Eddie was about to ask the lieutenant what had happened to the eggs, as the cook began to fry the meat for the men's suppers, when he recalled where the man had put them!

The order came later to attack the village, as it concealed many snipers who had hidden in there. The taking of it turned into a nightmare. The enemy had had time to establish themselves before the platoons arrived and had placed machine guns at strategic points, installed snipers with telescopic glasses and rifles that were strapped to the trees, ready to be set off in an instant.

It took two days of heavy fighting before any progress was made. They dug in deeply, although Eddie being a country man was chosen to go out on reconnaissance patrol at night time; being light on his feet he didn't make any noise, but they were subject daily to constant shelling, which took its toll in lives.

They moved out of that place a few days later, having buried their dead and restored the village to peace again. Orders had arrived via messenger, which directed the men that were still left standing to reconvene at the army's new headquarters.

The chateau, a large white impressive structure, no doubt once owned by minor French gentry who had been forced to give it up by their German conquerors, was situated at the bottom of a hill, which they had called 'Hill 60'. It was a death trap for the men who had been ordered there, as there was constant shelling from the enemy who had the exact range of the place, as they had recently been in residence there.

The Major had been wounded and so had the stretcher bearers, so Eddie and another soldier volunteered to take them to a safer place. There was continuous firing, as the terrified party wended their way along a footpath through the garden at the back of the house, where the French owners fearing for their safety had built a type of Anderson shelter into the hill. Remembering the first aid from the army course which he had taken in his down time during his training in Scotland, Eddie was able to tend the wounded with proper care.

They began to lose three to five soldiers every day, dug in the lawns and woods around the property. The enemy was accurate with their shelling and nifty with their hand grenades and Eddie began to wonder, like every one of his comrades there, if their luck would hold out until tomorrow. His thoughts, before he tried to sleep each night, were of Irene and little Gina and if it hadn't have been for the hope in his heart of seeing them once more, he didn't think he could have made it.

A few days after the Major had been shot, when the enemy had perhaps gone quiet through lack of ammunition, a truck arrived and as many injured were loaded upon it as possible. There were still a few walking-wounded, but the driver handed the lieutenant orders that he was to lead the men in the direction of Caen, where they would be met by a senior command. They were to join a platoon from a tank regiment and would be advancing towards the city.

Eddie's old soldier pals were to be diverted behind the lines and the younger soldiers were to be under the command of a new major. They worried for Eddie and every time the rations and ammunition were sent over, there would be an inquiry as to how their 'boy soldier' pal was faring.

Still on the outskirts of Caen, with nice houses in a prosperous area, Eddie rattled up on the front of one of the tanks that he had hitched a lift on. The tank stopped as a middle-aged Frenchwoman hailed them from her garden and the crew, forgetting that Eddie was sitting on the top, swung the turret around in case she was shielding a sniper. He was knocked to the ground and sat there dazed, as a senior officer, speaking in French, translated her words to the men. She was inviting them to join her for a glass of red wine and an apple each, wishing to celebrate their coming. Eddie was especially favoured after he had been dusted down and set to rights again, earning a large glass of 'Vin du pays' and getting a kiss as well.

Further on as they advanced into the city they were met with continual sniper fire, as the enemy had taken up advantageous positions from houses in the back streets. The lieutenant was shot in the shoulder and Eddie and another soldier dragged him to the nearest shelter, a roughly constructed bunker of wooden logs, which might have been used as an enemy observation post. Eddie was amazed to see a load of women's handbags and wondered why they were there?

After Eddie had fixed up the lieutenant's shoulder as skillfully as he could, the officer asked him to try to take word to the major that he had been wounded. He was to take the sergeant with him, a rifleman too, obviously for cover from any sniper fire. They set off at a pace and were preparing to run between the houses when Eddie, who was ahead, heard his companion shout for him to take cover, just as a bullet whizzed past his head! He worked his way around to the rear of the house and lobbed a grenade through the open window, thus making it safe for the pair of them to continue.

Moving closer to the centre, but becoming lost in the maze of streets, dangerous because every step could be their last if a sniper had his way, they met up with a French girl who spoke perfect English. Drawing them into a wooden shed at the bottom of somebody's yard, she told them that she hadn't seen any soldiers who wore their badges, but offered to take them to the Canadians, as she knew where they were. *What could they do?* She could have been offering to lure them to their deaths, there was no way of knowing, but they followed her anyway as she lead them through the gates of a large house to a rear garden, where they went through a gap in the hedge. Walking with the girl, Eddie took stock of her, wondering why she had no trace of a foreign accent, wearing a light blue summer dress, black stockings and a matching blue headscarf that hid the colour of her hair and he realised that she reminded him of Irene, who was the same height and build. He guessed that she was a member of the French underground known as the Maquis, as these were very active in helping the invasion troops.

She directed them to where the Canadians had established their headquarters, smiling as she left the soldiers, wishing them good luck. They were just in time to witness the Canadian Commanding officer, along with three of his men, chasing a German shepherd dog down the street. He was convinced that the dog was carrying messages to the enemy and it was certainly adept at dodging bullets as it ran.

The C.O. turned his attention to the raggedy appearance of the two British soldiers, who had suddenly appeared at the top of the narrow street, one wearing uniform trousers that were hanging in ribbons and holding a rifle butt that had been split in the middle from a bullet hole. They were taken to safety, that is, to another derelict building, this time with half its roof hanging off, but it gave respite and a new pair of trousers to Eddie, though both the men felt quite shaken by the turn of events.

The next day, Flags of Fighting France were hung out from the houses, as the people of Caen began to celebrate their liberation. Many homes lay in ruins, many fine buildings had been shattered, but the city was free again, but at the cost of many lives.

Eddie, now wearing a pair of British army issue trousers, as the Major wouldn't allow him to wear the Canadian trousers, helped an elderly Frenchman who was pushing an apple barrow to collect the dead. It was also a day of sorrow and of trauma, especially when one of Eddie's comrades was found and could only be identified by the chain with Our Lord's picture hanging around his neck.

CHAPTER ELEVEN

Before moving out of the city, Eddie and two soldiers were sent to check out a farmhouse, which was on the way to the next place where the enemy was said to be. The farmer wasn't there, but his wife and two daughters looked terrified, when suddenly they were confronted by three uniformed men with rifles after the mother had timidly opened the door.

One of the daughters ran to the piano, which was sited in the open plan room at the side of the garden windows. She began to play her country's national anthem, then followed on with the English one. Neither the soldiers nor the women knew a word of each other's languages, so the resourceful girl was trying to use her music to communicate with them. Her mother offered them soup and they tried to reassure her that they meant her no harm, but they had to search the house and the outbuildings.

When it was time to move on again, the city was quiet and there was a fresh task ahead. The company were to march through farming country until they reached a river, where it was understood the enemy had dug in.

The weather was just the right kind for marching and Eddie wished that he hadn't lost his bicycle. It would have been pleasant riding along the country lanes, as some of the men were doing. The farmers whom they passed along the way were friendly, willing to trade their Calvados for any cigarettes that were going. Eddie didn't smoke, but was still allowed a ration as everyone else in his platoon were and really appreciated the apple brandy he was given in return.

He was also an early riser and would slip into a field to milk a cow. He got to like a morning drink of fresh milk laced with brandy, which set him up for the day. However, all good things come to an end, and when there was a bottle inspection he had to rinse his water bottle out with some Dettol that Irene had sent him to combat any infections. The officer gave him a suspicious look and after Eddie had hastily come up with a plausible reason, he was given a lecture on hygiene.

The enemy were established in a brick works some miles away. The weather began to get even warmer and the going got hard along the dusty roads. Towards evening they caught up with the company ahead of them and dug in for the night.

The next day proved to be a disaster for Eddie and his mates. They were taken completely by surprise when a German Tiger tank came swiftly down the track towards them. The lieutenant shouted to get the six pounder gun around quickly and a soldier had to lean on the flash eliminator of it to make the tripod legs come up. Eddie went to the wheel of the gun to pull it around and the shield saved his life, as the shell from the tank hit the six pounder, killing all the soldiers around.

When Eddie picked himself up after lying dazed with shock, he found that all his mates but one were dead. One fellow, who was lying on his side, had just had his hair cut by Eddie only an hour before. The tank having done its evil work had reversed back up the track and disappeared from sight.

Eddie tried to pull himself together, though tears were coursing down his cheeks as he took in the pitiful scene. Looking around he found two survivors from the other platoon. One soldier, who was unhurt, was helping the other who had been wounded in the leg. Eddie recognised the wounded man as the officer's bat man. The soldier who was unscathed, had ripped off the tapes from his gas cape and was making a tourniquet to put around the wounded soldier's leg, and Eddie ran along a hedgerow to fetch help.

A bit further on in a clearing, he found the medical officer who was tending the wounded from a previous skirmish that the stretcher-bearers had recently brought in. Eddie gave him the news of the tank attack and the stretcher-bearers were dispatched along the track.

"You are wounded yourself," said the M.O. quietly, who had been listening to the news from Eddie in grim silence. "You'll need a dressing on that."

Sure enough blood was oozing and staining his shirt, but Eddie hadn't even noticed, he was still in shock. His Irish mates, those good simple men, some who had taken him under their wings, would be buried forever under foreign soil.

He wondered how much longer his own luck would hold out.

In the days that followed, as they moved on nearer to the brick works, then cleared out the enemy who were easily overcome, the lieutenant who had accompanied Eddie to find food lost his life. Then further on, another of his comrades was hit in the face by a spent bullet, which caused it to swell up like a balloon.

Eddie stood by him when a jeep, which was taking casualties off for medical attention, came by. It was full to capacity, but Eddie knew if the soldier's face didn't get seen to straight away there could be problems. He had to use strong arm tactics to persuade a soldier, whose injuries weren't so bad, to vacate his seat and was rewarded a week later, when his comrade came back with his looks intact, except for the removal of a tooth.

The following week, Eddie and his platoon were relieved from duty and were able to spend a couple of days resting in a row of old cottages that had been abandoned by their owners. In their blind panic, they had left behind a lot of their possessions, so the soldiers found the place to have the makings of a comfortable billet.

There were cows in the fields nearby and all wanted milking as their udders were swollen and uncomfortable, so Eddie spent a satisfactory couple of hours supplying his fellow soldiers with frothy buckets of milk. Though the next day, when he had picked up his bucket intending to milk the cows again, it was rudely snatched from him by another soldier who wanted to try his hand.

Eddie watched as the man ran across the road and stepped onto the verge, putting his foot on a shoe mine that the Germans had laid under the grass. Eddie ran, along with the others, to give the man some help and later that day the M.O. on duty had to remove his foot.

It wasn't until the platoon moved out next day, that they saw the notice, "MINES NOT CLEARED IN THIS AREA", which had been out of view behind the hedge.

The following night they caught up with another company who needed reinforcements. There wasn't much rest that night, as the enemy had positioned themselves in strength at the new objective. It was another bitter battle to take command of a turreted chateau, which was to be Command headquarters and officer billets. This time after forcing the Germans to flee, though there was substantial damage to the property, they were given a little longer to rest their tired bones.

It was August, the sunshine was welcome and this was a period where there was nothing much to do. Eddie was free to look around the countryside and, as he had always been interested in how other folks lived, he went to an abandoned farmhouse.

In the garden of the dwelling he came across three straw beehives. He had never seen anything like them before and, picking up a prop from the washing line, he knocked one over. Next minute he was running for his life, as a swarm of angry bees chased him around the farm yard. He dived under the lower half of a stable door to escape, where they fussed and fumed outside for a while then flew off to find their hive!

A horse was still in the stable. Eddie went to make friends with him and as he was patting the horse he noticed a pile of straw in the corner. He went to get an armful, as the horse must have been starving with the owners running away.

As he moved the straw, there was something hard on the ground beneath and he found it to be a barrel with a tap on it. He turned the tap slowly and a trickle of liquid came out. Lo and behold it was cognac! Not being a greedy man, he filled the water bottle that he always carried with him, and covered the barrel with straw again. It was just his secret (and the farmers).

One of the other soldiers, called Ernie, had accompanied him that day, but had been chasing another horse around a nearby field to get a ride. The horse was being way too smart for him and Eddie shook with laughter as he saw the poor man's attempts. He gave up trying when Eddie showed him the contents of his water bottle and was a much happier man when he'd had a swig.

On their way back to their billet, they found a lone cottage, again it looked as if the owner had abandoned it. Ernie had his eye on the wooden shutters that covered the windows, thinking that they could be the very thing to cover over their slit trenches, which they often had to dig. He went inside the small gate and pulled out his bayonet in order to tackle the rusty nails that held the shutters in place. He was working away at loosening the shutters when the door of the cottage flew open and out shot a little Frenchwoman. She was in a terrible temper and was shouting away at Ernie in her foreign tongue. He stood rooted to the spot, until she flew at him with raised fists ready to thump the perpetrator and when he suddenly realised her intention, he took to his heels and fled!

Eddie, who had gone ahead, leaving Ernie to his own devices, looked back over his shoulder at the sound of running feet. He turned around fully and began to shake with laughter again, as he saw the soldier pounding away in his army boots, chased by a woman half his size in hot pursuit. She nearly caught him, as her short legs clad in thick black woolly stockings and wearing wooden sabots, made better time than Ernie in his heavy boots and carrying his rifle. When she caught sight of Eddie, she must have decided not to take on two of them and turned back to the cottage much to Ernie's relief.

An elderly Frenchman went past their billet every morning. Starting as soon as it was light enough he would work in his fields from dawn to dusk. He carried a long loaf, a piece of cheese and a bottle of wine. Eddie watched him, marvelling that the man could work all day on such simple fare, returning only in the evening to his farm house and the meal, which his equally hard working wife had prepared.

As his company were not in action but resting, Eddie had set up an area for haircutting. He had finished his duties and every soldier after his short back and sides, looked neat and trim, when he received special orders to attend the officer billet and give the Brigadier and two sergeants a hair cut. He was cleaning his tools to put them away when the French farmer, who must have followed Eddie back along the country lane, asked one of the lieutenants who spoke fluent French, would Eddie give him a haircut and a shave? He agreed to do this and set to work getting soap and hot water.

He sat the farmer down on a box first and trimmed his hair, then he arranged a cloth around his neck and proceeded to strop an old fashioned razor, before lathering the man's face. Eddie had never shaved another man before and when he started to get to work the razor wasn't sharp enough and pulled at the hairs.

The farmer jumped to his feet and shouted, "Nix coiffeur, nix coiffeur."

The lieutenant laughing out loud said, "He doesn't think much of you as a barber."

Eddie apologised and, knowing that his reputation was at stake, ran to his billet where he took out his own safety razor. Returning quickly he shaved the man and was rewarded with his water bottle being filled with cognac again.

On that same afternoon, the farmer's son, a man of about twenty-two, had left the farm and returned at dusk. He was riding a beautiful black horse, which was sweating from being ridden over a great distance. Eddie was still with the farmer when his son came to speak to him. It appeared that the horse had been sent to a safe place whilst the Germans had been in occupation. Now it was time for the farmer to have him returned again. After the horse had cooled down, Eddie was allowed to feed it and help bed it down for the night. Along with the family, he felt the pleasure that the horse could come back to the farm again.

Eddie was often out at night on reconnaissance patrol as he was extremely good at moving silently though woods and thickets. He was always in his element, as he could walk like a cat at night time and, like them, seemed able to see in the dark.

One night when there was no moon, a fighting patrol had failed to return at the expected time. An hour went by and the officer in charge came to the billet to see Eddie.

Eddie had just returned from guard duty and was lying on the bed after loosening his boot laces. This officer wasn't on good terms with Eddie because he had refused to take on the duty of being the lieutenant's bat man and, on this occasion, Eddie was curtly ordered to get out and look for the missing patrol.

So he made his way quietly along the route that he had been given, until some muted voices came into his ears.

"He's got us lost..." someone began to shout loudly and there came a muttered reply.

It was then that Eddie realised this was the patrol he was looking for and, creeping up quietly, he touched one of the men on his shoulder with his bayonet.

"I'm Eddie, I've been sent out to fetch you in," he whispered, as the small group of men turned frightened faces towards the interloper. "Get word up to your corporal, then come with me."

Eddie was getting more and more anxious at the noise that the soldiers were making, as they shouted to their comrades that someone had come to take them back.

"Thank God you've come," said the corporal in a relieved voice, when he arrived later after his unit had been rounded up. "We've been wandering around for the past half hour."

"The noise your patrol was making could be heard from some distance. You were lucky not to have been picked off by the Germans," Eddie couldn't help but say.

His errand successfully carried out, he received no praise from the waiting officer. Instead he was put on a charge for being improperly dressed in the billet, as his laces had not been done up!

At the next town that they were marched to, Eddie didn't usually know the names of these places at the time, the platoon was billeted in a grain warehouse. The lieutenant had taken the office for his quarters, so he slept there as well and half of the soldiers had chosen to sleep on the upper floor and the other half downstairs.

Eddie had placed his bedding under the grain chute which ran from the upper floor to the ground, thinking he would have a bit of cover from any possible shelling. This could come at any time, as the enemy was still lurking on the outskirts.

Eddie had arranged with a local baker to heat up a tin of water the next morning, so he could have a bath. In return the baker was given fifty cigarettes for his trouble, but Eddie had to be there early before the man started to make his bread.

He turned in early and it wasn't long before he fell into a deep sleep. In the middle of the night he was awakened by water dripping onto his face. He assumed that it was raining and began to move his bedding out of the way, then he realised the real reason for the water and began to bawl at the top of his voice!

"You dirty bastards," he shouted, and went on about the unclean habits of the men upstairs, until the rest of the men told him to shut his mouth and go back to sleep.

He awoke from a fitful sleep at dawn and, remembering the hot water that he had been promised at the bakery, hastily dressed and went out to claim it. It was good to wallow in the warmth of the bath and, feeling refreshed after he had given himself a close shave, he wandered into the street again.

A soldier stood at the top of the street, bleary eyed after a stint on night duty, and jumped at the chance of having a bath when Eddie explained he hadn't emptied it. They exchanged rifles, as Eddie had promised he would look after his.

The lieutenant came out of the warehouse and wearily walked along the street. He had spent a most uncomfortable night on the office floor, wedged into something like a cubby hole and seeing Eddie, who shouldn't have been standing on guard, rather he should have been with the others in the grain store, he immediately pounced on the situation to make the most of it.

The soldier, hearing the lieutenant berating Eddie, snatched up his clothes and disappeared leaving Eddie's rifle by the pump. The officer, seeing the rifle by the pump walked along and picked it up.

Later that day Eddie was ordered to attend the Major's quarters to answer three charges. "Shouting in the night and causing a disturbance." "Changing the guard without an officer's permission." "Leaving a rifle by the pump unattended." Eddie felt fed up.

The next time he was told to report to the Major because of another petty thing he was being charged with, Eddie took his hairdressing tools with him. He asked for permission to speak and told his superior.

"With these extra guard duties I am constantly receiving as punishment, I can't do my duties as a rifleman and my other job as a company barber. I will have to give my job as a barber up."

The Major took this very calmly.

"Do you realise, Dockerty, if you went into action tonight and I lost you in that action, I would have to replace you. I would have to find another barber and he might not be as good as you, but he'd learn, as you did."

Eddie's sergeant was upset. He had become aware of the tension between the two men after his private had refused to be a bat man for the newly arrived officer. As Eddie had remarked that it took him all his time to look after himself, he was after all a trained rifleman and first class marksman.

A week later, much to Eddie's relief, the lieutenant was transferred to another company and the Major gave him his hairdressing tools back.

CHAPTER TWELVE

It was a bitterly cold day, one of the coldest in wartime. Eddie was on guard duty and blew constantly on his hands in an effort to warm them. He wished he had a glass of cognac or a tot of rum to drink. He walked around the area that he was guarding, up and down, stamping his feet, trying to bring some feeling back. He checked his army pocket watch, he'd be relieved from duty in five minutes time.

A few minutes later as Eddie saw the relief guard in the distance, he heard a child screaming from one of the cottages nearby. He quickly handed over to the hurrying soldier and ran to the cottage as fast as he could. Smoke was billowing from the open door and, as Eddie rushed through it and into the foggy front room and beyond to the kitchen, he noticed an open door that had steps going down to the cellar. The smoke was coming up from the cellar. Coughing and choking, Eddie landed at the bottom of the steps to find an old lady with her clothes on fire, too helpless to move from the overturned oil stove.

He took off his greatcoat, rolled her into it, thus smothering the flames that had enveloped her thin body. He carried her to safety, then went back to the cellar to stamp out the flames. The oil had been used up by then, so it had been quite easy.

Leaving the old lady and the trembling child in the care of concerned neighbours, Eddie carried on to his billet to find that his army greatcoat was beyond repair. It took a while and a little soft soaping for the store man to give a replacement for him to wear.

A few days later, when his platoon was in line in readiness to move out of the area, an elderly Frenchwoman ran along the line of soldiers. She stopped when she recognised Eddie and pressed a small item into his hand. He slipped the small tissue wrapped object into his jacket pocket and forgot about it until night time. He was surprised to find a small gold cross, obviously one of the woman's most treasured possessions and decided to give it to Gina when he got home.

The company was now in Belgium on the outskirts of the city of Louvain. The store man had gone on leave and Eddie had been ordered to mind the store while he was away. They were not in action, but behind the lines at the time, so Eddie combined his duties as the company barber, cutting hair for the H.Q. staff that were billeted nearby. The villagers who lived around the area were very friendly and Eddie cut the hair of an elderly Belgian and was rewarded with a pretty lawn and lace handkerchief from the man's wife.

After the store man came back, Eddie was given a forty-eight hour leave. He took the money he had been saving and went to Brussels, as he planned to take home a pair of Continental shoes for Irene. There were lots of girls in the city as Brussels had not suffered the effects of the war, as the King of Belgium had given in without fighting and allowed the German Army through the land without hindrance.

The city was a Mecca for all leave parties who wanted to enjoy city life and buy from the well-filled shops. Over a cup of coffee in a busy café, Eddie talked to a couple of the friendly locals and told them he was going to buy some shoes for his wife. They offered to help and Eddie found himself in a shoe shop, where one of the girls who had a shoe size the same as Irene's, chose a beautiful pair of black calf leather with wedge heels and sling backs.

It was in Brussels that Eddie met up again with Charley. Charley was a coloured soldier who was born in Liverpool and Eddie had first met up with him at the battle for Caen. The platoon had fought their way towards the city and were waiting for more ammunition at a crossroads when Charley, who was the driver of the truck, turned up with it. He was a big man and extremely handsome, he seemed to be completely without fear, standing there laughing and kidding as if there wasn't a horrible war on, the wind blowing through his black curly hair, whilst he had watched them unloading. "Come on you fellows, move it!" he had shouted when the soldiers didn't seem to be putting their backs into lifting off the heavy boxes. "Get this stuff off my carrier. This isn't my war, mine starts when we coloureds takes over."

Charley had greeted Eddie with open arms and he seemed to know his way around Brussels, as much as he would have known his way around Liverpool. His uniform was pressed with the professional touch, with knife edge creases down his trousers and it appeared that he had many good friends living in the city. Eddie asked him for directions to a jewellers shop, where he could buy a thin gold chain for the cross he was keeping for Gina.

Whilst he was walking around the city and looking in the windows of the well-stocked shops there, he saw a familiar face in the crowds of civilians. It was a soldier posted as a deserter. The soldier's mother was a French woman and her son could speak the language fluently. He had disappeared after a major battle and had completely vanished. He stared at Eddie for a few seconds, raised his hand in a salute then quickly disappeared into the crowds.

The company was on the move again when Eddie got back from Brussels. They marched along through the countryside until dusk was falling and then they were called to a halt.

The soldiers had found temporary shelter, whilst an advance party went out silently through the fields and woods to look for a better place to stay.

A little later, whilst the cooks were serving up a hasty meal of tinned meat and a hunk of bread, the enemy commenced to throw up flares, vivid sheets of light that lit up the countryside. The watching soldiers went hot and cold at the sight, but one wag, an officer who was trying to keep their spirits up, suggested that as it was Guy Fawkes night, the 5th of November, the Germans were putting on a display.

The advance party returned and they followed them to what turned out to be a centuries old castle. Whilst Eddie marched with his platoon across the drawbridge, through the huge wooden doors and into a courtyard, he had the strangest feeling that he had been there before. Not in his life time as he remembered it, but he certainly had a feeling of deja vu.

The kitchen had a stone flagged floor and was dimly lit, with a huge fireplace that stretched along the far wall with a wooden beam above it. It felt as if he had returned home with everything looking so familiar and he knew where everything was in the place, which was very uncanny.

The old castle stretched its arms around the weary men that night, and the sound of battle didn't penetrate the centuries old stone walls. The soldiers slept like infants under the thickness of the army blankets. There were no beds to sleep on, but enough blankets for all.

They felt so safe, probably safer than they had ever felt since leaving England.

In the morning the cooks were up bright and early, serving porridge, bacon and eggs and sweet tea to a well rested company of men. After their meal they gathered their kit together, then forming into their own platoons they were on their way again.

Back at home, there wasn't the fear of nightly bombing anymore, although London had been experiencing the nasty doodle bugs, it seemed that Hitler had his mind elsewhere.

People were tired of the rationing, shortages of food and clothing, with restrictions like the blackout still being enforced, but there was a feeling of hope that it wouldn't be long before it was all over. Soldiers were given leave, now that the enemy was putting its energies into the Russian campaign, including Eddie, who was able to catch up with the news and family gossip and visited the Club at night.

He liked to listen to the news on the radio, it was a focal point in their home at the time. ITMA was very popular and the gags and sayings were quoted widely. Tony Hancock, Elsie and Doris Waters and others of their time had a great following. Lord Haw Haw was the broadcaster for a German propaganda programme. He had a very British accent and he dealt in half truths, so that people might believe the most outrageous of his statements. Some people took him very seriously and it was said to have smashed their radio sets to pieces in their rage, but most people looked upon him as a big joke. They usually switched him on if they were feeling bored with other programmes and knew it for what it was, propaganda, but it was easy to fall into a depression if your morale wasn't very high.

During Eddie's time in Belgium, Irene had written that one of her Australian cousins called Frank had come over with the Australian Air force. She had got to meet him when he had looked his family up and there had been a get together at Isabel's house in Southport. He had looked very handsome in his navy uniform. They had assisted the British Air force, flying in Wellingtons and Lancasters across to Germany, which had become a nightly occurrence as they bombed the hapless cities to Hell.

He had been there when his best friend's plane, which was flying ahead, was the target of anti-aircraft fire, being blown to pieces as his horrified mate looked on and although Frank took the Distinguished Flying Cross back to Australia, he also would have taken bad memories back as well.

Returning from his leave in England, happy that his Gina hadn't forgotten who her daddy was and had been delighted with her pretty cross and chain, Eddie found that there had been another big battle and the company was preparing to move on again.

They marched at dawn along a road that seemed to stretch for miles into the distance. On one side the woods were thick with pine trees, on the other farmers' fields, with farmhouses and small cottages dotted here and there. Most of the cottages looked abandoned, with gardens thick with weeds, but they found one place with tomatoes growing up the outside wall. The skins were cracked through lack of watering, but some of the men dropped out and picked handfuls of the delicious fruit.

The Irish lads from the Free State, drawn from depleted platoons to make a bigger one, started singing, 'The wearing of the green' 'The sash me Father wore' and 'Kevin Barry'.

The officer in charge shouted to them to keep quiet, not because he didn't enjoy their singing, but further on he warned them of the perils of being heard by the enemy. There was silence from then on and only the sound of marching boots could be heard.

Many miles were covered before they were called to a halt, as the ration wagon had caught up and was about to dispense tea and sandwiches in a small wooded clearing. As there was plenty of shelter the officer decide that they would dig in and spend the night there.

Next morning it was misty and once the camp came to life again, they found it wasn't very far to their next objective.

In the distance they could see a large body of water. On closer inspection they found it was a canal and there were engineers waiting on the water with boats. The platoon crossed without incident, except for a hail of bullets that had rained upon them as they prepared to land on the other side.

The attack came soon. A fierce attack which gave the gunners they had joined up with and themselves a very bad time, but the enemy was eventually repelled, which allowed another platoon to make the crossing.

Eddie spent the night in a ditch and by dawn, not having had any sleep, he could hardly keep his eyes open. He desperately wanted to close his eyes again, but stiffened when he saw a bicycle passing him by on the road above. It was a lady's bike, but it wasn't a woman who was riding it. A German soldier was astride it, peddling away furiously, hoping his luck wouldn't run out.

A rifle cracked and he fell off, with the bicycle clattering across the road. It had a carrier fixed to the handlebars and the soldier had put a round red Dutch cheese in it that had fallen out and was rolling into the gutter.

On the other side of the road, a door of a cottage had opened and a woman stood transfixed by the scene, petrified with fright. A little child ran from behind her and she automatically bent down and picked him up.

Later, Eddie confessed that he must have been off his head, as he broke his cover and ran across the road, picking up the cheese as he went. Reaching the woman, he put the cheese into her arms, then pushed her, the child and the cheese back into the cottage and slammed the door on them!

He was lucky enough to be back under cover before the next happening. A horse and cart came racing up the road, it had broken out suddenly from a farm gate further along. The cart was loaded with soldiers, guns and food and the driver was hoping by its speed to get by without hindrance. The men came up from their cover and one of them lobbed a grenade, landing in the rear of the cart as the vehicle passed them by. The horse escaped injury, but the surviving enemy gave themselves up.

In that action the platoon lost one of their best loved lieutenants when a machine gun had gone into action at the end of the road. Some of the men were ordered to silence it and the lieutenant had led them to do this. In the fighting that ensued he lost his life.

It had been strange that Eddie and he had been talking only a couple of nights before; the officer had been rather depressed while they had sat together enjoying a drink of cognac each after they'd dug in.

He had asked Eddie to promise to get in touch with his relatives if he died in one of the next few days' actions, as Eddie only lived a stone's throw from where the lieutenant's mother lived.

Later he carried out his mission with great sorrow, for as he said to Irene, "He was one of the nicest lads I had ever met. People read about these things in books about wars and brave men, but they are just ordinary men who are prepared to do their duty as they see it. They stick their ground because of their high quality of training and the discipline in the months of preparation and no praise can be high enough for them."

It took all of Eddie's courage to go and see the lieutenant's sorrowing mother, and thought about his bravery often in the months to come.

"Golden lads and lasses too, all go down to dust."

After this action was finished and mopping up operations completed, they were marched on to Holland. Once across the border they found it to be very flat country with thickets of trees running along each side of the road. They had an ecstatic reception from the Dutch people whom they met as they marched in. There they found another canal that had to be crossed before they came to grips with the enemy; an enemy who had by then become well organised.

It was there that Eddie came nearer to a town named Cuyk, a place that brought him a lifetime of memories.

At a small village on their way, they took over an empty house, checking it over very carefully as they did so, as the Germans were well known for booby traps. Once it was established, Eddie was put on a spell of guard duty and he noticed a young girl moving swiftly around the little farm that was opposite to their billet. She was looking about her as if she was fearful of being watched, making in the direction of what appeared to be a collection of pigsties, then disappearing suddenly behind a haystack. Eddie had noticed that she carried a bowl in her hand and was puzzled, because there didn't seem to be any livestock on the farm.

When he was off duty he went to the place to investigate. He had to be very alert and careful as there were still pockets of snipers around, who had been taking up positions in the most unexpected places. To his amazement, after he had carefully examined the haystack, he found a boy, who looked to be around the age of eight or nine, hiding in its centre. He had obviously been living inside it and even had an observation hole from which he could see the world around him. Eddie took the frightened boy back to the farmhouse, where the girl was waiting for him by the front door. She looked terrified, but explained in halting English that the boy had been hidden in the haystack for quite a long time. Even now she expected the Germans to come back and find him.

It appeared that both children were Jewish. Their parents were dead and the man who owned the farm had kindly taken them in when they had nowhere else to go. The girl didn't have any trace of her Jewish origin, but the boy unmistakably had. Eddie looked at his olive skin, dark hair and features and could immediately see the difference between them.

She began to cry and Eddie did his best to comfort her, assuring the sobbing girl that the Germans would not be coming back again and he would take her brother to his superiors, who would undoubtedly want to know what had been going on.

The boy, who had valuable information due to what he had seen from his peephole in the haystack, was escorted back to his sister later on.

It must have been a wonderful feeling for both of them, when they realised the nightmare was over and could resume the happy life they'd had before the coming of the Germans.

CHAPTER THIRTEEN

The months wore on, leaves were coming up more regularly and Eddie came home to a peaceful England. Any bombing now was being done in reverse, it was the German cities that were getting the hammering and only London had been victim to the last doodle bugs.

To his wife and family, Eddie was full of fun again, miraculous when one contemplates the baptism of fire that he and his fellow soldiers had been through. He had said that he had lost touch with many of the regular soldiers whom he had trained with in Ireland. They had been together in the invasion, but many had been lost in the fighting that followed, or had been transferred to a different company.

However, after one of his leaves as he was marching along with his platoon, he met up with some of them, much to his delight. His company was passing through a heavily shelled town and, as they did so, Eddie saw some familiar faces, as some of the regiment were still quartered there.

Most of the houses and shops were in ruins and the roads were ankle-deep in mud. He dropped out when he noticed some of the men he had come over with, his first inquiry being where was Mick? The soldier, with a big grin on his face, told Eddie the man's whereabouts, pointing to a still standing warehouse further along the track.

There was a big department store that Eddie had marched past, its windows all smashed and the doors hanging off their hinges, but he had noticed some beautiful models lying in disarray in various stages of undress. He selected a model clothed in the scantiest underwear, tucked it under his arm and went to find Mick.

He snuck into the billet where Mick, who liked to catch up with his rest when he was able to, was lying fast asleep. He placed the pretty model into the bed beside him and tiptoed out again, sorely regretting that he couldn't be there to check out his friend's reaction.

In months to come he met up with a soldier who had been in the billet when Mick awoke. His first question had been, "Has that Eddie Dockerty's company been through?"

The billet had been in an uproar, as Mick had put the model in another sleeper's bed, who happened to be a sergeant, then the sergeant awoke and put it into another sleeper's bed. In this way the model travelled around the billet, until a grumpy man put his boot under her and she was tossed into the bushes.

Deep into the Dutch countryside, Mick and the town were left far behind as the company marched on. Although still very flat, the area was thickly wooded. Many areas could only be described as thickets, where vast stretches of un-penetrable slender saplings all reached up to the sky for a place to live.

They were nearing a river, where the woods were giving way to farmer's fields and a big black mill stood sentinel at the side of the road. In the distance there was the outline of a small town. At this point the company was halted and a reconnaissance party sent out. Eddie was one of them.

An earlier recce had reported that there were snipers in the area and another factor was the sandy soil around there. Vehicles couldn't operate on the sandy tracks, so everything had to be brought along by hand.

Slipping through the streets of the quiet town of Cuyk, situated as it was on the West bank of the Dutch Meuse, Eddie came upon a convent. A nun was outside getting water from a copper boiler and looked up in alarm when Eddie spoke to her. She backed away, spilling the water from her flowing bucket in her haste. He spoke gently and, although she was afraid, she pointed to the convent and motioned him to stay. She returned a little later with a priest.

Eddie was not much better placed with a priest as he didn't speak English either and kept talking away in French. When he made no headway, he too went away. He came back accompanied by a tall, thin girl in her early twenties. She looked sternly at Eddie through her steel-rimmed spectacles before she spoke to him in perfect English.

"Who are you and what do you want?" Her voice sounded quite chilly.

"I want some information," Eddie answered simply.

He explained to the girl that he was an English soldier who had been sent to find out the enemy's position. Where they still in the town or had they evacuated? The girl looked at him with a blank expression on her face.

"Where are the Germans?" he asked urgently. "Are there snipers in the town? If so where are they placed? Please tell me if you know, the information is vital to us!"

The girl turned to the priest and spoke to him quickly in Dutch, translating what the soldier had said to her. She waited for his reply, then turned again to Eddie.

"The priest said that if we give you the information and the Germans come back, then they will take reprisals. They have already shot two Americans who came here asking questions."

"I am here with a regiment which has never been pushed back since we invaded the Normandy beaches," said Eddie proudly. The priest listened carefully as the girl translated. He looked at Eddie standing there. He saw a thin, dark, weary man, but he sensed the determination that would brook no refusal. He heaved a great sigh and spoke in Dutch to the girl again.

"Give him the information he wants… but first we must tell him about our refugees."

They took Eddie down to a dimly lit cellar. He saw about a dozen people, mostly the elderly and small children lying around on rough bedding.

"These people are here for sanctuary. We are putting them as well as ourselves at risk in telling you what you want to know. Tell me again what it is you want."

They started to talk. The girl gave him all the information he needed. "There are snipers in the church steeple, in houses all around the town. Some have already gone across the river and they shoot at the people if they walk down the lane to buy food from the farms."

She spoke rapidly, telling him everything he needed to know.

Eddie thanked her and the priest, smiled gently at the nervous-looking onlookers, then left the convent, hoping that he wouldn't be seen by the enemy. He used great caution and what cover he could find, bearing in mind what the girl had said about the Germans being in the town.

Back at camp, he found his sergeant who listened attentively, then the man sent a runner with a message for the C.O. The message came back that they should all take cover as they were going to shell.

The platoon fled to the nearest shelter and as he ran Eddie's thoughts were on the church steeple, glad he wasn't up there when the guns started up.

The enemy retreated over the Meuse and at last the town was clear again. There were more troops moving in before Eddie saw the Dutch girl again. He found that her name was Anny and she had learned to speak her excellent English when she had been at college.

He went back to the convent as often as he could and on his first visit there he had found a young novice lying unconscious by a heap of fuel at the rear of the building. He summoned help, then carried her into her cell. She was very frail and Eddie thought that she may well be suffering from malnutrition, so he went back to the billet and collected all the chocolate rations from the men who would part with them. He went back and inquired how the young novice was doing and took the chocolate with him as a present for her. From then on he was made very welcome, even allowed to work in the kitchen where he found it was a hive of industry. The sisters were quiet as they worked on their various tasks of cooking and cleaning for the convent residents.

It was actually quite a large community and Anny, only too happy to practice her English, was often there.

One day, a small accordion was being played by a young boy in a corner of the kitchen. Anny invited Eddie to try the Dutch style of dancing and gave him a pair of clogs to dance in. He found it much faster than the ballroom dancing that he was used to, but it was bouncy and exhilarating and he found himself out of breath when the music stopped.

The convent washing hung down from a pulley suspended from the ceiling and Eddie and Anny had brushed it several times as they had danced around the kitchen. Finally a pair of stockings fell off the pulley and into a pan of soup that was bubbling away on the stove. Eddie glanced around the kitchen apprehensively, but as no one was looking, Anny fished the stockings out of the soup, wrung them out in the nearest sink, then placed them back on the pulley.

Eddie remarked that the soup may taste a little different than usual. Anny just smiled, it was not going to be her supper.

When more troops moved in and occupied the town, Eddie's platoon was billeted in the hospital wing of the convent. Eddie was really out of order, when he asked in a jocular tone, that the young novice he had brought the chocolate to should give him a kiss. The young girl blanched, dropped the cleaning bucket she was holding and fled.

She must have complained to Anny, who came posthaste to give him a lecture on his bad behaviour. He didn't appear to be very repentant, as when she had finished, he asked her to give him a kiss instead. He came as near to having his face slapped as he ever did!

She forgave him later when she got to know him a little better, becoming good friends. There was no language barrier, so he could talk freely and she came to understand the kind of man he was.

The people in the convent were the only Dutch folk that Eddie had met at first. He supposed there must have been others, but he never met them. After the troops had conducted house to house searches in the town, more people started to appear. Eddie never found out where they had been to, whether they had been evacuated by the Germans, or gone into hiding, he never knew.

By the time that Eddie's company moved out, the town had

come back to near normality, or as near as possible in war time. The Canadians were the next troops in, but by that time Eddie's regiment were some miles south of Cuyk. When they had made camp, the Major asked Eddie to give him a haircut.

The Major sat on an upturned jerry can by a slit trench, while Eddie snipped away at his hair. A shell came out of the blue sky and buried its nose in the soil some yards away, but it didn't explode. Eddie had thrown himself into the trench in two seconds flat! The Major, with the towel still around his neck and the comb in his hair, looked down at him from above.

"My word, Dockerty," he said mildly. "Your nerves must be in a terrible state, we will have to do something about them."

Eddie expected to be given leave, or at least be sent to the M.O., but instead the Major, not given to running a one man welfare state and convinced that therapy was the best thing, sent Eddie to cut hair in a place called St. Anthonis. He was instructed to open up one of the empty shops there, but he was only to cut the hair of his own 'A' company men.

It was night time when Eddie arrived in St. Anthonis. He was hungry, thirsty and very tired, having had to walk fifteen miles to get there. He could hear a cook's blower going as he passed a building, so he tapped on the door and, after explaining his mission and how far he had travelled, asked for food and drink. The cook, who was a surly man, refused him saying that his rations were up the line and there'd be nothing for him there.

Eddie went to bed in an empty shop that night feeling very hungry, but in the morning, after he had folded his blanket, had a wash, dressed himself, then opened the shop, putting a sign outside which said he was the 'A Company Barber'; the door opened and in came his very first customer. He sat down in the chair provided and waited to have his hair cut.

"You can get out of that chair and clear off," Eddie said when he came in from the privy out back and saw the cook had come for a haircut.

"I want my haircut!" The cook said angrily.

"Can't you read? My sign says 'A Company Barber'. So clear off, you're not from 'A' Company."

The cook fussed and fumed, but he had to leave without a haircut.

Eddie cut the hair of everyone available in the company and when he had finished he asked the sergeant in charge if he could go to visit friends in Cuyk. Anny had extended an invitation to him as he was leaving, that he should go and meet her parents if he was ever that way again.

The sergeant said that he could, but he was unable to give him a pass. There was also no transport available, as the vehicles were all engaged in taking supplies up to the front line. He had to make his own way back again and found it hard going, as tracks had been made in the soft sand by heavy tanks and trucks and, as there had been a recent downpour, there were lots of pools of rain. He had to take all his possessions with him, as the hairdressing tools were too precious to be left behind.

Eddie walked through miles of the flat Dutch country with its long flat roads. Had he been at home, there would have been shortcuts he could follow, but in this foreign country it was safer to stick to the roads. He changed his mind, though, as he got nearer to the town and the area became more familiar.

He walked some way down a dark high-hedged lane, looking forward to seeing his friends at the convent, especially Anny, but suddenly the hairs on the back of his neck stiffened. He stopped in his tracks. Was that a row of gun barrels poking out through the hedge to the right of him further along the lane?

After a few frozen minutes, he noticed that all was silent, no one had moved or spoken. He forced himself to move forward and investigate.

He moved himself up to the first of the gun barrels, only to find on closer inspection, that it was just a big bluff. Slim tree trunks had been trimmed and shaped exactly like guns, then placed in position in the hedges. Eddie had experienced tricks like this before, but this one was clever and had really scared him. He continued along the lane walking on the vehicle tracks, in case there was an unexploded land mine.

It was getting really dark when Eddie finally reached his destination. He only had verbal permission to be there by the sergeant, so as the Canadians were occupying the town by then, he was nervous of encountering their Military police or any English ones for that matter. He had sped silently through the deserted streets towards the convent, which was the only place he knew.

His heart sank, as he knocked on the thick oak of the convent, when he realised that it was possible that Anny had gone back home for the night, making conversation impossible with the convent dwellers and he didn't know where she lived.

After a short interval the door was opened by a nun and, without speaking, she beckoned Eddie to go inside, then ran quickly to fetch the priest to see him. Eddie managed to convey to the priest that he wanted to speak with Anny and the small boy on the bicycle was dispatched with a message.

Anny came quickly once the priest's message had been given to her. She had many calls on her services as a linguist now that the Canadians were billeted in the town. She was surprised to see Eddie in the courtyard, possibly because he had taken up her invitation so quickly, but now his duties as a barber were over, he had been left to cool his heels.

He was made very welcome by her parents, though they couldn't speak a word of English, but with Anny interpreting, they were able to communicate.

Anny also had other brothers and sisters who had learnt to speak English at school, so they were really happy to practice the language too. He never found out, though, why Anny had introduced him as "Jimmy" but he was happy to be called just that.

When the meal was over, a simple meal, but enjoyed by all as they had only recently been reunited as a family, the daughters got up to clear the table and Eddie offered to help with the washing up.

They were horrified. It wasn't done for a man to do a woman's job, he was to sit with the father, a small grey-haired man, whom Eddie had been told was a businessman, but if he hadn't known that, thought he looked like a professor. The matter was settled and Eddie sat with Father who had produced a stone bottle containing schnapps to share. Eddie, who was used to drinking brandy, found the spirit very palatable and he settled back quite comfortably with his new found friends.

As the evening wore on, Anny told Eddie that as every bed was occupied at their house, she had made arrangements for him to stay in their neighbour's home and, when the parents showed signs of wanting to retire, she took him across the road, where again, he was made very welcome. It was all very quiet and peaceful, far away from the noise of battle and he got to sleep in a real bed again.

Anny called for him next morning when he had woken, refreshed after sleeping like a baby and took him back to eat breakfast at her home. He was welcomed by Anny's mother, a quiet little woman, who had given Eddie the impression she was deeply religious and the family, much taken with the chance of plying him with questions in their best English, found once again it was a heaven sent opportunity to speak with an Englishman.

After breakfast was over and Anny had the opportunity to speak with Eddie again, he found that one of her many jobs included delivering the mail. It was her day, opportunistically for Eddie, to drive out to St. Anthonis, where she had a parcel to deliver. He drove back to his barber's shop in style, although he had to lie on the floor of the vehicle as they drove through the streets of Cuyk, as he hadn't got a pass.

When he got back, he went straight to the sergeant who had given his permission and handed over a bottle of cherry brandy that he had found in a small abandoned brewery on their way. Anny had said the owner hadn't been seen in the district for quite some time and it appeared that a lot of his stock had gone with him.

Eddie felt much better for the short break, as it was a return to normality for a while. It had been sheer luxury sleeping in a real bed and taking his meals with a family. He opened the shop, preparing himself for business again, but nearly all the soldiers had had their haircuts, and Eddie began to realise that it was time to join his company again.

In the next few days, his only sighting of Anny was when she came by with a friend, this time on Red Cross duty, and there was not much time to talk. Then the Major sent a messenger telling him he had to return.

CHAPTER FOURTEEN

His company had moved behind the lines when he rejoined them. They had been in action for some time and were due for a well-earned rest. Eddie had noticed a horse trough in a nearby field and as the weather was getting a little warmer he decided to have a bath. He had to clean the trough out first, which he painstakingly did with clumps of hay. Next he carried bucket after bucket of clean water, done with a cheerful heart as he liked to smell nice.

When he had prepared everything to his satisfaction, he stripped off and lowered himself into the trough, he left his rifle and towel in easy reach and began to give himself a good wash with a piece of soap. He gave a sigh of satisfaction and lay back.

Two German soldiers had been hiding in the bushes at the end of the same field. They were deserters from the retreating army, not really Germans, but they had been pressed into service and were determined to give themselves up at the first opportunity. They both emerged from the bushes and walked over to the centre of the field, shouting loudly as they ambled along with their hands above their heads, "Kamerad... Kamerad."

Eddie, lying back with his eyes shut in the makeshift bath, opened his eyes and sat bolt upright in horror. His reaction was to reach for his rifle and towel as he stood up quickly in the trough. His apprehension was short lived as his own soldiers on guard duty had spotted the Germans and ran up to take charge. They accepted their formal surrender and were passed on to H.Q.

It was discovered during interrogation that the men were Polish and had been pressed into service or shot and had been determined to surrender to the Allies when they could.

After his bath, Eddie got dressed and went back to the billet. Many soldiers were there, some playing cards, pontoon and Brag, some were writing home, some were resting on their beds and some were boning up their boots, with thoughts of going out to the nearest town.

Eddie wanted none of these things, so he decided to go for a stroll. He was joined by two of his mates as he walked down a village street and as he was interested in the houses and cottages that were built in the Flemish style, he stopped to ponder on them.

It was hot and they were all wishing for an English pub to materialise so that they all could have a refreshing pint of beer. Wine they could have in plenty at that time, but it was country wine, sour and dry to the palates of the English and Irishmen that made up their company.

It was a real country village, typical of the Continent and Eddie had noticed that, apart from the war damage, the cottages were badly in need of repair, with gutters hanging from the roofs, shutters and gates needed re-hanging, with everywhere having an air of dilapidation.

They came to the end of the street and found themselves in the centre of the village. There were a few houses on the outside of the square, which were built to a better standard than the cottages. A dog rushed out at them from a gateway, barking as he ran, then a child which was pursuing him, stopped short at the sight of the three soldiers. A drift of cooking smells came on the air from one of the houses, probably from what the locals called *frites* and it suddenly made them all feel homesick.

On their way out of the village, their attention was drawn to a lovely house with a colourful garden. It was ablaze with flowers of every hue and the lush green lawns that swept around the house were in a well-kept condition. The soldiers leaned on the gate the better to see and admire, then as they walked a bit further, they saw a ditch that ran along the boundary hedge.

At the top of the lane stood a farmhouse and, seeing that their way was blocked, they turned to walk back through the village again. It was then that Eddie's sharp eyes noticed something lying amongst the marshy plants and ferns that grew in profusion in the ditch. On closer inspection, they found it to be the body of an English soldier, lying face down in some water. He had been dead for some while and must have lain there unnoticed, which was puzzling, as mines had been cleared from the area and there was nothing to say how he died.

Later Eddie and his company were stationed near another city. Tents had been erected to accommodate the swell of soldiers and they had a little free time and transport for a spot of sightseeing. Whenever they could, they would spend their off duty time there, as the King had given in without a fight, so there were no ravages of war and his people were not harmed in any way. It was a very ancient city and the buildings were built in local cream-coloured sandstone, so from a distance it looked like a fairy tale city.

One day, Eddie climbed into the lorry, which had been waiting to take them into the city. They had a few hours break from the camp, so some soldiers were going sightseeing and Eddie was going to a café for his dinner, where he had established a good relationship with the proprietor.

He and Eddie had an arrangement. Eddie would exchange his ration of fags for a meal and a bottle of excellent wine. That day he spent a couple of hours there and when he had finished his tasty meal, the proprietor came to have a chat with him.

It appeared he was having problems with the Military police, who were going to close him down. He had broken the law, on this he wouldn't elaborate, but cheerfully he announced to Eddie that he was going to reopen next door. He explained that he would have a different name above the premises.

Eddie had to smile at the man's optimism and next time he went for his usual dinner deal, he concluded that the man was still having a hard time from the Military, as the shutters weren't up on either of the places.

Later, about half an hour before he was due back to be picked up by the lorry, Eddie left the café and walked along the cobbled street. When he got to the compound where the lorry was parked, he met the driver who asked if Eddie had a spare rotor arm.

Eddie looked mildly surprised as he was not in the habit of carrying spare parts with him on his off duty time, but then the driver explained, putting Eddie into the picture.

The soldier had driven the lorry into the compound and was halfway through his meal in a favourite restaurant, when he remembered he hadn't disabled his vehicle. By now the 'Redcaps' would have removed and confiscated the rotor arm themselves.

Eddie thought over the problem, then came up with an idea. They would ask the other driver, who had come in a bit later, to go and collect his lorry, drive it out, then loan this driver his rotor, so that he could drive *his* vehicle out.

The idea was a good one and all went well, the rotor arm was returned to its rightful owner and the first lorry load went back to camp. Then the second lorry got a tow back again.

When the driver went to see the fitter next day, "Rotor arms," the fitter said, "there's loads of them, the Redcaps keep on bringing them in."

"I'll have two then," said the driver thankfully.

Back on the Belgium side of the river, Eddie's company waited for their orders, whilst the action was across the border in Holland.

The men were not used to such inactivity, so they decided to visit the city, but that evening there wasn't any transport. They looked at the boat that was tied up by the river bank. It was used to carrying troops across the water, but using it was a bit of a risk, as it might be needed later.

They decided to take a walk and passed a café that was popular with the soldiers, but it only sold soft drinks, and tonight the men were in the mood for wine.

A brightly painted caravan passed them as they walked. It was being driven at speed, with the driver whipping the horse in an effort to make it go faster. The van swayed from side to side, lurching with the excessive speed.

After the van had passed them and was some distance ahead, the watching soldiers saw it turn over and fall into a ditch. The horse was struggling to get free of the van, as the three men ran to assist, managing to free it from the shafts and get it on its feet again.

Eddie opened the door of the caravan with some difficulty, but he had been alerted to the sound of a woman's voice screaming in the back. He found a young woman in the advanced stage of labour and then understood the urgency of the situation.

The gypsy man had been thrown free of the van as it tipped over. He had struck his head on a stone and was still dazed as he staggered to his feet. White-faced and haggard, he manfully did his share in dragging the caravan free of the ditch and placing it upright on the road again. The horse had been tethered to a gate at the other side of the road, so the soldiers helped the gypsy to put it back in the shafts again. The gypsy gripped the hands of each in silent gratitude, then jumping in his van, began to brandish his whip again.

The woman had stopped screaming, Eddie hoped she hadn't passed out, as they watched the vehicle careering along in the distance. All were hoping that he had the kind of luck that would see his wife safely at the hospital in time.

Walking back after a few glasses of wine at a place a little further, the three men turned into the fields where they were camped. There was a noisy argument going on between two men outside one of the tents.

"I'll mark time on you, me lad," Eddie heard one yell.

"Not if I can help it, yer an eejit," came the reply.

Eddie and the other men walked on. They had learned to mind their own business when battles broke out between the men, especially on a Saturday night. They'd had a good briefing once by one of the Irish sergeants, who seemed to be full of wisdom.

"No politics and no religion and yer can't go wrong with that."

The whole camp was in an uproar the next morning, as it

appeared that someone had stolen the wheels off the Major's jeep. Eddie emerged from his tent to find everyone talking in groups instead of going about their business as they normally did. The jeep had been left propped up on oil drums and the main speculation was how had the thieves achieved it? They could not have got the wheels through the gate during the day, as someone would have seen them and at night time the gate was well guarded. The guards were prepared to swear that no one had passed through the gate in the hours of darkness.

Speculation was rife; everyone had an answer. The culprits, if they came from inside the camp, must have planned it well ahead and it had been a well-kept secret, but Eddie's own theory was that they must have used the boat. To load it with the wheels and float it down the river would have been a simple matter and there could have been a shed or something where they could have stored the loot.

Other items had gone missing from the camp previously, so Eddie supposed that the wheels would be hidden until the receivers could safely dispose of them and then make a nice profit. To Eddie's mind it meant that the thieves must be in collusion with some soldiers.

The drivers from the camp were talking amongst themselves in the lorry compound when the sergeant who had been responsible for the jeep came up to them. He pointed to his sleeve which normally displayed the three stripes denoting he was a sergeant, saying that he had lost his stripes because of the bloody business. He was back to the ranks, one of the boys like them again. They stared at him in silence as they didn't know what to say.

He didn't get his stripes back until a few months later, he served as an ordinary driver, but he was always talking about the theft. Eddie, who was on loan for a while to that section, felt it was becoming an obsession and the drivers steered clear of him. He was always probing, asking questions and seizing on any clue that may lead to the thieves' identity. It made the men feel nervous, they could unwittingly betray a comrade, a much more serious offence.

Later, whilst back in action, he earned his stripes again, but one of the unsolved mysteries of the war was who had stolen the wheels off the Major's jeep?

Eddie was recalled back from the driving job soon after when the Major had decided that his men needed the services of a barber again. He was kept busy on that first week of duty, but when he had finished, he had to go back to Louvain again.

He liked Louvain, it would have been a nice place for a holiday in peacetime. He was ordered to take over the store-man's duties, whilst the soldier went on his leave back in England.

One evening after Eddie had turned in for the night, two soldiers knocked on the store room door, wanting him to go along with them to sell used boots and blankets to the local people.

Eddie declined and was asked by one of them if he would like his head kicked in.

"Do you want to try and do it now?" Eddie said, knowing that these were a couple of bullies and should be fighting up the line instead of making a nuisance of themselves. The fellow backed off, noticing that Eddie had picked up a cricket bat, though at the time he wondered what it was doing there. The men slunk off and Eddie reported their threat to the Major, who had them packed off on active duty.

The platoon was billeted in a school-house and Eddie got to know the caretakers who lived in a cottage down the road. The old lady was very charming and practiced her English with Eddie if he was passing by. She told him that when she was a young girl during the First World War, she had learnt her English from the soldiers who were stationed in Louvain.

One day as she was talking to Eddie, she pointed to her pretty niece who was standing talking to a young soldier nearby.

"Yvette seems to be very taken with this soldier," she said. She glanced back at Eddie and asked him directly. "Do you know anything about him?"

Eddie groaned inwardly. He knew that the soldier was married with two young children. He was in a dilemma, but he was determined to get it over with now.

"Are you talking about the man that is talking to your niece? He will have probably told her that he has a lovely wife and family."

He saw the old lady's face change as he spoke, but it was better she knew then than later. There were plenty of unattached men that the niece could get friendly with. The old lady kept her own counsel and Eddie didn't get any repercussions from telling the truth.

She met him again before the platoon moved out and, as they said goodbye, she gave Eddie a present for his wife. He had a strong feeling she wanted to say something, but instead she kissed him in Continental fashion on two cheeks. He opened the parcel later to find a beautiful lace-trimmed handkerchief.

"She got the message," said Eddie to himself with a smile.

CHAPTER FIFTEEN

Back with the regiment, Eddie was on rifleman's duty again. His company was now in the area of the Escaut canal and their aim was to cross over it and join up with another company on the other side.

Their orders were to clear the area so that bridging could begin. This they did without much trouble, moving after this to an area north of a village to await further orders. When they moved again, it was across the border into Holland.

Heavy mortaring and shelling had to be endured before they came to a wood, which had been their aim to reach. The wood was very thick in parts, so in places it was almost impossible to move through it. In other parts the thickets were non-existent, but everywhere there were signs of German occupation.

Their own Company Major had been wounded and so a Major with a rich Irish brogue came to take over. He walked with a limp and with the aid of a stick, as he had been injured in an earlier campaign. He was very handsome with black, wavy hair and blue eyes. His Irish brogue was so thick you could cut it with a knife.

Their sergeant had marched the platoon up to the doors of a small convent and as previous arrangements had been made, a nun let them into the courtyard to await the arrival of fresh orders and the new officer.

The Mother Superior came out in person to invite the men into the kitchen. Once in the kitchen, she motioned them all to sit at the table and she asked the sisters working in the kitchen to make them a meal. They looked to her for instructions on what to make them.

She suggested that the nuns make apple and pear fritters, which they willingly did, and soon the men were eating them hungrily, finding them delicious.

Eddie, who was a little more watchful than the others, saw that they were using up their meagre ration of flour.

The sergeant returned with the new Major and after being presented to the men, he gave them a briefing. They had to penetrate the enemy zone to find out if a certain bridge had been blown up, as this knowledge was essential to the forward plans. They were told to look for a railway line and a signal box as landmarks on the way to the bridge.

They set off from the convent, moving forward and using what cover they had available. They came to some rough common land that was covered in thick stubbly grass. A hedge ran along one side and the soldiers made for this as they intended to use it as cover.

They had hardly been there a few minutes when a burst of fire opened up, sending them running behind the hedge for cover. They all threw themselves to the ground and Eddie could feel the bullets going over his head, as he lay with his face pressed into a clump of dock leaves.

A calm Irish voice reassured the men, telling them to lie flat for a while, then each man was to try and make his way back to the convent. The soldiers listened carefully to what he said, then all of them jumped to their feet as one, forgetting his words of warning. They all bunched together, making a black silhouette against the darkening sky. It may have been a miracle, or the height of the hedge, that prevented a massacre.

Eddie stayed with the Major. By this time his experience had taught him the dangers of mass exodus. The new man was furious, he swore he would send every man back for re-training. The two of them stayed there for a while until they felt sure it was safe to move. Only then and very cautiously did they make their bid to move away.

The Major was still determined to execute his mission and get the necessary information back to H.Q., so the two men moved forward and found that the bridge was still intact and, on the way back, they encountered some snipers who had been out on the same mission as themselves. The Major was ordered back to his own post at Headquarters once his work had been completed, but unfortunately on the way back his jeep overturned and he was killed. They were all very upset in the company. Although he had only been with them for a short time, he had earned great respect from those who had been in contact with him.

The Mother Superior welcomed the soldiers back. Eddie had been so touched with her kindness that he had made a special trip to see the cook so that he could replace the nun's rations. They were delighted by his thoughtfulness and invited him to take part in the rosary service they were holding that evening.

The Mother Superior took him aside after the service and said to him, "I knew that you would return and I see a long life ahead of you and much work for you to do." Eddie could only agree with what she had said, as he felt as if 'someone up there' had been looking after him. As each day had dawned he had thought to himself that this could be his last on earth, then in the evening, the fact that he was still there constantly amazed him.

About a day's march from the convent and some miles behind the front line, Eddie had a brilliant idea for making himself a brew of tea. An empty biscuit tin with one side bashed in and a number of empty butter tins with lids and bottoms cut off, provided a few yards of piping when threaded together. He had concealed the pipes, which would take the fumes away under the earth, with an old bush thrown over it and he used special candles which heated without smoke. He had successfully heated some water for his first brew and was about to enjoy drinking it when the Major from one of the other companies happened to be passing by.

"What's that you've got there, Dockerty?" he asked, standing there with one eyebrow raised quizzically, as he stared hard at the impromtu stove and the collection of butter tins leading from it, his keen eyes noting the tea.

"It's for making myself a brew of tea, Sir," Eddie said, standing to salute the Major, something he never forgot to do now.

"Well, I think the whole damn thing should be patented,

161

Dockerty. In fact, I'll put you in charge of making the tea for the incoming patrols. Well done, soldier."

An accolade indeed, except each morning when the patrols came in, Eddie had a hard job keeping up with demand and he was glad to leave his tea maker behind when the company moved on.

The water waggon arrived and the men were able to have baths. There was very little water to wash the soap off, but at least the soldiers felt a little cleaner. A change of clothing was issued too, but Eddie was reluctant to hand over his homemade socks for washing, which Irene had sent him, but he took the fresh socks anyway and washed and dried his own.

The platoon marched down the road to a small village. Eddie was feeling sleepy, as he and three other men had been on reconnaissance duty the night before. Stealing quietly through the night, they had lain concealed at the back of a stone wall and watched with incredulous eyes as another platoon of men with a sergeant put up their arms and surrendered after they had been caught in an ambush. Within the hour, the Germans were packing up their kit and loading a horse and cart with the unlucky soldiers. This had been reported back to H.Q. and next day their platoon was ordered to move into the village.

Eddie talked to the leader of the men who had been on another patrol. He said that they'd been making a house to house search in a village which looked as if it was deserted. At the far end of the village the slim figure of a young woman appeared. She came out of a house and stood in the doorway looking down the street at them for a moment or so. The men hurried down the street, looking around them as they went, then followed her into the house. They were just in time to see her heading down some cellar steps and quickly followed her. As they got to the bottom of the steps they saw her climbing out of the basement window and, realising she may be a decoy, they ran across the cellar and climbed out of the window themselves. Within seconds, guns had opened up by the enemy, who were hidden in a place nearby. No one would have lived to tell the tale had they not followed her, as substantial damage was done to the house.

The girl had disappeared from sight. It was as if she had never been there.

The officer in charge of the company issued orders for his men to clean up. Boots, kit and all gear were to be given a once over and then they were to assemble in the square to give a good impression to the people in the village where they were to be billeted.

After the display they found themselves to be billeted in the local schoolhouse. They found it very chilly in there, but they rummaged around until they found some wood and made a fire. They had to be careful not to make much smoke, as the Germans might shell the village if it looked different from usual.

There were no beds, of course, just a rough, hard, wooden floor, with the wind blowing through the gaps between the planks. Eddie said after the war had ended that he never did recover from his army days: he possessed the coldest bottom in the district – a legacy from sleeping rough.

The cook's truck came up next day and brought welcome supplies. He fetched them some army blankets, which they used to sleep on, as well as to cover themselves. They had a hot meal of meat, vegetables and potatoes and also one treacle pudding to two men. The cook would bring supplies and any news he could pick up as well.

This day he had a word of warning. There was a well-dressed schoolmarm who was to be left severely alone. She had been collaborating with the Germans while they had occupied the village before and she was hoping to get on the same good terms with the English.

She had gone up to the cook's wagon and asked him for rations, speaking to him in perfect English, but she had made a few suggestions to him which had given him a bit of a shock. He expected a schoolmarm to be the model of propriety and this young lady was not.

The head scarf slipped from her head as she talked to him and whether it was the Germans or the villagers that had cropped her hair, he couldn't say, but it made her stand out amongst the rest as a collaborator with the enemy.

Eddie was used to eating well at home and sometimes he crossed the Major, who had firmly stated that the company should live on their rations. The regiment was stationed some miles away from the river Rhine at the time when Eddie fell from grace.

They had dropped back while other troops passed through their lines, as often happened. They all enjoyed the break as the weather had turned warm. They sunbathed and went swimming and Eddie was able to pursue his favourite occupation, looking for food.

They were in farming country, with many farmhouses around, but they were nearly all deserted. He looked around an abandoned farm where hens were clucking and strutting around the yard. Eddie caught several of them and took them back to the billet. By the evening he had organised a few of his mates and they proceeded to pluck the birds, and Eddie, ever resourceful, had found an old washing boiler in one of the outhouses, as the cooking range in the farmhouse had been smashed to pieces.

Eddie set to work with some old bricks, mud from the tracks in the lane and a corrugated sheet. He fixed a washing pot in the centre and soon had a fire going. The birds cooked all night and by the morning, the flesh just fell away from the bones.

The hungry men gathered around the pot as soon as they could and ate the birds with relish. They didn't turn up for breakfast and it just happened to be the day that the cook was giving them bacon and eggs!

The Major tucked his stick under his arm and set off to find the absentees. He found them sitting around in front of the makeshift cooking range enjoying the last of the chicken. He took in the scene at a glance and said, "Find Dockerty for me." Eddie had looked out of the window and spotted the Major coming, so he had disappeared.

When he was finally found and brought in front of the Major, he got a first class lecture on the subject of living on the land. The Major ended with the words, "You have killed the birds who laid the golden eggs."

Eddie was very penitent and he promised not to go hunting anymore, but secretly he was amused that the cook had been before him on the previous day to collect the eggs.

This was not the first time that he had a lecture from the Major on the subject of finding his own food. This was the Major who had been away from the company, recovering from his wounds that he had received at Caen, and he had rejoined them when the fighting was very intense up the lines and the shelling was very heavy on both sides.

Eddie had found a sheep that had been wounded having been caught by a blast of shrapnel and the merciful thing to do was to shoot it. He didn't see the sense in burying it when food was in such short supply. With the help of his young friend, Johnny, who had been with Eddie in the same company since they landed at Caen, he managed to hang the sheep in the doorway. He was no butcher, but Eddie never let any job get the better of him and so he skinned and dressed the sheep to the best of his ability. He rewarded himself with two of the best chops and prepared the rest of the meat to send to the cookhouse.

He and Johnny found it too heavy to carry it to the cook, so they looked for transport. Johnny found an old pram in an outhouse and Eddie found a sheet to cover it. The sheep was put in the pram and Johnny started to push it in the direction of the cookhouse, making good progress though the wheels on the pram were a trifle wobbly. He was in the middle of the village when the Major stepped out of his office.

His eyebrows shot up again when he saw the scene before him; one of his best men pushing a pram down the village street. He glanced quickly up and down the street to see if anyone else had seen him. He was a very calm man and he merely walked up to

Johnny and mildly inquired, "What have you there, Rifleman?"

Johnny became a bit incoherent, but he managed to convince the Major that he was on his way to the cookhouse. The Major gave him a thoughtful look, then said, "Find Dockerty after you've delivered the meat to the cookhouse, then send him to me."

He found Eddie himself when he was making his rounds. He was standing in a small trench that he had dug and had a small fire going in the bottom of it. He was using the sulphur candles to cook the chops on, but it was a slow business. Unable to attract Eddie's attention, the Major tapped him on his steel helmet with his stick.

"What have you got there?" he asked in a deceptively mild voice. Eddie launched into the same explanation as Johnny had just given the Major. He listened carefully and then said, " You don't seem to realise that these people are our responsibility. If they have no food, then we have to find it for them. We have our rations and we must live on them."

He walked away and Eddie got on with his cooking. The cook welcomed the fresh meat with open arms and all the men, including the Major, had a good hot meal that night. It made a change from the tinned food that they normally had. Eddie was very careful to obtain permission before he dispatched any more animals after that. Many animals were casualties between the two warring factions. Their bodies were left in the fields until the owner came back to the farm to bury them and dairy herds were left unattended and dripping with milk. Eddie did his share of milking when the occasion arose.

CHAPTER SIXTEEN

While they were still some miles away from the river Rhine, Eddie and some other men were sent back for a mile or so on an errand. The driver of one of the lorries bringing supplies had been wounded and his vehicle had been left abandoned in a field until a replacement driver could be found. The unit urgently needed blankets, so a lieutenant and two men, including Eddie, were sent to collect some from the lorry.

Eddie saw that it was the same kind of lorry he was used to driving for his father when the building firm had still been operating, so he jumped in the driving seat to see if it would start up. The engine roared into life as he started it first try, so he was allowed to drive it back to the camp. His fellow soldiers were delighted, as they had anticipated a long trudge back laden with blankets.

When they reached the camp the lieutenant had a word with the C.O., after Eddie had put the lorry in a nearby field for the night. In the morning, having been put in the picture by the lieutenant, Eddie's Major asked him to carry on with driving the lorry, until a new soldier was sent over to pick it up.

Some time elapsed before the new driver was sent up and, for a short time, as Eddie had no regular duties, he was sent on a leave trip to Amsterdam, which had been liberated for a while. Eddie loved the picturesque city with its fine old buildings and busy canals. He joined a tour which included the house where the young Jewish girl, Anne Frank, was hidden from the Germans, then was finally betrayed when the Dutch people were so near to liberation.

He walked around on his own later and stood for a while on one of the bridges, looking down into the water, lost in thought. He felt a touch on his arm and turned to see a Dutchman smiling at him.

"Have you any money, soldier?" he asked. Eddie just stared at him.

"Would you like to spend the evening with my charming daughter?"

He fled when he saw the dangerous look in Eddie's eyes; he was lucky he wasn't chucked off the bridge.

The company had moved to some dugouts which the Germans had recently vacated and the nearest building to the riverbank where they were situated was a small cottage occupied by an old lady. With her age and the terrifying sounds from all around her, she must have been totally confused. She sat all day in her neat little front room in a daze.

Eddie's platoon took over her cellar for cooking meals and brewing tea, otherwise they didn't trouble her and left her in comparative peace. There was no one who could speak her language amongst them, so they could not ask why she had not been evacuated with her own people.

The Germans had also occupied the cottage and the cellar for cooking purposes. It was a sturdy basement room with a beautiful brick arch. For cooking the meals on, an old army stove had been installed with a pipe passing through the wall.

Eddie was elected cook by the lieutenant. He made the breakfast which consisted of a thick porridge known to the men as 'Burgoo' and cups of hot sweet tea. He did not reign for long as the cook. In the long journey up to the front line, the tea had got mixed up with the sugar. If Eddie had left the men to sweeten their own, it would have been all right, but he added some to the porridge from the new sack and the porridge went a funny colour. Eddie asked the lieutenant to taste it first of all before it was served to the men. He tasted it thoughtfully then he said, "It tastes all right, but I don't think the men will like it."

He was right of course and there was a near riot by the men, so that Eddie lost his job as the platoon cook. He didn't mind as there had been a dangerous aspect to the job anyway, as on two mornings some German "comedian" had awoken him by hitting the wall where he had been sleeping with a six pounder shell! Eddie thought it was probably the last fellow who stood in as cook when the Jerries occupied the cottage and he was making sure that Eddie wasn't late with the breakfast.

When Eddie came out of the cottage one morning, there had been a fall of snow. It lay thick on the branches of the pine trees, which stood around the area where they camped. The air smelled so good, but as he looked around appreciatively he noticed some marks in the snow. There must have been some activity in the night which had gone unchallenged, for there were big paw marks, followed by big boot marks behind.

Eddie concluded that it had been a single soldier with a dog patrolling the area and they must have come very quietly over the river in a boat during the night. How it was managed without the soldier and his companion being noticed by the men who were on guard duty, Eddie would never know. He was just thankful that the soldier hadn't lobbed a grenade into the cottage. He must just have been out on a reconnaissance patrol and not wanted to draw attention to himself; he also could have been one of the previous occupants of the cottage. He would have known that the old lady would be in there as well as the soldiers.

She had got used to them being there after a while, it was just a change in the colour of their uniforms after all. She started moving around the cottage and to the wood shed and Eddie noticed her one day walking out carrying a band saw. He watched her in surprise as she upended the saw, slipping her foot into the end part and gripping it between her knees. This way she was able to roll the slim tree trunks up and down the saw blade. Eddie watched in fascination, he was really impressed by the method she was using and impressed that she was able to keep her fire going in the cottage. She had a sizable amount of logs by the time she had finished.

He took the idea home with him, purchased a band saw and, by the time he had returned after his next leave, he had Irene sawing wood up like a professional. One of the many skills she'd had to learn, besides poultry and pig keeping, and how to dress fowl and fillet fish while Eddie was away.

He went on another trip to Brussels the next time he had a forty-eight hour leave. He went with a group of soldiers who were all bent on enjoying themselves. Eddie enjoyed the rest and the comfort of a real bed in the private billet to which they were sent. He didn't want to visit any of the places where the other men went and got into disfavour when he wouldn't hand out his money after they had run short of their own. He didn't realise how unpopular this had made him until they left him sleeping in the billet while they boarded the lorry that was taking them back to camp.

When the landlady roused him to let him know that they had gone and left him behind, he dressed, had a hasty meal and before leaving the lodgings asked where the nearest Military Police office was. After Eddie had told them his tale of woe, they stamped his pass and then he had to find a way to get back to camp.

He stood by the main highway later and watched out for an ammunition lorry to go past in the right direction. The first vehicle to come up the road though was a staff car, the officer sitting in the back was obviously of a high rank because of his uniform. He had a fur-lined coat draped over his shoulders. Eddie saluted and then he signalled to the driver to stop the car and then explained why he needed a lift so urgently. The officer leant forward and asked to see his identification and, after this had been examined, Eddie was allowed to sit by the driver and the journey continued.

The officer decided that as the camp was still rather far away by evening and Eddie still had a little leave left according to his pass that he would take him to H.Q., as that was where he was going himself and then the driver would take him back up the line in the morning.

He was given a meal, a beer and a bed for the night and woke refreshed the next morning, feeling truly grateful to his benefactor, who was in fact a Brigadier.

He got on well with the driver and didn't want him to take any unnecessary risks, so when they heard the sound of gunfire as they came nearer to the battle front and the car was now driving through three feet of water as a dyke had burst and flooded the road, Eddie told him to go no further or he could be driving along the enemy lines.

"My lot are over there in those trees," said Eddie, getting out of the car after thanking the driver for getting him out of his predicament. "At least they were two days ago. Anyway, thanks again, Mate."

"Oh you can thank the Brigadier for this, Eddie. I just had my orders to get you right back to camp." And so with a friendly wave he turned the car around and was gone.

"You're back early," said his sergeant when Eddie reported back to him, "the rest of your party haven't got back yet."

Eddie was mystified by their non-arrival, until he heard that the leave lorry had broken down and the men had spent the night in very uncomfortable quarters. He had really come out the best from that little disagreement.

They had moved on to Blitterwijk and a small Dutch farmer came to the door of the billet one morning. He couldn't speak any English, but he got the soldiers to understand that he had children and he needed milk for them. The lieutenant asked Eddie to go with the man and find out all he could while he was with him, as there was not supposed to be any civilians in the area.

The Dutchman led Eddie to a dug out shelter in the corner of a field, where his family, a woman and two small children, were living. A rough canvas sheet roofed it over and there were some food supplies, which included a flitch of bacon hanging from a hook.

The man turned to Eddie and pointed to the children, then he went through the motions of milking a cow. Eddie nodded and they both went back to some farm outbuildings, where the cows lived in comparative safety. Eddie helped the farmer to get the milk he needed, then escorted him back to his family.

Whether the enemy had been watching, Eddie would never know, but as soon as they had started on their way back, then the shelling started up. He took a flying leap into the nearest shelter, then when he looked up, he found he was in the pit of a small sawmill with the cutting wheel dangerously near the top of his head. He waited there until the shelling had ceased before he made his way back to the billet.

They moved into a big Catholic church that night and guards were posted in the village at strategic points. The next morning Eddie and others were ordered out on a reconnaissance patrol. They were to meet up with another platoon, but somehow they missed them.

They came to a grassy meadow stretched out to a concrete road beyond, where a small farmhouse stood. The lieutenant ordered them to cross the meadow, but as they did so, guns opened up and after lying flat they wriggled for the nearest cover. Shells hit the road as they lay there, sending lumps of concrete into the air above.

Eddie lay flat whilst the shelling was going on and, when he could, he made his way to a pile of brushwood which he dived under. It provided temporary shelter, but when he surfaced again, he couldn't see any members of the patrol anywhere.

He made his way back very cautiously, taking any cover he could find and eventually he came to a small stream. Looking around to see if there was any land that looked as if it could be mined, he decided it might be better if he waded down the stream, rather than take the chance of being blown up by a land mine. Eventually the stream ran under a bridge in a village, but as there was no sign of his platoon there, he carried on. At last he came across the company headquarters where the Captain directed him to wait until his platoon turned up. There he learnt that the meadow they had crossed was mined and it had been a miracle that any of them had survived.

An enemy patrol had made their way under cover of darkness

to the little Protestant chapel at the end of the village, where they were able to command a good view of the village. They used the chapel as a post for their snipers until they were winkled out. This was at the cost of many lives on both sides.

Miles past Blitterswijk they camped for the night in a thickly wooded area. The guard was placed at the edge of the road, which gave a good view in either direction. Eddie was on the first spell of duty on the front post where he would be for the next few hours. The night was very dark and he shivered with the cold, despite the heavy greatcoat he was wearing.

He had been there for about an hour when his sharp ears heard rustling in the ditch some yards away on the other side of the road. He stiffened and brought his rifle up ready for action. At that moment his sleeve was touched by the duty sergeant, who had come up very quietly.

"All right, Eddie?"

"Rustlings in the ditch, up on the left, about eight yards away."

Visibility was very poor, neither of them could see anything at all. It was still very dark and all sounds had ceased around them. The sergeant was carrying a Bren gun and minutes later the stillness was shattered as he opened fire with it, spraying the ditch along its length for a dozen yards. The matter was settled as far as the sergeant was concerned and he walked away.

Eddie stayed at his post without further incident and no investigations were made that night. He completed his spell of duty, handed over to the relief soldier, then turned in to sleep until the morning.

The sergeant went personally to investigate as soon as there was enough light to see by, going straight to the place where he had fired upon the previous night. There in the ditch lay five dead Germans, four soldiers and an officer, remnants of a fighting patrol, who had come very near to success in their mission last night.

Eddie was in the camp cleaning his rifle when the sergeant came to tell him about his lucky escape, and it was the same sergeant who had saved his life before in the back streets of Caen.

Things had begun to start easing up, as the enemy had put their all into the fighting previously, but were now in retreat. The weather had turned cold and it was raining. It was on this night that Eddie, along with the sergeant and another soldier, had volunteered to go out on a mission. Two strange soldiers came to accompany them and they were the scruffiest men Eddie had ever seen. The two men looked at them, seeing the army issue denims over pristine khaki shirts and asked, "Have you ever done this sort of thing before?" Eddie and his fellow soldiers were too amazed to answer that question.

They were ferried quietly across the river in an engineer's boat. The object of the mission was to capture some enemy soldiers, two at least, and take them back for questioning. Their faces had been blackened, slippers were worn instead of heavy boots and small camouflage nets were carried by each man. Few soldiers like to part with their boots once they had got used to them, but the slippers ensured a noiseless approach.

They arrived on the opposite bank and climbed up the steep side, which was slippy and muddy. Once on the grass they made for the nearest cover and after a period of cautious watching and waiting they came within sight of a small cottage. They got into positions of surveillance, shivering in their wet clothes, as at that point the rain was still pouring down. The sergeant and the two strangers were to make the 'snatch' and Eddie and his mate were to provide covering fire if necessary.

After what seemed an eternity, the door of the cottage opened and two figures were outlined in the shaft of light that shone out. The German soldiers made their way along the road, then two other soldiers passed them by to take their places in the cottage. Before the first soldiers were able to settle down to their guard duty and before their eyes could become accustomed to the darkness of the night scene around them, they were seized and taken prisoner. It was all done so quickly that the two Germans in the cottage were unaware of the fate of their comrades.

Their mission successfully completed, the little party returned to base with the prisoners, handing them over to H.Q. where they were duly interrogated. Eddie was most impressed with the strangers, as he felt they had really known their job.

Eddie took off his soaking wet denims and shirt with relief and dried himself as best he could, seeing as he didn't have a towel. He searched around for dry clothing and put them on, glad that they were sleeping in a warm and cosy barn that night, where the hay was fresh and sweet smelling. He set to work to make himself a comfortable bed, stacking two straw bales on either side and two bales on top to make it snug and draught proof. He searched for some army blankets, found two and, wrapping them around him, he fell asleep almost immediately.

There was a terrific banging noise going on and it penetrated through the haze of sleep into which Eddie had fallen. He awoke very reluctantly back to his world at war. The enemy must have found their positions, they continued to shell for some hours and Eddie found it near impossible to get back to sleep again. He welcomed the sergeant who had come into the barn to talk to him, as Eddie was to be the first guard that day, and spoke of his grief over a fellow sergeant, who had accidentally been shot by a new recruit while inspecting his rifle that day.

Eddie sought to divert him from the tragedy by talking of civilian life and the sergeant stretched out on the hay beside him and asked him what being married was like. They spoke for a good hour and the shelling had stopped, but neither man noticed, as Eddie spoke about the honeymoon he never had.

The light of dawn filtered through and the sergeant, who was in charge of setting on the guard, told Eddie to continue his story, whilst another man was sent instead.

CHAPTER SEVENTEEN

After his night time expedition Eddie was allowed to go on leave again. He liked Brussels and he and a group of soldiers were dropped outside the civilian billet by the lorry in which they had travelled.

The host and hostess were very hospitable and, after checking in with them, Eddie went straight up to bed, savouring the clean sheets and blankets after all the nights of sleeping rough.

He was awakened in the early evening by his pal called Jock. He had to shake Eddie awake as he was so soundly asleep, but Jock was determined to go out on the town.

"Come on… wake up," he persisted, as Eddie opened reluctant eyes. He was still half asleep as he dressed to comply with Jock's demands.

The Belgian lady met them in the hallway.

"You go out? You must eat something first," she said in her heavily accented English, leading them into her dining room to wait for a meal. She was an excellent cook and they really enjoyed the food that she placed before them, making a nice change from army food. It was a good hour afterwards before they stepped out into the street to make their way into the city.

They were wearing their best uniforms, which had only cost them fifty cigarettes apiece to have them professionally cleaned and pressed. They both looked very smart as they set off down the street.

On one of the main streets in the centre was a large café and the two men went inside for a drink. At the front entrance there was a large glassed-in cash desk and an equally large elderly lady, dressed in resplendent black satin with pearls in her ears and around her neck, sitting behind the desk. She was a formidable-looking lady and her hair, which probably should have been the same colour as her pearls, was an improbable shade of black.

There was a bar at the end of the large room and, after both men had walked over, Eddie ordered a bottle of wine between them, which he took with a couple of glasses to the table where Jock now sat.

An attractive young lady, who had watched them as they came in, had got off her bar stool and followed him and, as he sat down, Eddie wondered why there were half a dozen women sitting at the bar, but no men. The young woman smiled at them both and asked if they would like to buy her a drink. Eddie, ever practical, said if she went to fetch a glass, she could help herself to one from their bottle.

Apparently he had said the wrong thing, as she ignored him and confined herself to talking to Jock, who seemed very interested in what the young woman had to say. Eddie strained his ears to listen and at first he couldn't hear what was being said, but when his ears became accustomed, he could hear that there was a bit of negotiating going on. He butted in at a crucial moment and tried to cut the price!

It was then that the young woman flew into a furious temper, stamping her feet and screaming at them. Eddie couldn't be sure what he had said to cause her upset, until she screamed that she had never been so insulted and she wouldn't be dropping her drawers for that kind of price.

And there were a good many more things that she said that Eddie considered extremely vulgar and he noticed that her thick French accent had suddenly turned into a 'Scouse' one.

Three young men emerged from the back of the café and advanced on the two soldiers purposefully. Eddie picked up his near empty wine bottle and swung it in his hand. They stopped dead in their tracks and while they were thinking about their next move, Jock and Eddie backed up to the front door and made a quick exit.

"What did you go and get her mad for?" Jock asked him reproachfully. "I really fancied her, she was a bit of all right."

"Go back then if that's how you feel, but count me out."

They parted company, whilst Eddie had a look around the shops and Jock went back to his prostitute. He was not in the billet next morning, nor had he slept in his bed.

A couple of days after their return from the Brussels leave, the company was on the move, making their way across Holland. Again the country was heavily wooded and everywhere showed signs that the Germans had only just moved on. Abandoned equipment was found as they progressed further and they had to be especially wary of snipers, whom they encountered now and again. Mines had been lain in the soft sandy tracks as the enemy had retreated, making it hard for the vehicles and extremely hazardous for the men.

They made camp late in the evening amongst the trees, aware that the enemy was very close at this point, but not sure how close. It wasn't until the next morning when the reconnaissance patrol went out that they saw the Germans were about to vacate their position in a nearby village and move on.

All food, supplies and blankets were being brought up by hand because of the transport difficulties. The food was stone cold when it reached the men and the porridge, which was hard and lumpy at the best of times, was uneatable. They managed to boil some water to heat the tinned food, but as the labels were loosened by the hot water, each tin was a mystery. However beans, stew, vegetables, spam, peaches and tinned milk went down in any order it was given to them. They were, after all, ravenously hungry.

Eddie got his fair share of night patrols and one night heard a lot of noise coming from the German position. The men crawled on their bellies and wriggled nearer for a better look, then saw a soldier leading a horse and cart up and down a cobbled street in the village, making clattering noises. It transpired it was to camouflage the work that the Germans were doing and it was being done on a dark night to prevent any watchers from seeing what they were up to. Later on they found that they were setting up a Dennet wire, a single strand of wire with mines and booby traps attached to it. The wire was dealt with by the Pioneers when the next attack went on.

St.Patrick's Day came around and, in spite of the push towards the crossing of the Rhine, the company feasted on geese, turkey and pork; food that they had nearly forgotten existed as they had become so used to McConachies tins. Beer and wine flowed to accompany the food in celebration, though Eddie couldn't remember if the traditional shamrock was distributed.

The whole battalion moved across two countries and into Germany in a day. Lorries and trucks rumbled through cities and towns in Belgium and Holland. They went over the biggest Bailey bridge ever built on the way there and across the border into Germany itself.

Eddie's company was camped in a wood by an old schloss on the river bank, waiting to be given the signal to cross themselves. Shortly after an attack started and his company was in this action.

They were backed in the attack this time by Churchill tanks, though unlike the advance into Caen, Eddie didn't get to ride on one. Many German soldiers were captured this time and looking at the age of the prisoners, they realised that the Germans were scraping the bottom of the barrel. Most of those that were captured were mere boys as young as sixteen and others were well above the 'call up' age. Eddie heard that near enough 140 prisoners were taken on this and other attacks that day.

The area around began to look like the scene on 'D' day, as the army, now up to full strength, began to establish itself. Much of the visibility was obscured during the day by an artificial smoke screen, used to veil the enormity of the preparations for battle being made. The sickly, choking smell hovered over the troops all day long and they were thankful to breathe clean air when it disappeared.

Eddie's platoon was designated to secure a station and a level crossing. This was their objective, while others went forward on the crossing of the Rhine. Thousands of guns opened up the attack, escalating in power, with 360 rockets in half a minute.

Eddie and his sergeant were on prowler guard that night, when they witnessed a signaler being captured by a platoon of Germans. The two watchers were only on spotter duty and were also outnumbered, so were helpless to intervene. They were totally frustrated being unable to help and had to watch them go.

When the company went forward again, a stream ran through the area ahead of them. It was ten yards wide and very shallow, so didn't prove an obstacle. However, the banks were a lot of trouble as they were very steep and, once they were over, they encountered the enemy as soon as they had dug in.

Another battle commenced which had a successful outcome and they were able to send their prisoners back behind the lines. They moved on to a village, where houses had been booby trapped, with small explosives being left in dressing table drawers. In the cottage that Eddie went in, a trap door lay in the floor. Two men could have hidden in the space revealed, but luckily no one was there. Shelves ran around the kitchen walls and were filled with jars of jam, bottled fruit, vegetables, pickles and bottles of homemade wine. It must have broken a housewife's heart to have left it all behind. On this occasion it was left for her to come home to, as the soldiers were looking for snipers at the time.

A farmhouse stood a little outside the village; it had a blue grey slated roof upon it. Eddie looked up, interested as he was in all things to do with buildings, and noticed that some of the slates had been disturbed. He went up to the door of the farmhouse and it was opened almost immediately by a woman. She spoke in German, then went to close the door. Eddie put his foot in the door, determined to find out why the slates had been disturbed. As an infantryman he had been trained to look for possible sniper positions.

When he had succeeded in gaining admission to the house, he stood in the hall. A man came from the kitchen and the woman pointed to her wedding ring. He was a tall fair-haired man, who looked as if he was a military man, not a farmer, but he was dressed in farm clothes, so Eddie indicated that he wanted to search the house. He had his rifle in readiness in case he had to enforce his demand, but the couple stood back and let him pass to mount the stairs. The attic was empty except for a pile of straw. He turned and went down the stairs, then into the garden where he found, after searching around in an old shed, what he was looking for. It was a German uniform, a rifle and Luger pistol, buried under a pile of tools and rubbish there.

Eddie walked back, carrying his evidence to where they stood waiting; the man had no expression on his face, but the woman burst into tears. She offered him a gold cigarette case, but Eddie refused it with a gesture. He was not afraid of any trouble from the man, as he had already taken the magazine and bolt out of the rifle, and the pistol, empty of its bullets, resided in his army satchel.

Eddie turned and left, supposing that the man must have been a deserter who had made his way home. In the same circumstances he would have probably done the same and his orders were to look for snipers, not farmers.

"But for the grace of God go I," Eddie muttered, as he set off down the lane.

Weeks later and many miles on, they were in Hamburg when peace was declared and there was no more fighting to be done. It was a wonderful day for war-weary men.

There were no celebrations in Hamburg: it was France, Belgium and Holland who celebrated their liberation, but the feeling was there just the same. War had ended, peace at last.

However, for Eddie and others, there were changes in the air. There was much work to be done by the Army of Occupation. Drivers were in demand and Eddie was sent on loan to the Dutch; he went to Emsdetten and began work on various duties there.

When he and the other drivers arrived at the camp they were taken to Holland to have a vehicle allotted to each man. There was a big field park there filled with lorries and other vehicles. They were all polished up and waiting. Eddie chose a Q.L. Bedford, finding it a joy to drive as it was so well maintained. It was very light on the steering, unlike others he had driven and which he had found very tiring.

When each man had been allotted to his vehicle, they started back on their long journey to Emsdetten. Eddie enjoyed this part of the detail most of all. It enabled him to see some of the villages and towns where he had either marched through or fought his way through during the campaign. It was a shame that he couldn't stop and look at the scenery, but he was now in the company of the drivers who were making up a long convoy.

Back in Germany with his new vehicle to drive, the days were filled with many duties. Part of these were spent transporting displaced persons from the camps where they had been confined, to other camps where they were able to have a bath, a change of clothing, eat regular meals and have papers prepared so that they could travel back home. When they were ready to go, the lorries were detailed to take them to the nearest biggest railway station and Eddie looked forward to each day's work.

It was nearer to his previous lifestyle before the war, as other duties included loading coal or delivering potatoes to the civilian population. As he drove along the road, he saw many displaced persons, a pitiful sight, trudging along with their feet wrapped in sacking as they had no shoes. All intent to get back home and to their loved ones, if they were still there of course.

One day he saw a young girl running along the side of the autobahn. It was raining in torrents and there was no shelter for miles. She raised her hand in the hope that Eddie may stop his lorry and give her a lift, but those were the days of non-fraternisation even if he had not been driving an army vehicle. As always he carried his gas cape, so he lifted it and threw it through the window to her. At least it would shield her from the rain until she could get a lift.

There was a small vegetable truck behind, which chose to swing out and try to overtake Eddie's trundling lorry, whilst he was throwing out the cape to the girl. In doing so the army vehicle had swung out a little and the truck smashed into the rear of it. Water ran out from its ancient radiator in rusty rivulets and fruit and vegetables slid from their boxes and rolled about the road. Eddie stopped just long enough to make sure that the driver wasn't hurt, then he drove as fast as he could to catch the rest of the convoy. He had been last in line and was already late for civilians waiting at the station.

A German shopkeeper and his daughter had been waiting at the station for the best part of an hour. When Eddie arrived, the daughter, who spoke fairly fluent English, made it very clear to this English soldier that she wasn't very pleased. Eddie got the message, then proceeded to shovel potatoes onto his lorry from a train truck, whilst the other drivers waited in line. This did not suit the German girl, as she wanted to sort through the potatoes and put the best ones in some sacks.

The drivers got impatient and started to hoot their horns at Eddie, but the girl was impervious to their hooting and carried on. Eddie, with the lorry eventually loaded, pulled out of the station with an angry girl and a Papa who was obliged to ride in the back.

The girl was most displeased that there was only room for one passenger in the driver's cab and spent the first part of the journey standing up and shouting through the window to her Papa. The wind blew up her skirt and Eddie, glancing sideways, pulled it down and made the remark that she was a big girl now. She shot him a furious look and sat down for the rest of the journey.

An army camp loomed up and without any explanation Eddie turned and drove the lorry inside. He pulled up outside the cookhouse and asked the cook if he could supply them with a meal. He had not eaten since breakfast and he thought that the civilians would be hungry too. The cook was very good and he gave them some food and cups of tea and Eddie filled up the father's flask.

When the cook heard that the lorry was carrying potatoes, he asked the young fraulein if she would be willing to trade him some for a few cans of fish. A deal was struck and she brightened up considerably for the rest of the way.

Eddie's day was not over when they got to the shop, as the customers were waiting there even though it was dusk. He had hoped that he could throw off his load at the rear of the shop and be on his way, but he was frustrated by the fräulein yet again. She wanted the shop scales brought out, the potatoes weighed and shared out equally. He dropped the backboard and she proceeded her weighing, but was horrified when he threw off some of the loose ones in effort to speed things up.

"People will run off with the potatoes and half of them won't get their ration," she wailed. Eddie explained that the convoy would be back at the camp now and would be tucking into a hot meal.

"Go into the house and have schnapps with Papa and Mama will cook a meal for you." She went on with her weighing, seeing that everyone got their fair share. When all was finished, he jumped into the driver's cab, waving his hand in a polite farewell and drove away as fast as he could.

It was late when he got back, but luckily the cook was willing to fix him a meal and he crawled into his bed totally exhausted, falling asleep immediately. When the order came to assist again, he made sure another driver was allocated to the fräulein's errands; one day in her company had been enough.

He was awakened from his deep sleep a little later, as noisy soldiers coming in from a night out banged about. One of the soldiers, seeing that Eddie was awake, broke off his conversation with a mate and came over.

"Your brother was here today," he said. "He's left a message for you to go and see him." Eddie had no idea that his brother Samuel was so near. As Samuel was the youngest of the four sons, Eddie had assumed he'd not been sent out of England, as he was only just of age to be 'called up'.

However the war was over now, so he had probably been sent to help with the clearing up. Eddie asked for his brother's whereabouts and was given a hastily scribbled note.

He realised he would need transport to make the visit, as his brother was stationed some miles away.

Eddie managed to get the loan of a jeep the next morning. It was a day when he had some free time so he could go to see his brother.

From the address he had been given, he realised that two of his platoon were in the same building, as they had been sent there for deserting their posts.

He drew up outside the building and was hailed by an officer who knew him well.

"What are you doing here?" the man asked suspiciously, no doubt thinking that Eddie was there to visit the two deserters.

"I've come to see my brother, Samuel Dockerty." Eddie was a little on the defensive, as they hadn't got on very well when they had served together previously.

"Good God," he exploded. "You mean to say there are two of you!" He still looked suspicious and accompanied Eddie whilst he looked for his brother.

Sam was in the Signals quarters and was now attached to Eddie's regiment. The sergeant was speechless when he saw that Eddie actually did have a brother in the building and went away without another word. They sat for some time chatting and then Eddie said goodbye as he had to get back to the camp. On his way out, he asked a soldier where the prisoners had been put and was told they were in the guardroom until a decision had been made regarding their fate. He had brought his cigarette ration with him and he left them these.

He thought about them on his journey back; these soldiers had been first class fighting men through Holland, Belgium and France. At the very last their nerves had gone and both had deserted, leaving their posts. If they could have hung on a little longer, peace had been declared only days away.

Eddie and the others were detailed to transport the occupants of a Russian prisoner of war camp. The lorries had to be covered with lice powder before they were used. The people were in a terrible state before they got to their new camp and would be pleased to get bathed, receive new clothing and eat proper food before they went home.

The majority of the inmates were quiet, dejected folk, who appreciated the help that they were to be given, but one man was inclined to be aggressive and very drunk on some homemade spirit that he'd been drinking. In this camp things had been a little different and, when peace had been declared, they had been allowed to acquire a few things of their own.

First a woman with a pram was loaded on, then bags of personal possessions and a vat of spirit that the men of the group refused to leave behind. The man, who somehow had acquired a gun, celebrated his freedom by continually firing it into the air. His companions, also aboard, were very uneasy, but no one dared to try to take it from him. The officer in charge tried to take it away from him without success.

Eddie realised that they would never get away unless the man was quietened, so he went around and took the two pins out of the backboard, which let the chains drop. Then he got into the driving seat, turned the engine on and jerked it on the clutch. The drunken man fell off the lorry and dropped the gun. The officer saw his chance and pounced upon it. The poor little mother fell off too, still holding onto the pram and screaming something abusive in her own Russian language. Eddie helped her back on the lorry and lifted the pram beside her, noting that the frightened baby had somehow escaped an injury.

CHAPTER EIGHTEEN

After a spell of duty in Germany, Eddie was granted leave to go home to England. It was a most unusual journey and it took some time to get there. He had to cross Holland and he stayed in an echelon camp on the way.

At Euston station, after a choppy ride across the English Channel, a lady was helped into the train compartment where Eddie was sitting by an officer and he asked Eddie where he was travelling to. Eddie replied that he was going to Liverpool and the officer asked would he look after his wife, as she was travelling to Liverpool as well and he was worrying about her getting there safely. Eddie promised that he would do his best and the relieved looking man, after saying goodbye to his wife, left. The wife on the other hand was very distressed and began to cry softly for a little while, then she pulled herself together and began to act normally.

In the beginning, after she had noticed his badge, she asked Eddie about his regiment, then she told him a little about herself and her husband. It was a relief that people were able to talk freely now in public, as before peace was declared, posters had displayed 'Walls have ears' and other grim reminders. The train sped off and the time flew by and they pulled into Lime Street station in record time.

As they got off the train and approached the barrier, an elderly man introduced himself and said he was there on voluntary service, and although he had no petrol to go any further than through the Mersey Tunnel, he would gladly take them over there. It was midnight then and, on the Birkenhead side, Eddie knew there wouldn't be any transport, but on this occasion he was prepared to walk.

Although he was already overloaded, Eddie being a gentleman offered to carry the lady's case and finally they compromised, by each carrying it for a spell. They must have walked miles from when they had been dropped outside the tunnel, as Bidston, where the lady lived, was quite a long way away. She invited him into her house and made him a meal, which he enjoyed with lots of cups of tea, then he said he must be on his way. He was offered a room for the night, as her mother was there as well, but Eddie was impatient to finish his journey, so he declined her offer and left.

His kit bag was heavy as he trundled along the quiet tree-lined roads, looking forward to seeing his wife and child again. In his bag lay a small box for Irene, in which lay a fine gold ring with pearls in an unusual design and a little Dutch doll he had bought for Gina, dressed in the national costume, which an old lady had made. The natural choice of name for the doll was Wilhelmina, after the name of Holland's queen.

This leave was longer than usual as it was called embarkation leave. After three weeks and on his return to Germany, Eddie was due to go out to the Middle East. It gave him time to get to know his daughter, as at five years old, he had sadly missed Gina's early years.

Rationing was still in place and there were many shortages in all the shops. Irene showed Eddie the pathetic piece of meat that the butcher had given her for their weekend meal. Eddie went to see the butcher personally and came back with a bigger piece than Irene had seen in a long time. He wouldn't say what had transpired between the two of them, but he did advise her to change her supplier if she could. Things could be had on the 'black market', but at prices that Irene's meagre army allotment wouldn't run to.

Back in Germany and returning to the army, but missing the comradeship of his mates in his regiment, Eddie sent word to his Major asking if he could be recalled. A prompt reply came back, asking if he would attend for an interview. He received a warm welcome.

"Yes," said the Major, "it is time you came back to us, but at the moment I haven't got a vehicle for you to drive. The carrier driver will be leaving soon, so you can learn to drive that and take his place."

Eddie found it was Charley's vehicle and he was sorry to see the coloured boy go. He could always be relied upon to turn up with fresh supplies, when essential things like ammunition were running low, however dangerous the situation.

The non-fraternisation ruling was for the troops own protection, but Eddie, a friendly man, found it very confining. The troops were continually thrown into contact with the German people and they found, like themselves, they were only too happy that the war was over.

On his return to the regiment, Eddie was billeted in a school. There were no comforts there, but he had been in worse places and during the day he was on guard duty at a hospital for the war wounded in the town. The patients were mainly soldiers who had been in action on the Russian front. They were in a pitiful state, many suffering from frostbite in addition to their wounds.

Before Eddie had been there a week, he had introduced himself to the Matron and he struck a bargain with her. He would cut the hair of the patients and, in return for his services, he should have the privilege of a hot bath whenever he wanted. He thought himself very lucky when she gave her permission and thought he was the only man to get it.

One night he went along for a bath and he looked around very cautiously before he entered the building to make sure he wasn't under observation. The hospital was shadowy, but there was a cheerful clink of dishes coming from the kitchen, along with the chattering of women's voices. He made his way to the corridor where the bathrooms were. He had stuffed his own towel inside his tunic, preferring to use his own than those of the hospital. He went into a cubicle, put the plug in the bath and started to run the water.

Movement in the next cubicle told him that someone else was there, but Eddie assumed it was probably a patient or a member of staff. He turned off the hot water after running a nice tub full, then cooled it down until it was just right. Then he got in and lay there, revelling in the luxury, relaxed and even dozing a little in the unaccustomed warmth.

A voice started to sing next door and made Eddie sit up sharply to listen. It was a deep, expressive voice and it was singing about the mountains of Mourne. Not in anyway a German voice, as the song demanded to know "did his mother come from Ireland?" Eddie thought it was time he got dressed and out of there, but before he left the cubicle, he lifted a chair into place, stood on it and looked over the wooden partition. A familiar figure was sitting in the bath, all soaped up and thoroughly enjoying himself. It was Eddie's own Sergeant Major!

Eddie had great difficulty in trying to control a fit of laughter, so he got down from the chair and made his way out as quietly as possible. There was still no one about as he passed through the outer door.

When he returned to his billet there was a light in the kitchen, which told him that his friend the cook was still there. He went for a chat and a cup of cocoa, but didn't recount that evening's encounter at the hospital, as he deemed it would be unfair. He went from the kitchen to the bedroom as he had a letter to write home. The censorship had relaxed since the war had ended and there was so much for Eddie to write home about. The girl at the reception in the hospital had offered a room where he could write in peace, but Eddie declined her offer, as well intentioned as it might have been. To get a bath was a necessity, but to break the rules of fraternisation for the sake of a letter was another thing.

Before the regiment left Germany for the Middle East, they organised a race for the occupation troops. Eddie was selected to run for his unit, the officer who chose him saying that as he was an infantryman he must be fit. Eddie had no pre-race training and as he had always been a good runner he had no worries on that score.

An ex-commando turned up to run in the race, coming along with the intention to win it. He said to Eddie when they had the opportunity to talk, "If you want to get a place in this race, then stick with me."

Eddie thought that the man sounded a trifle big-headed, but he spoke with such conviction, that he was impressed in spite of it, thinking that the man would probably win it anyway. He watched his tactics closely and noted that the commando ate very little, spent a lot of time on the toilet and exercised. He did seem to be an old hand at the racing game, so Eddie, thinking that his advice was logical, tried to do the same.

At that time, Eddie was undeniably fit, as the time he had spent in training for the Normandy landings and the fighting that soon came after, had brought him to his peak. There was not an ounce of superfluous fat on his body.

The day came and the crowd gathered to watch the race, with those taking part in good spirits. They were jumping around, laughing and joking with each other, then the starter's gun cracked and the race was on.

Eddie got off to a good start, keeping to the commando's heels as he had advised him to. He kept up this position for some time and found that they were well ahead of the rest. Both of the men kept up their speed, then put on an extra spurt to get them past the winning post. The time registered was four minutes and twenty four seconds for the mile, a record at that time.

Years later, a young man named Roger Bannister was to run the first four minute mile, however the two men were pleased with themselves that day.

CHAPTER NINETEEN

The men had been told that the full Battalion would be going out to Egypt and Palestine and other regiments would be taking over the occupational duties. Liberty ships were sent to take them on their journey up the Mediterranean.

The first port they docked at was Port Said. Eddie had often heard of it, but never dreamed that one day he would be actually there. The Egyptians came out in small boats to trade with the soldiers as soon as the ships dropped anchor; they were piled high with fruit and bottled drinks. The traders threw ropes up to the ships and, when these had been secured, baskets of fruit and bottled drinks were attached to them. Eddie bought a bottle, but was not impressed, thinking it tasted like warm pop.

When the ships were finally docked, the soldiers disembarked and formed lines on the quayside whilst they waited for further orders. They were then marched to a transit camp where there were a number of tents and marquees erected for them. Here they were given meals and the opportunity to rest and wash before moving on to the railway station.

A train pulling a number of cattle trucks was waiting for them and the soldiers made themselves comfortable on bales of straw. The Egyptian traders were climbing all over the train as it pulled slowly out of the station.

One vendor had a tray of rings and Eddie noticed a pretty ring with a blue stone in it. It was small, so he thought he would buy it as a gift for Gina. He indicated to the youth that he wanted to buy it, but after taking Eddie's money, the youth pressed a worthless washer into his hand and dropped off the train.

"Get your knees brown, Johnny," he laughed mockingly as he went.

He got a shock as Eddie dropped off the train after him and was punched in the face and the tray of rings snatched off him. Eddie threw the box to the soldiers on the train and just had time to grab the handle on the guards van, as the train puffed along on its way.

Once he was safely on the train, he looked back and saw the youth being grabbed by a large Egyptian in a fez and carrying a whip. Eddie thought he might be the local bobby.

Their destination was a place called Ismailia and when they arrived there they were marched to a camp outside the town. Here were more tents for them, but this time there were also some Nissen huts, which gave the place more of an air of permanency.

Eddie was picked for a special squad of twenty 'hardened troops' who were driven to Haifa, where they were dropped off at a camp that overlooked the sea. After a while they were marched down to the quayside to where a refugee ship was moored. Only the sick on board were allowed to land and the soldiers escorted them to an Israeli camp. The rest of the people had to stay on board and sailed on the next tide. Eddie didn't get to know why this was before they were driven back to Ismailia.

There had been an influx of immigrants from the ghettos of Europe at this time. They all hoped for a new life in the future state of Israel. Life on those ships was appalling, conditions that the passengers had to live under were terrible and, even if they managed to reach Palestine safely, these pathetic people could be turned back and not even be allowed to set foot in the Holy Land. There were limitations on the number of people accepted, though pregnant women and their husbands had the best chance of being allowed. There had been a lot of unrest and sabotage, with the King David hotel being blown up.

Detail at the camp involved driving duties for Eddie. At first he picked up rations for the company, became a substitute driver for the C.O. and did a lot of trips to Cairo. He never did any guard duty and spent his free time swimming and sunbathing at the local Lido.

The constant sunshine worked wonders on veterans like Eddie, who had fought the war in cold, muddy conditions.

His favourite job was to drive parties of soldiers on sightseeing tours. They went to places that were names in the Bible to the average man. He made constant trips to Jerusalem, Bethlehem, Nazareth and Galilee. They saw the Garden of Gethsemane, the Mount of Olives and many other famous names.

One sightseeing tour left its mark on Eddie. It was when he took a party of soldiers to see the Pyramids and the Sphinx outside Cairo. There was a leakage of brake fluid, which hadn't been noticed when the lorry was made ready for the trip. It wasn't noticed until Eddie was driving down a hilly road that led to the ancient monuments. He put on the brakes to hold the lorry on the steep hill and found that there were no brakes to hold it. He had to resort to desperate measures and warned his passengers to drop off the vehicle when they could, as he was going to try and slow it down through the gears. As this did not stop the headlong flight down the road, he pressed the horn to warn pedestrians that the lorry was out of control. It blared all the way down the hill with the soldiers dropping off like flies. Miraculously Eddie avoided injuring anyone, as the Egyptians scattered for safety as they became aware of the lorry in its headlong rush.

"Jump off with the others," he had said to the officer accompanying him on the trip. Had he jumped then he would have jumped to comparative safety, but he hung on grim-faced, gripping the passenger seat with his hands. They came to a stop when the vehicle hit rough ground around the Pyramids, much to everyone's relief!

As luck would have it there was a second lorry waiting and word was sent back to the depot about the incident. Eddie finished the day in ignominious fashion, being towed through Cairo, a frightening experience in such a busy city. He was without a vehicle for a week and missed his trips out very much.

The men found that fruit was abundant there and it made a

welcome addition to army rations. Eddie enjoyed eating dates, which he bought in large chunks from the fruit seller. The soldiers would buy dates and take them in with them to eat, whilst they watched film shows in the camp.

"The very best dates were put on the stones which marked the graves in the local cemetery," Eddie said to a friend when he got back home to England.

"How do you know that?" she had asked. Eddie left her guessing.

One of the new sergeants fell in love with a pretty girl that he met on the beach. She was a French girl and very friendly to him. Starved as they had been of female company, the soldiers found that the Europeans they met in Cairo were very pleasant. They had all been warned to treat the Egyptian women with respect and not to make friends with any of the young ones.

"Isn't she a smasher," said young Lennie eagerly to Eddie. He agreed with the man, she was really quite sensational with a lovely figure and lovely legs. Something tugged at Eddie's memory though, as he felt he had seen her before. He listened while Lennie told him that he had written to his parents to tell them that he was going to be married, although he was already committed to a young lady back home and did not know how to break the bad news to her.

Eddie made some visits around the camp, asked some questions and found that most of the soldiers had a photograph of the same young lady. What was more to the point, they knew her better than the young sergeant did. She was in the habit of hiring a room for the day and taking her boyfriends to it.

Eddie had a hard time talking to Lennie. He took a lot of convincing that the love of his life figured in the love life of a lot of his fellow soldiers. His mother had written from home saying how disappointed she was in him, if he persisted in the marriage, then she advised him to make a career of the army, as she would not wish to meet his wife. Later, he forced himself to go and see the photos that Eddie had told him about and listened to the stories that the other men had to tell. Finally, he decided he'd had a lucky escape and wrote off to his mother to say that the situation had resolved itself.

The staff car driver went on leave to Ireland to visit his family and Eddie was given the job while he was away. The work wasn't hard, but the hours were long and he didn't get much free time. He mainly drove the C.O. around on his official duties and in the evening drove him to his club. There he would wait outside until the officer came out with friends and, after driving them home, he would be dismissed for the night.

One afternoon he was waiting outside a building where a meeting was taking place. The officer had been there for around an hour, whilst Eddie sat inside the car that was like an oven, as there was no air conditioning. He mopped at the perspiration that was running down his neck and prayed that the officer wouldn't be much longer.

A hand rapped on the window nearest to Eddie and he turned to see a face grinning at him through the glass. It was a young Egyptian who made quite a decent living from the troops as a 'shoe black'.

Eddie asked him what he wanted, though he knew what he would say straight away.

"Clean your shoes, Johnny?"

Eddie, who as usual was attired in an immaculate uniform and wore shining army boots, opened the door to show the youth. To his dismay he received the entire contents of a bottle of blacking down his uniform front. He went red with rage and, getting out of the car, he raced after the youth, who was running down the street. Though the youth was swift, Eddie was swifter and being in such a temper at the insult on his uniform, he gripped the young Egyptian and bundled him, shoe brushes, blacking and all, into the Sweetwater Canal. He then ran quickly back to the car and went to change his uniform, as although the soldiers had been told to keep a low profile with the locals, he had been badly provoked.

Eddie returned to his quarters, changed hurriedly into a fresh uniform and hoped that the C.O. wouldn't be waiting outside the building when he returned. He didn't report the incident, but told his sergeant when he saw him next. He was told to forget the incident, but he would have done the same.

The driver came back from Ireland and Eddie returned to the depot and to other duties.

He was assigned to garbage disposal and he and another driver took the camp rubbish to a disused sand pit, which was being used as a dump.

They tipped the contents of the lorry into the bottom of the pit and stood back to watch, as a swarm of women and children descended upon it. They picked up empty boxes, discarded items and anything else that took their fancy. Then they laid it in small piles at the top of the tip, with a child left to guard it.

One woman had left her baby at the top while she rummaged and it was crying pitifully for its mother, whilst flies buzzed around its eyes. A large Egyptian rode up on a donkey, his legs dangling on either side of the small animal. When he dismounted, he kicked the baby out of the way and it rolled over and fell to the bottom of the pit.

The large Egyptian received one of life's little surprises then, when Eddie kicked *him* on the backside and it was his turn to go rolling down to the bottom of the dump. Eddie just had time to look at the women who stood around watching, Bedouin women who didn't wear the yashmak, but drew their black veils over their faces instead, as he hastily jumped into the lorry with his mate to make a run for it. They were tittering discreetly behind their veils, enjoying the discomfort of their fellow Egyptian. It seemed to Eddie that life there was very cheap.

Driving on the desert roads were hazardous in daytime and at night it was even worse, but Eddie chose it as the lesser of two evils at the time. He had been chosen to drive an armoured car to Gaza and he was accompanied by an officer who had to take a test on driving the vehicle before he could drive it around the area.

When he got to the camp at Gaza and the officer had taken his test, Eddie asked permission to return back to his billet in Egypt. He had seen the mosquito nets that hung ready for use in the night time and knew he wouldn't be able to sleep.

He set off at dusk along the sandy tracks of the desert, the road was very rough and he met no other vehicles on the way. He drove as fast as he could until he got to the Sweetwater Canal and flashed his headlights across the canal to attract the attention of the boatmen. Two Egyptians poled a raft across and Eddie drove onto it. He was very late getting to bed that night.

The following morning he was on a duty trip to Cairo and had no money, nor an inclination to sample the delights of the place. He had a late start back after a holdup, whilst dropping the soldiers off for their sightseeing, as another lorry should have been there to bring them back.

He drove along the desert road, appreciating the sound of a well-tuned engine as it was performing well, when he noticed that a set of headlights behind his vehicle had come into view. Remembering the time when a tall, thickset fellow had jumped onto his running board, asking for guns to sell and noticing the knife sheathed in the scabbard dangling from the Egyptian's waist, Eddie put his foot down on the accelerator. He had been lucky that the man had been content with his explanation, that he was just a driver and didn't carry guns.

Feeling apprehensive, he began to drive faster, knowing that there was nothing but sand as far as the eye could see. The headlights disappeared from view and Eddie heaved a sigh of relief.

There was a small café at the halfway mark and, when Eddie saw the building, with its lights shining into the darkness like a lighthouse on the edge of a rocky coast, he pulled into a parking space. The driver of the vehicle who had been worrying Eddie again for the last few miles, came to a stop beside his. He had gone inside the café by then, where he had ordered a coffee.

"What have you got under that bonnet of your lorry, wings?"

asked a girl dressed in an American uniform, as she came in through the door and joined Eddie at the counter. "I've been trying to catch up with you since leaving Cairo."

Eddie laughed, knowing that she had probably been nervous and had just wanted to follow him on the lonely desert road. He offered to pay for her coffee, but she ordered egg and chips for both of them and said it was her treat. He agreed to drive at a speed that she could keep up with, as she was driving a staff car and her destination, like his own, was Ismailia.

CHAPTER TWENTY

The days in the sunshine were coming to an end for many of the men and the swimming and sunbathing at the Lido was beginning to pall. The weeks were flying by and thoughts were turning to home. There was no longer a goal, a war to be fought and won, and the windswept summers and the green fields of both Ireland and England seemed so desirable in contrast to the desert sunshine. Eddie wrote to his wife that he would soon be coming home.

But first he was to go on loan to another unit, where he was detailed to drive the staff car there for a week.

On the first night of the transfer, Eddie found that he had to, as usual, wait outside the officer's club for a number of hours. It seemed longer than the normal spell of duty and he was feeling very thirsty. The door of the club opened and a young officer and a pretty girl walked down the steps towards him. The officer appeared to hesitate, then seemingly having made up his mind, he came to the car and asked if Eddie would run the young girl back to the hospital where she worked as a nurse.

Eddie was reluctant. He was waiting for a senior officer who had the official use of the car. There would be trouble for him if he wasn't there when the man came out to be driven back to camp.

"Have you had anything to eat or drink?" asked the officer. He had hit on a sore point with Eddie, as he was absolutely parched. On getting a reply in the negative, he disappeared back up the steps and came back five minutes later with a brimming glassful of beer for him.

"Your officer will be some time yet," he chuckled. "He is in the bar drinking with some of his friends."

Eddie handed the glass back when he was finished; his thirst was slaked and, in gratitude, he was willing to agree to the officer's request. The officer, who decided to accompany the young lady and not intending to return to the club, threw the empty glass into the bushes nearby and Eddie drove the pair of them to the hospital.

It was past midnight when the senior officer appeared at the door of the club. He was holding up a fellow officer and growling about the state that the fellow was in.

"Bloody man, can't hold his drink," he grumbled, pushing and pulling at the man until he got him onto the back seat of the car. The officer rose up again crying in anguish, he had been pushed right onto the spike of the armrest.

They finally moved off with the staff car now loaded to capacity. Eddie was directed to drive down a road and on to a field dotted with tents. His officer selected a tent that still had its flaps up and the inebriated man was helped from the back seat and put to bed. His boots were removed and he was left to sleep it off in peace. Eddie thought he wouldn't like his head in the morning.

He was ordered to drive on to another unit and after his passengers had alighted, he asked the senior officer for permission to go off. He was so tired by the time he reached his quarters that he didn't even go for a cocoa and a natter to his friendly cook.

Next morning, having slept the sleep of the dead, Eddie ate his breakfast, then grabbed his swimming trunks and towel, intending, as it was his day off, to spend his time at the Lido. Later he would read a book in the billet and have a day of rest. He was just about to dip his toe in the water to see how warm it was when a voice shouted his name. He recognised the man as one from the driver's unit and it appeared he was wanted at the transport office.

"It's my day off," said Eddie.

"You're wanted to drive the staff car."

What else could he do, but dress and go?

When he got to the office, it appeared that a new recruit that had been detailed to drive the staff car just for the day to take Eddie's place, had parked on the 'holy of holies', the parade ground, where no car was ever allowed to park. The senior officer had come out and torn a strip off the unfortunate recruit, then asked for Eddie to take his place. After a few minutes, Eddie, dressed in a hurry having come straight from the pool, found himself on duty again. He came to loathe the staff car duty spells and was happy to hand the duty over to a man who'd been on leave.

There was a new batch of soldiers who had come out from England. These men were to be the future drivers of the army vehicles, when the '39 group were demobbed. Eddie was one of a number of drivers who had been selected to teach the rookies how to maintain and drive the vehicles.

There was plenty of space on the hard sand at the back of the camp for the drivers to practice on. Eddie discovered that one of the men came from Birkenhead and back in Civvy Street he had been a milkman, and so Eddie found him very easy to teach.

Eddie's brother, Sam, who belonged to the Signal regiment, was attached to their regiment at the time and came to see Eddie in his billet where he was having a rest. He asked why Eddie and the other veterans were excused from going on long exercise runs like he had to. He was feeling a bit underprivileged at the time. Eddie explained that because so many of them were to be demobbed in a very short time, it was now not necessary for them to keep on training.

A party of soldiers were chosen to go up to Bethlehem at Christmas. They would have the privilege of visiting the Church of the Nativity on Christmas Eve. It was a long journey from Ismailia and Eddie had volunteered to drive one of the lorries on a journey he never forgot.

It was dusk when they reached the city and they drove in with the stars coming out and shining, as they had done nearly two thousand years before.

When the soldiers arrived there, the streets seemed very quiet. They parked the lorries and went in an orderly fashion to the church. There were many devout Catholics amongst the men and they were awed by the solemnity of the occasion. They were actually in the city where it all began... it was a sobering thought and emotions began to get the better of them. They took off their caps prior to entering the church.

The church was dimly lit and they could just see inside. A doorman barred their way and asked to see their passes. No one had mentioned the need for passes and Eddie and the sergeant, who were in charge of the party, looked at each other in despair.

The rope which barred their way was unhooked to let a party with passes go through and they could see that there was plenty of room inside for all of them and, having come all that way to attend the service, it seemed very unfair.

"Line them up," said the sergeant, "just march them straight in."

The doorman couldn't argue with that, as two lorry loads of soldiers pushed by him, determined to attend the service anyway. It was a 'Fait Accompli' in the best tradition and they had their Christmas in Bethlehem where Jesus was born.

One trip that Eddie remembered well was to the hill of Calvary. The chaplain was recounting the trial of Jesus before the Roman, Pontius Pilate, and the subsequent events after. The chaplain spoke then of our Lord carrying the cross, how he had stumbled and fallen with the weight of it. An Irish voice came from the back, simple and sincere:

"And sure, your Reverence, I'd have stumbled and fallen meself if I'd been carrying the weight of it!"

On the occasion of the trip to Galilee, Eddie was able to buy two necklaces made of delicate green and mauve shells to take home. Another souvenir was a small trinket box made by a German prisoner of war. The box had been made out of mess tins, the only available metal which the craftsman was able to get. Eddie thought that the man must have been a silversmith at least, for the quality of the work merited a much more precious metal than tin. It had been made with loving care, with a spray of roses on the lid, flowers and leaves adorning the sides of the box, with a pair of doves standing beak to beak, as though kissing. Engraved under the lid, a pair of doves stood on a leafy branch. Small pieces of glass had been inserted at intervals, colours that simulated precious stones. Had the whole work of art been in silver and precious stones, it would have been a collector's piece.

Eddie had wished to pay the man for it, but he refused, though accepted fifty cigarettes from him. Neither of the men had sufficient command of the other's language for conversation, but Eddie felt, like him, he had been conscripted into army service. Like Eddie, he would be only too happy to leave the war years behind him and pick up the threads of his civilian life again.

Eddie had other souvenirs, besides these, to take home. There was a pair of sparkly sandals for Irene and Egyptian bracelets, which were square pieces of metal with Pharaoh's heads on them, linked together with thin chains. They seemed unique until Eddie saw that nearly all his unit had them. Some Egyptian entrepreneurs had been very busy supplying souvenirs for the British troops to take home with them.

Eddie was still on driving duties in Egypt and Palestine as his demob' date drew nearer. Many of the older men had already gone, some of these had been regular army men, the ones with whom Eddie had trained. He would have liked to keep in touch with them, for they gave him comradeship that he had never known before or since. Many came from Southern Ireland and Eddie was Irish, by descent, but born in England. They had been his comrades; he had fought and endured hardship with them.

The regiment's Quarter Master was due for demob'. His fellow officers put a rope on the staff car and drew it outside the main gate in traditional style. Eddie had the privilege of driving him to Port Said, which he deemed an honour, as this man had been very good to him during his time there. The first part of the journey was to a leave camp and afterwards he would board a ship for England. Eddie said his own farewell and was really touched to see the tears running down the elderly soldier's face. Parting from the army where he had been so happy for many years was a very emotional time for him.

At the leave camp there were many leaflets blowing around in the wind. Eddie picked one up so he could study it. The king who had never been crowned had been there to visit the soldiers, the men who could have been his subjects had he fallen in love with a woman who had been acceptable to the monarchy. The paper said, "We visited here". The date had been some months before and was signed by the Duke and Duchess of Windsor.

Many of the veterans, like Eddie, were being asked to sign on again after their discharge, but most of them were weary of war. Civilians at heart, they could not wait to get back to their homes and families.

The men were marched onto the Parade ground one morning, but Eddie had refused to take the ribbons. The sergeant who was inspecting them said he was improperly dressed without them, so Eddie had to fall out and borrow the store man's set of ribbons, before he passed inspection.

He had been very put out about the campaign medals. No distinction had been made between the soldiers who had taken part in the Normandy landings and who were in the bitter fighting in the months to come. The same medals were issued to the men and women who came after in the noncombatant roles and miles behind the battles that were being fought. He meant no disrespect to them, as all had played their part in winning the war.

The Major presented him with a copy of the regiment's history book, pointing out Eddie's own name within it, for bringing in the wounded at one time.

"Take your leave and rejoin," he urged. "There will be nothing for you in Civvy Street yet, it will be years before Britain gets going again." Eddie didn't commit himself, although it would be with great regret that he would leave the seasoned warrior behind.

Eddie took the book and read it through carefully, finding it very accurate on the battles that were fought, but he also thought that a good thing would be for a common soldier to tell the story, mentioning things that wouldn't be shown in army records.

Eddie was demobilised in the Autumn of 1946, he felt that the twelve months he had spent in the Middle East seemed more like twelve years. At first it had been a novelty as it was so different from his lifestyle back home, but now he was tired of Egypt and Palestine.

The demobilisation took place in an orderly fashion, the men who had been called up before Eddie went first. At last his number came up and he was free.

The journey home was not a comfortable one. They travelled on an old ship, which had seen better days. Eddie learned how to play Crown and Anchor with the sailors and spent his nights on deck in a hammock, as the weather was humid and the Mediterranean was placid as they sailed.

They were landed at a French port and travelled over the Channel where they were sent to a centre for demob'. Here Eddie had to part with his precious Luger, a good friend and companion he'd had for many months. He was given a suit, a striped suit that became very fashionable as army men poured back into Civvy Street, and a share of his gratuity money which amounted to sixty quid.

So that is the way Eddie ended his war, with a striped suit that he wouldn't be seen dead in, £60 and a suntan!

EPILOGUE

Eddie didn't go home to a land fit for heroes. There was still rationing, still mass unemployment, a huge amount of money owed to the U.S.A., soldiers returning to broken homes and children who had grown up in their absence and resenting the appearance of an unfamiliar father telling them what to do. Once the celebrations were over, the population again began to wonder what this war had cost them. Hadn't they fought a war to end all wars in the Great War? So Hitler had been defeated, but it had been at the expense of the lives of the country's younger generation, who should have been there to make Britain great again.

Eddie, affected by the sounds of battle, the night sweats, horrific dreams that woke the family with his shouting, managed to find work on a local housing estate that was being built for those that had lost their houses in the air raids, but it was heavy going for the once fit man. The M.O. presiding over the demob' medical had pronounced Eddie fit to resume his life in Civvy Street, ignoring the heart that was stressed and weakened, as it didn't really matter much to him.

As the years went by, with a wife and a growing family, Eddie struggled to make ends meet. His dreams of a big house in the country, private education for his children, holidays and a luxury car to ride around in, were shattered. He was reduced to fixing creaky gates, broken walls, replacing rickety fences, as his health broke down and he was unable to hold down a full time job. He was in and out of hospital until he passed away at seventy-one.

And his thanks for joining others in the fight for freedom? A poxy government retirement pension, which, upon his death, they found he'd been given an overpayment and snatched back the small amount from his grieving widow.